TAN

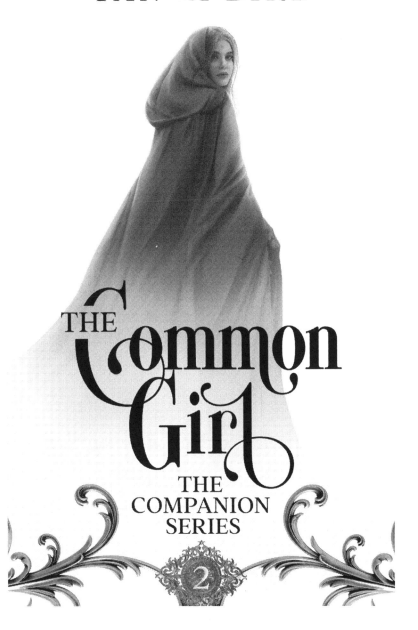

THE Common Girl

THE COMPANION SERIES

2

For Mum.

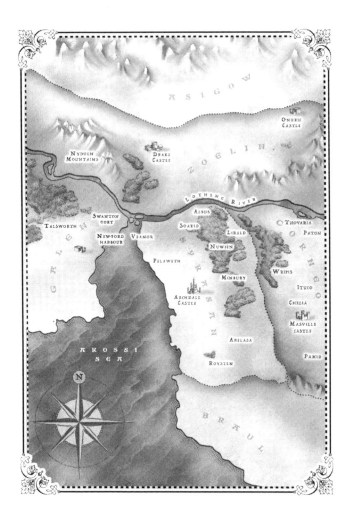

PROLOGUE

Tyron refused to join in. He stood with his back to the weak sun, watching Aldara concentrate. Small puffs of steam came from her mouth whenever she spoke or laughed, a reminder that the cold season lingered. He was about to suggest that she put her cloak back on but thought better of it. She had enough people telling her what to do. He tried to give her the freedom she craved in the small ways he could.

Sapphira had convinced Stamitos to teach her self-defence, and it had not been long before Aldara had asked Tyron to teach her also. He had said no.

'I want to know how to protect myself,' she had said, 'in case the need arises.'

What she did not say was *again*. Instead, she had looked away.

His chest had constricted as he thought back to the night when two Zoelin men had done as they pleased with her. They had left her a bloody mess. 'I'm sorry, but I can't even pretend to be violent with you.'

Her eyes had returned to him. 'What if Stamitos taught both Sapphira and me?'

Now there they were, gathered in the abandoned butts, away from the disapproving stares that bore down from the castle windows. Stamitos was holding Aldara's left wrist, while Tyron willed himself to stay still.

'If you leave one mark on her, you will have a very different fight on your hands,' he called to his brother.

Stamitos smiled at Aldara. 'Block out everything else and focus on me,' he said, loud enough for Tyron to hear. 'Bend your other arm and put your elbow level with your shoulder. Now you are going to thrust your forearm directly into my throat.' He pointed to the part of her arm that should make contact with him.

Aldara moved her arm towards his throat.

'You need to step into it,' Stamitos said, 'so your body weight is behind it.'

She tried again, that time making contact. Tyron smiled to himself.

'Sorry, did that hurt?' Aldara asked, glancing at his throat.

'No,' Tyron answered for him. 'He has let go of your wrist. Now thrust the same elbow straight into the centre of his chest.'

Aldara stepped in and pushed her elbow between his ribs. 'Now what?'

'Now your shin goes straight to his groin,' Sapphira said, a smirk on her face.

Stamitos's hands immediately covered his crotch. 'No. That is what's referred to as a dirty fight.'

Tyron stepped closer to Aldara. 'And that is exactly what you will do if the need arises.'

'I thought you did not want to be a part of it,' Aldara said, eyes shining.

Tyron put his hands up. 'Forget I am here.'

Aldara and Stamitos exchanged a glance.

'What if someone goes for my throat?' Aldara asked, the smile on her face fading. 'Has me in a choke?'

Tyron blinked away the vision of her sitting in a tub of blood-tinged water that had long gone cold. He could still remember four rows of bruises down the right side of her neck, left by the hand of a Zoelin guest who he had never met and prayed he never would.

Sapphira stepped forwards and gently pushed Stamitos out of the way. 'Choke me,' she said to Aldara.

Aldara looked at her, unsure. Her eyes went to Stamitos, who nodded for her to go ahead. She stepped up to Sapphira and wrapped her hands around her throat, reminding herself to breathe through the memories the action evoked. Sapphira pulled Aldara's arms over her shoulders so her hands slipped from her throat and she fell forwards into her. In the same motion, she brought her knee to Aldara's stomach with just enough pressure so Aldara doubled over with the force.

Tyron stepped between them and pulled Aldara upright. 'That's enough for today.' If Sapphira had been a man, he would have broken her nose.

'It's all right,' Aldara said, slightly breathless. 'I want to learn.'

If Tyron had his way, she would not need to learn, but he was acutely aware of the fact that he had been unable to protect her in the past.

'Go back to the castle,' Aldara said, her tone gentle. 'I would really like to learn, and I cannot do that with you clutching your sword.'

Tyron glanced down to where his other hand was gripping the hilt of his weapon.

'I promise we will be gentle, my lord,' Sapphira said, pressing her lips together to stop from smiling.

He glanced at her, a hint of anger in his expression. 'Next time you teach her the moves before you use them on her.'

'That *was* a little savage,' Stamitos said to Sapphira.

Sapphira jabbed her elbow into his ribs while Tyron looked between them all. He did actually trust them as far as Aldara's well-being was concerned.

'All right. But I meant what I said. Not one mark on her.' He faced Aldara. 'I'll send Pero for you later.'

She curtsied, and Sapphira mirrored the action.

He resisted the urge to reach out and touch her face as she returned upright. He rarely touched her in the company of others. He was not entirely sure why. Perhaps he was afraid of what it gave away. He kept his hands at his side and glanced at Stamitos before turning and leaving them.

In the month since his return from the Zoelin border, he had felt like nothing but a burden on her. His inability to sleep, concentrate, or be mentally present would no doubt be taking a toll on her also. She insisted on staying with him through every nightmare and, every time his mind turned on him, talking to him until the air returned to his lungs. She would sit by his bed on the days that he could not leave it, stroking his hair while he lay trapped somewhere between conscious and dead. He had stopped trying to push her away; it only hurt her more, and he could not bear the idea of that.

As always, he felt himself improving as he found a place within him for the memories: a screaming woman covered in her dead husband's blood, a small boy burned alive, the feel of a blade passing through Zoelin flesh. He began spending more time outdoors, where he could watch

Aldara come to life for both of them, and then at night, they would return indoors so she could breathe life back into his tired lungs and heal him in ways she would never understand.

Each morning, his mother, the queen, would visit. She would pass Aldara in the doorway, saying nothing to her but always observing, no doubt trying to gauge if he was better or worse with his Companion at his side.

When Tyron reached the trees, he turned to watch Aldara again. She was nodding as she listened to what Stamitos was saying, and then she stepped forwards, arm striking out at him. Stamitos leapt back and she stumbled forwards. They all laughed then. Open-mouthed, unfiltered laughter, with no consideration as to who might hear them. He let the sound warm him. Stamitos had come to care for Aldara like a sister. The idea should have pleased him, but it was just another heart that would break when it all came to an end.

And then there was Sapphira. Stamitos had met his match in choosing her as his Companion. Fierce, funny. Complete disregard for the rules. Tyron had overheard some of their whispered conversations; they spoke of love without fear and made plans for a future that could never be.

More laughter reached him from across the lawn. Sapphira had taken Stamitos's legs out from beneath him and he lay flat on his back, half laughing, half winded. Tyron wondered whether they would all remember this time. When they were finally forced to live the lives set out for them, would they recall the small moments they stole beforehand? Their futures had already been decided; all they could do now was hold on for a while and pray they all survived the fallout.

'Tyron,' a voice came from behind him.

He turned to see Pandarus standing a few yards away. He rarely stood close anymore. 'What is it?'

'He is here.' Pandarus looked past him, through the trees, towards the laughter. He shook his head. 'Companions used to be a collection of the kingdom's most refined and educated women. What happened?'

Tyron looked back at Aldara, who glanced in his direction. 'Stamitos is educating them.'

'I see that.'

Tyron faced Pandarus. 'Where is he?'

'The throne room.'

Tyron nodded. It was time to sit down and share their best wine with the man who had taken Syrasan women in the north and killed the men who stood in his way.

'We can handle it if you would prefer,' Pandarus said, seeing his hesitation.

Tyron walked alongside his brother. 'I don't trust you to handle it. I will be the one fighting when it all goes wrong, so I would prefer to be kept informed this time if it is all the same to you.'

Pandarus shook his head. 'I heard you were feeling better, but you sound as though you need a lie-down.'

Tyron kept his eyes on the grass. The snow had stopped falling, but patches of ice remained in its place. 'When you prove that you can manage relations with our neighbouring kingdoms, I will gladly opt for a lie-down.'

Pandarus said nothing as he looked about.

'I suppose it is pointless to remind you that I remain against the trade agreement,' Tyron said.

'About as pointless as me reminding you that we have no choice but to honour it.'

Tyron shook his head slowly. 'I will never understand why you signed it in the first place.'

'You do not have to understand. You just need to

support my decision, which is backed by your father and king.'

'He was not left with much choice.'

'Do not start. We need a united front in that room if we are to see the children returned. King Jayr is finely tuned to conflict. If he gets so much as a sniff of a doubt from any one of us, he will take action to protect his interests.'

Tyron watched his damp boots. 'Yes, I have witnessed his logic firsthand.'

'Then you understand what is at stake.'

Tyron nodded. 'I understand.'

They walked in silence, with plenty of distance between them, and their eyes ahead.

CHAPTER 1

Two hundred voices vibrated through the church, echoing the bishop's words. A priest walked amid the guests below the royal family, a thurible in hand, swinging gently from a gold chain. The burning laurel leaves emitted smoke that carried their prayer to God. Queen Eldoris closed her eyes and let the words wash over her. It was a traditional Galen blessing, spoken at the end of wedding ceremonies—a blessing from home. It had once been sung at her own wedding, many years before, and now for her firstborn son and his Galen bride.

Seeping hearts, transcending human thought,
  We kneel in prayer before Thy throne,
  May their love know no ending in this life,
  Join their hearts,
  O perfect love.

. . .

Love. Eldoris opened her eyes and looked at Pandarus, who stood tall in front of the bishop and next to his new wife. He wore a red tunic, as well as a sash of green in recognition of his young bride.

Her name was Salome. The fact that her name translated to "peace" was surely a sign from God. She was a plain girl, but draped in cream silk and lace with gold trim, she was something more. She had been hand selected for her royal Galen bloodlines by Eldoris's father, the king of Galen, who by God's will remained alive in his seventy-second year. The marriage had been planned in their early years, a decision that ensured the strong Syrasan and Galen alliance continued. With Corneo a constant threat, and King Jayr of Zoelin tightening his grip on Syrasan, the young bride had been shipped across the Arossi Sea at the conclusion of her education. While she barely reached Pandarus's shoulder, she did not wilt next to him, despite the fact that she hardly knew the man she had sworn before God to honour and obey until her death. 'What is to be gained by courtship?' her husband had said. Delays were pointless. They would both play their roles, like every royal before them.

O perfect life, be Thou full and fertile,
  Tender charity and steadfast faith,
  Patient hope and quiet, brave endurance,
  Trust not fears nor pain or death.

Eldoris glanced at her husband, the mighty King Zenas, who now rarely left the walls of Archdale Castle. He was looking much older than his fifty-one years. His skin was now as grey as his hair, and the endless feasting did little to help his ageing body. She could tell by the shifting of his weight from foot to foot that he was already tiring from standing for so long. Syrasan wedding ceremonies were lengthy occasions, and sombre in comparison to the festive Galen celebrations she remembered from her youth. The bishop had spoken the vows as a warning, threatening eternal damnation for those who stray from their promise before God. His eyes had remained on Salome as he spoke so she might live in fear of it.

King Zenas glanced at his wife and gave her a small smile. Eldoris returned the gesture. They allowed themselves to share a moment at the wedding of their firstborn son. They had not shared one in years.

Bring joy which brightens earthly sorrow,
O may peace calm earthly strife,
Grant them a glorious morrow,
We pray Thou bless thee with sons.

She looked past her husband to where her other sons stood, so handsome in royal dress—tunics of red with sashes of black and silver. Tyron's head was turned, his eyes reaching beyond the noble guests to where the Companions were tucked behind the stone pillars at the back of the church. They were purely decorative on such an occasion, though Tyron was not viewing them as a collection. His gaze fell only on Aldara, whose eyes remained respectfully ahead. Companions knew better than to let their gazes wander where they should not.

For weeks, Eldoris had passed the girl in the doorway when visiting her son, whose troubled mind saw him confined to his chambers, sometimes for days on end.

Every day the girl went to him. Eldoris had tried to figure out if the visitation was helping or hindering his progress. She could not fathom a woman who could care for him more than she. But there she stood, petite, quietly rebellious, and not meant for this life.

The girl next to her had a reputation for being *openly* rebellious. Sapphira had been hand selected by Eldoris's youngest child, Stamitos, who took full advantage of being the furthest from the throne. He was as wild as they came. The girl seemed to have the same hint of mischief on her face, until her eyes met Eldoris's; her smile vanished and she immediately looked away. Stamitos turned his head and locked eyes with his mother. He was still the same young boy who she had been reprimanding in church his entire life. Complete disregard for propriety and the sweetest soul she would ever know. Her expression softened when he smiled at her.

Hear us, our gracious God,
  Bringing blessings through life,
  Now and to endless ages,
  Always forgiving of our sins.

'Ironic, is it not?'

The sound of Cora's voice pulled her attention back. She turned and studied her daughter next to her, wrapped in yellow silk, her dark hair dotted with black pearls. She was breathtaking in her nineteenth year. 'What is ironic?'

Cora nodded towards the back of the church. 'Pandarus's whore invited to witness his sacred wedding vows.'

Eldoris gave her a disapproving glance. 'Really, Cora,

we are in God's house.' Her daughter's manners were not what one might guess looking at her.

'Would you prefer that I call them by name?' Cora whispered, a smile flickering.

'Call them what they are—Companions.'

Cora kept her eyes ahead. 'Companions… groomed for Syrasan's royal men, whose sins are overlooked because their impulses are so difficult for them to control.'

'Still your tongue,' Eldoris said, keeping her eyes forwards.

Cora pressed her hands together in front of her and bowed her head in a feigned act of prayer. 'Yes, be silent. We would not want any men hearing their truths.' She glanced at her mother as her hands returned to her sides.

Changed from glory to glory,
As we worship at this place,
Till we lay our crowns before thee,
Casting sin aside.

Eldoris's eyes wandered back to the Companions. She knew them by name and had studied them closely enough at social events to see beyond the exteriors shaped by their mentor. Six remained from the recent eight. Her husband's Companion had died from an infection caused by an unsuccessful termination. She had been prepared to take the life of her unborn child in order to prevent being cast away, sold off to the highest bidder, to decay outside of the castle walls. Eldoris knew her death continued to weigh on her husband, for he was yet to select another. The other missing girl had belonged to Pandarus, a political pawn sent to Zoelin to mentor once her son had grown bored.

His waning interest was not uncommon, and the women knew better than to complain—at least not out loud. It was still a better life than the one from which they had come, and the gold paid for them saw their families through famines they may not have survived otherwise.

She glanced again at Cora, who always appeared composed but whose resentment and bitterness bubbled just beneath her surface. She could not blame her daughter. They lived a life built by men, for men; a life that took away their choices and consumed their youth.

Eldoris looked forwards and closed her eyes again.

God, Thou art all compassion,
    Pure unbounded love Thou art;
    Visit us with Thy salvation,
    Enter every trembling heart.

CHAPTER 2

*P*rince Tyron sat upon his horse on the frosty banks of the Lotheng River. He was far enough from the bridge to go unnoticed by the crowd that had gathered to welcome back Syrasan's stolen children.

Leksi was beside him, loose rein and flask of water in hand. 'I'm still trying to understand what is happening.' He spoke loudly, competing with the angry roar of the river.

'You and me both.'

Leksi's eyes went to the bridge where King Jayr was leading the small party over violent waters. 'The trade agreement is going ahead?'

Tyron nodded. 'The trade agreement is going ahead.'

The young king was draped in blue, head shaved to reveal the ink that covered his scalp. Tyron wondered what he had done to deserve the markings given to him. What had it taken to be honoured in such a way by the king before him? Protect his family and people? Fight for their beliefs and honour? Kill for them? They were not so different.

King Jayr rode onto Syrasan soil as though such an

invitation had always existed. His expression was relaxed and his body loose. A few months earlier, Tyron would have shot an arrow through the neck of any Zoelin man who crossed that bridge. A few months earlier, they had been under attack by the very man who now paraded himself as though he were their saviour. The man was a monster, but as far as the Syrasan people were aware, he was practically a hero.

Children began to leap from the backs of the horses that had carried them from Onuric Castle. They rushed into the open arms of loved ones who were still grieving the men who had died trying to stop them from being taken. The part that made Tyron look away was that the men who had followed King Jayr over the bridge were probably the same men who carried out the violent acts. And now they stood holding flags of blue in a kingdom with open wounds. If only the families knew the truth. If they did, perhaps they would take the swords that had been given to them by their king, for the purpose of self-preservation, and drive them through the chests of these Zoelin men. But those thoughts were self-indulgent and pointless; what mattered now was that the Syrasan people were safe from further attacks.

Tyron looked at Leksi. 'This is an embarrassing display. I can practically see him calculating the worth of the goods he has just returned.'

'Just to get this straight,' Leksi said, putting away his flask and resting his hands on the front of his saddle. 'Pandarus signed an agreement with King Jayr for the trade of Syrasan women.'

'Correct.'

'And when our king learned of the agreement, he refused to honour it.'

Tyron's eyes went back to King Jayr. 'And then our

friend over there, afraid of what his disappointed Asigow buyers might do, took what he needed and killed any Syrasan man who stood in his way.'

It had been one of the most difficult fights of his life. Never had an enemy attacked unarmed common people and ridden off with their daughters. He had suspected all along that the unmarked attackers were Zoelin, despite his brother's efforts to have him look east to Corneo. But it was from the north they came, burning villages and slaying men armed only with farming tools. He closed his eyes at the memory of it.

Leksi glanced across at Tyron. 'Lucky us, there to do the dirty work while your father and Pandarus figured a way out of the mess.'

'We are still in that mess.'

Leksi eyes returned to the scene before them. 'At least the younger girls have been returned.'

'We would not have agreed to it otherwise.'

'I am surprised that your father let even those of age remain at Onuric. They should have all been returned regardless. Let the families decide if they want that life for their daughters.'

Tyron swallowed. 'Those of age have already been sold.'

'That's what he said?'

'That's what he said.'

Leksi shook his head. 'Not a chance those girls were ready that quickly. He is either lying or simply selling women, not Companions. And what does our king tell their families?'

Tyron watched as King Jayr received thanks from a crying mother. Her gratitude saw her hands come together in front of her face, as though in prayer before God. 'The story goes that, after learning of the proposed trade agreement, Nydoen rebels crossed the border and took women and children for illegal trade. They were caught by King Jayr's men before reaching the Asigow border, and the women and children were taken to Onuric.'

'These people must be fools if they believe their daughters would want to stay in a foreign land after such a traumatic event.'

'They were invited to enjoy King Jayr's generosity during their stay and sample the opportunities available to them.'

Leksi laughed. 'That sounds like Pandarus's logic.'

Tyron nodded. 'He financially compensated each family, handing them a letter written by the hand of their once-illiterate child.'

'Do the letters mention a dagger being pointed at their back as they write?'

Tyron gave a weak smile. 'The letters explained their choice to pursue a privileged life as a Companion.'

He was against the trading of Companions outside of Syrasan, and had his father not been sure they would lose a fight against the Zoelin army, he felt confident it would not be going ahead.

'Would you sell a daughter for coin if your family were starving?' Leksi asked.

Tyron thought of Aldara. A few years before, her family had sold her as a Companion so the rest of them could survive. Now she lived what was considered a privileged life by common standards. Yet outside of himself and the Companions she was forced to live with, she would be alone for the rest of her life. His mind was always thinking ahead, and he could not help but think about how much lonelier she would feel when the time came for him to take a wife. Could she live with the pain of sharing him? They rarely spoke of the future because it was unbearable, yet a life apart was more so. 'Hopefully I will never have to find out.'

King Jayr was surveying his surroundings, no doubt looking for Tyron, who had been sent to escort him and his men to Archdale. The fact that his father had sent him and not Pandarus showed how little he trusted the king.

King Jayr spotted the two of them downstream, beneath the cover of trees, watching the performance. He said something to the man seated on the horse next to him, and Tyron knew he could no longer hide away from it all. He kicked his horse into a walk and Leksi followed.

'That must be one of his advisors,' Tyron said, voice low. 'Look at the size of him.'

Leksi narrowed his eyes on the man. 'Tyron, that is Grandor Pollux.'

Tyron's eyes went to him. 'Is that supposed to mean something to me?'

Leksi slowed his horse. 'I met him during his last visit.' When Tyron did not respond, he added, 'And so did Aldara.'

Tyron stopped his horse and let the information filter through him. His eyes went to his hands, clenched into fists around the reins, as though trying to decide what to do with them. He breathed through the memories and impulses that flooded him before finally looking across at Leksi. 'Do not let me kill him.'

CHAPTER 3

*P*anthea and Rhea were seated in the armchairs in front of a blazing fireplace, books open on their laps for appearance. Aldara and Sapphira had been seated in those same chairs just a few minutes earlier, but when the others had arrived and lingered, they had reluctantly surrendered the seats. Aldara had said nothing about it, while Sapphira had huffed and groaned at the enormous inconvenience.

'When do my needs stop being less important than theirs?' Sapphira said to Aldara, loud enough for the others to hear. 'I too like to warm myself in front of a fire on occasion.'

They were seated opposite each other at the table now.

Aldara leaned in. 'They are just chairs,' she whispered.

'It's not about the chairs.'

Aldara knew it was not about the chairs. She was trying to defuse the conversation before Sapphira got herself in trouble again. She was doing that a lot lately.

'I am Stamitos's Companion. Those girls belong to no one.'

'*Prince* Stamitos,' Aldara corrected. 'Lower your voice before Fedora hears you.'

'Let her hear. I'm tiring of her lectures.'

'Put her back on her leash,' Panthea said to Aldara. She did not even look in their direction when she spoke.

Aldara looked at Sapphira, eyes pleading silence.

'All right, all right. But next time I stay in the chair.'

Aldara turned and checked the door to make sure Fedora was not standing there listening to them. Their mentor had extraordinary hearing, and the women had a habit of always saying the wrong thing when she was in proximity. Aldara was also waiting for a messenger to arrive and tell her that Tyron had returned from the border. He had gone to ensure Syrasan's children were safely handed over to their families, and also had the responsibility of escorting King Jayr back to Archdale. It was the second time the king had visited Archdale since the attacks in the north, but this time he would be an honoured guest, and one of the noble Companions would no doubt be expected to share his bed. Aldara could see a change in Tyron since the honouring of the trade agreement. His silence came at a personal cost to him.

When she turned back to face Sapphira, her friend had a mischievous look on her face.

Aldara was almost afraid to ask. 'I know that look. What are you planning?'

Sapphira dug a hand into the pocket of her dress and produced two dice.

'Where did you get those?' Aldara asked, keeping her voice low. 'Dice games have been banned by the church.'

'Everything is banned by the church. And since when do you live by the rules of the church?'

Aldara exhaled and looked at her for a moment. 'Never.'

'Exactly.' Sapphira shook the dice in her hand. 'I'll teach you how to play Hazard.'

Aldara glanced at the other women by the fire who were pretending to read. 'I know how to play Hazard,' she whispered.

Sapphira stopped shaking the dice and raised an eyebrow. 'Then let's play.'

Aldara sat forwards, a hint of a smile forming. 'All right, but you hide those things the second you hear footsteps.'

'Fedora's feet don't make noise. That would be a sign of imperfect walking or something.'

Aldara smiled. 'Well, you better watch the door.'

Astra appeared in the other doorway that led through to the bedchamber and they both jumped at the sight of her. She narrowed her eyes on them.

'What are you doing?' she asked, already walking towards them.

'You're as silent as Fedora when you walk,' Sapphira said, turning back to Aldara and shaking the dice again.

'I walk normally. You are used to the sound of your own heavy steps. Every time you walk into a room it is as though a yoke of oxen has entered. Are those dice?' Astra looked to Aldara, knowing Sapphira's answers were usually unreliable. When she did not immediately get one, she added, 'They are banned by the church, you know.'

Sapphira smiled. 'Seven,' she said before throwing the dice onto the table. Two sixes appeared.

'Outs,' Aldara said. 'Roll again.'

Astra moved closer to watch but held her expression of disapproval. Sapphira collected the dice and rolled again. A one and a two appeared on the dice.

'Outs again,' Aldara called.

Panthea stood up and wandered over to the table. 'Is Sapphira losing?' she asked, sounding pleased.

'Not yet,' Sapphira said. She picked up the dice and rolled again, a three and a two. 'Chance,' she called, scooping up the dice and smiling at Aldara.

Rhea stood and walked over to join them. 'What does *chance* mean?' she asked.

'If she rolls another chance, she wins,' Aldara replied. 'If she rolls the main, seven, she loses.'

'What if she rolls neither?' Rhea said, leaning in to watch.

'Then she keeps going until she rolls one or the other.'

Sapphira scooped up the dice and threw them onto the table, giving up on her attempts at being discreet. A four and three settled on the table in front of them.

'Outs,' Aldara called.

Rhea and Panthea clapped their hands together.

'You don't have to be so openly pleased,' Sapphira said, glancing sideways at them.

'You cannot blame them,' Astra said. 'It is refreshing to see you lose at something.'

Aldara was enjoying the lift in mood and the banter between them. It had been a long time since they had done anything together that was not a compulsory, scheduled activity.

'What are you doing?' came a voice behind them.

They all turned to see Fedora standing in the middle of the room, her eyes on the dice.

'We were just playing a game, my lady,' Aldara said, hoping to prevent Sapphira from having to speak at all.

Fedora walked over to the table and the women standing in front of it stepped to the side. 'Where did these dice come from?' She picked them up and looked straight at Sapphira.

'Prince Stamitos gave them to me, my lady,' Sapphira said unapologetically.

'Are you trying to lead the others to Hell with you?'

Sapphira shrugged. 'The company might be nice.'

Everyone stopped breathing except Fedora; her lungs continued to work perfectly. She slipped the dice into her pocket and kept her cool gaze on Sapphira.

'I believe it is time for you to do your chores,' she said.

'My chores are done, my lady.' Sapphira lifted her chin as she responded. 'That is why I was enjoying some leisure time.'

Fedora did not even blink. 'No, they are not.' She stepped forwards and picked up the jug of water off the table, then walked over to the fireplace and tipped its contents over the flames. Thick smoke rose from the blackened wood. The room instantly grew cold. 'Your first job is to clean the fireplace and then build a new fire. After that, come and see me. I have a few more things for you to do before you get to eat.' She walked off through the door towards the bedchamber, leaving Sapphira silently fuming at the table.

The other women retreated to their corners.

'Why do you insist on making things harder for yourself?' Aldara said, shaking her head.

'It was a joke. That woman has no sense of humour.'

'I'm sure she's laughing now.'

'I'd like to fight her someday, with something other than words.'

Aldara laughed. 'That is very brave of you, even with all of your combat skills.'

'And she took my dice.'

'Because they are banned by the church.'

'Every man in this castle has a pair in his pocket.'

Aldara tilted her head. 'I'm sure every *man* does. Fedora is trying to make you a *lady*.'

Sapphira crossed her arms and looked over at the wet fireplace.

'Quickly now, Sapphira,' Panthea said, smiling into her book. 'We are not getting any warmer over here.'

Sapphira turned back to Aldara, mouth pinched and head shaking.

'The easiest way is Fedora's way,' Aldara said. 'Just get it done, and keep your mouth closed next time.'

Sapphira stood up and walked over to the fireplace, brushing past Astra, who was making her way back over to the table.

'Where is Violeta?' Astra asked, keeping her voice low so the others would not hear.

'Entertaining,' Aldara replied.

'Entertaining whom?'

'I honestly don't know.'

'I do,' Astra said. 'Prince Pandarus must be growing bored from his efforts at producing an heir.' She turned and walked from the room, head high but body rigid with rejection.

And just like that, everything had returned to normal.

Friendship seemed an impossibility among them. Especially when the noble Companions continued to share a bed with Prince Pandarus. Hali's absence did not seem to be helping Astra in the way she had hoped.

Aldara stood up and pulled a book from the shelf on the wall without looking at it. She left the main room, passing the bedchamber, the bathing room, and found refuge in the abandoned dressing room. She sat in her usual spot on the floor, with her back against the mirrored wall to prevent self-examination. She let the book fall open to any page and exhaled loudly as she studied the words in her lap. As she began to read, she realised it was a Galen prayer book. She was tempted to close it and spend her few precious moments of quiet examining the construction of the cover instead. But given that she was still not fluent in the language, she decided to persevere with reading it.

O most sweetest spouse of my soul, desiring heartily ever more to be with thee in mind and will, and to let no earthly thing be so nigh to my heart as thee. I beseech thee heartily, take me, a sinner, unto thy great mercy and grace.

She closed the book. It was one thing to be force-fed the sentiments at church, quite another to seek them out in her personal time. Thankfully the expectation of daily church attendance had diminished to weekly visits within a few months of her arrival at Archdale. She had soon found ways to be busy at the right times. The scolding glances from the priest every time he mentioned the *burning fires of Hell* were enough to make even Sapphira look down into her lap.

'There you are,' Fedora said, stepping through the doorway. 'Clean yourself up. Pero is waiting to escort you to Prince Tyron's chambers.' Fedora glanced down at the book in her lap. 'When was the last time you attended church?'

She had been so busy attending Tyron that she could barely remember. 'I was planning to in the morning,' she lied. Tyron rarely let her out of his bed before noon. The Companions often attended a smaller service in the mornings, while the noble and royal men they had entertained were washing away their sins from the night before.

'Be sure you do,' Fedora said. 'We cannot have the prince thinking you have turned away from God. Just remember who he prays to when he is fighting on our behalf.'

Aldara swallowed down her shame. 'Of course, my lady.'

Fedora was still looking at her. 'I understand the last few weeks have been very difficult for Prince Tyron. I am pleased that you have been of help while he recovers.'

Aldara waited for the rest.

'Just remember that your presence and support are part of your role. You are not a member of his family. And you are not his wife.'

Aldara kept her face as neutral as possible. She had not told a soul about the days following his return from the border. They had both mentioned love in a particularly vulnerable moment. While they had not repeated the senti-ment, or brought up the exchange since, it was still very much there between them. The only armour they had against each other was to not speak it aloud again. 'I understand my role.'

Fedora nodded. 'Good. I will send Sapphira in to help you once she is done with her… chores.'

A smile flickered on Aldara's face. 'Yes, my lady.'

When she was alone again, she stood up and walked along the hanging dresses, hand gliding over each one. That was how she selected a dress nowadays, imagining the feel of the fabric through Tyron's touch. It was far too cold for silk; it would be velvet that would soon slip down her skin, while his warm hand slid up her leg. She pulled the green dress from its hanger, held it against her, and turned to face the mirror. Something had changed in her appearance of late and she was having difficulty figuring out what. She was beginning to see herself through Tyron's eyes. The person reflected back was not the same sixteen-year-old girl who had arrived at Archdale two years before.

She lowered the dress and studied her reflection. There stood the woman who Idalia had promised she would become. The memory of the king's former Companion, dead in a blood-soaked bed, hit her sharply. She looked away from the mirror. The role had a way of destroying strength and beauty, and seeing herself as one of them forced her to acknowledge the cost of this life. She had lost her family, friends and freedom. Her identity. She needed to focus on what she had gained or she would break again. Into the dress, fix hair, paint face. Don a thicker skin than the one she lived in. That was how she would survive.

CHAPTER 4

They lay facing one another, naked aside from the bed linen that was twisted about their feet. Even with the fire lit, Aldara had her leg tucked beneath his for warmth, and for something more. A familiarity had crept in. She evoked a feeling that he was trying to place—the feeling of family. It was the easy silences, the shared observations, the jokes. It was raw and honest. Except for the lie they told themselves. One stifling lie. *There is no love between a prince and his Companion*. It was a rule, and the rule existed for a reason. They held onto it in hope of protecting the other.

Now there was another lie. Grandor Pollux had arrived at Archdale that afternoon, and because Tyron did not want to see that broken expression on Aldara's face, he was going to keep it from her, and had instructed Fedora to do the same.

'What are you thinking about?' he asked, his hand tracing her collarbone and throat.

'How easy this moment feels.'

He scooped her up with one arm and pulled her on top

of him so he could have her closer. Her hair fell to one side and she brushed it away from his face. He looked at her lips, which were slightly swollen from those moments before. He ran his thumb across them and she took it into her mouth, watching him, aware of the effect she had. Every day he lost a little more control in her presence.

She released his thumb and tilted her head. 'What are you thinking about?'

His eyes were still on her lips. 'I think you know what I am thinking about.'

She smiled and kissed the side of his face. 'Would you like me to stay here tonight?'

He wanted her to stay every night, even the nights that she did not. But they were always being watched by someone, and he was determined to keep a casual appearance so as to not draw the attention of his family.

When he did not answer her straight away, she pulled back and looked at him, trying to read his expression. A smile flickered on his face as his hands slid along the backs of her thighs.

'Who said anything about you leaving?' he said, grabbing hold of her legs in a way that always made her squeal and laugh. Her entire body jumped and her head went back as she laughed and begged him to stop. He released his grip and brought her head down so he could consume the open-mouthed laughter. That was all it took to ready him. His body fed on her laughter. It triggered a need that drove her own, consuming them both until they could no longer think through it.

'We need to sleep,' she whispered afterwards, her eyes closed and body limp.

He pressed his forehead to her chest and his body twitched with the arrival of sleep.

From the moment Aldara opened her eyes, she knew something was wrong. The sound of Tyron's sword being pulled from its sheath made her sit up. It was still dark, and the fire had diminished to embers that did little in the way of light.

'Tyron,' Aldara said, trying to focus in the dark.

Tyron's hand came across her mouth and she went still beneath it. 'Don't move. Don't speak.'

She nodded and he took his hand away. She felt the bed shift as he left and watched through blinking eyes as he crept towards the door, sword in hand. He was listening for something, something Aldara could not hear. She realised then that he was still trapped somewhere between sleep and reality. She remained still, not wanting to panic him further. He would come back to her as soon as his mind cleared. He walked back to the bed, naked, eyes blazing in the darkness.

'We need to get you out of here,' he said, looking around for her clothes.

She breathed deep and long. 'Why?'

'I need to take you somewhere safe.'

Aldara crawled across the bed towards him. 'Tyron, come here. Sit on the bed.'

He bent down and picked up her dress, then felt around with his bare foot for her undergarments. 'He's here.'

'Who is here?'

'Pollux.'

Aldara went still. She had not been prepared to hear his name. They had never spoken it between them.

'I was trying to protect you. I should have told you.'

Aldara shook her head. 'He is not here. You need to stop. Sit down so we can talk about it.'

Finding her undergarments, he bent to pick them up. 'He *is* here. Now get dressed.'

'Tyron, stop,' she said, moving towards him.

He did not see her in the darkness, and when he turned to thrust the clothing towards her, his fist made contact with her shoulder, knocking her backwards on the bed. Neither of them moved for a moment. Tyron's hands went into his hair.

'Are you all right?' he said, his voice breaking.

Aldara swallowed and sat up, staring at the black form in front of her. It had not hurt in the slightest, but it was something she had not been expecting in the middle of the night.

He lowered himself onto the bed and looked at her. 'I'm sorry, I didn't realise you were so close.'

'I moved. It's my fault,' she said, wincing at the conversation.

After a long moment, she picked up her clothes and began to dress. Tyron went to the fireplace and poked at the embers before adding a log to it. A soft glow filled the room.

'I am going to take you to your quarters,' Tyron said.

Aldara finished the buttons on her dress and looked at him. 'I can stay.'

He shook his head. 'Let's go.'

When the two of them opened the door, Pero leapt up from his cot, trying to wake himself up. Tyron said nothing, simply placed a hand on Aldara's back and the two of them continued past him.

By the time they arrived at the Companions' quarters, the sky had begun to lighten. The eerie glow of dawn filtered through the window in the corridor. They stood just outside the door, where the heat from the main room could reach them. Aldara glanced at the fire that Sapphira had built. It was still going strong. She was looking everywhere but at Tyron.

'I'm sorry,' Tyron said, watching her. 'I hope you know that I would never hurt you intentionally.'

Aldara looked at him now. 'You didn't hurt me. I was just a bit shocked.'

Tyron glanced down at the shoulder where his fist had made contact.

'Not about that,' she said, reading his thoughts. 'Is Grandor Pollux really at Archdale? I thought perhaps you were dreaming.'

His eyes went to hers. 'I think I was. But Pollux is at Archdale. They are only here a few days. I thought it might be best if you did not know.'

She hated standing so far apart, not touching. 'It was inevitable that I see him again. He is one of King Jayr's most trusted advisors. He will be at the feast tomorrow night. I will see him then.'

Tyron shook his head. 'You are not going anywhere near the man. It is bad enough that I am forced to be civil.'

Her stomach tightened as she thought about the next few days. 'I want you to know that it is my own fault that I got hurt that night.'

Tyron was silent for a moment. 'What?'

'They just wanted a good time, a Companion. And I wasn't prepared.'

He held up a hand to stop her. 'Don't—'

She kept going. 'They would not have hurt me had I just complied.'

'Aldara, stop.' He shook his head. 'I know what you are doing.'

'I just wanted to explain…'

He exhaled because he was getting worked up. 'You are

playing it down in hope of defusing me. I don't need your protection.'

She shook her head. 'I'm not—'

'You are. You are worried that I might retaliate, so you are playing down what happened.'

She crossed her arms in front of her. 'Moments ago, you were running about with a sword in your hand.'

He groaned. 'Is it so unreasonable that I want you safe?'

'Is it so surprising that I want the same for you?'

He looked down at his hands. 'You know everything, the importance of this alliance and why I cannot jeopardise it. I am in control as long as you are safe.'

She said nothing.

'I want you to remain in your quarters for now.'

She swallowed. 'For how long?'

His eyes returned to her. 'Until I tell you otherwise.' The volume of his voice made her jump. He looked away when he saw it. 'Can you please just do this for me?'

Before she had a chance to respond, Fedora appeared in the doorway, wrapped in a gown. She glanced between them and then dropped into a curtsy. 'Is everything all right, my lord?'

Tyron was silent for a moment before speaking. 'Aldara is to stay within these quarters until I tell you otherwise.'

Fedora glanced at Aldara's crossed arms. 'As you wish, my lord.'

Aldara curtsied and walked past Fedora into their quarters. She went through the main room, past the bedchamber and into the dressing room, where she collapsed into a heap on the floor.

CHAPTER 5

*T*yron and Pandarus sat on either side of their
father in the throne room. Stamitos was off
enjoying his youth, and no one had the heart to tell him
otherwise. Across the table, King Jayr was leaning back,
hands resting comfortably on the leather arms of his chair.
Tyron could not help but admire his ability to keep his face
void of expression. On King Jayr's left sat Grandor Pollux,
inked almost beyond recognition, his muscled arms resting
on the table in front of him.

Tyron glanced at his large hands before looking past
him to where two bare-armed, blank-faced Zoelin guards
stood. The number of weapons strapped to various parts
of their bodies suggested they were ready for any outcome.
Tyron's sword sat on the table to the side of him, as was
customary when meeting under peaceful circumstances.
He resisted the urge to hold it, given how disadvantaged he
already felt. His father had warned him not to speak unless
called upon. In fact, he had been warned a number of
times. He was allowed to disagree with their decisions as
long as he did so internally; the agreement was already in

place, so as far as King Zenas was concerned, further debate was just unnecessary noise.

'I trust you are pleased with the quality of women arriving at Onuric Castle?' Pandarus asked.

Tyron noticed his father shift next to him, the only evidence that playing diplomat was difficult for him as well.

'I cannot speak for all of them, I have only sampled a few,' Jayr replied. His nostrils flared at his own wit.

Pandarus coughed.

'Much of their worth is in their virtue,' Zenas said, leaning forwards. 'Your actions devalue them.'

'I would be surprised if our Asigow buyers notice or care,' Pollux replied.

Tyron closed his eyes before looking at him. 'Not only do your actions devalue the women in your care, your words devalue your buyers.'

Jayr's dark eyes went to him, but his expression did not change. Zenas glanced sideways at Tyron, a warning.

'Is there anything else you wish to discuss?' Zenas asked.

Jayr looked at him. 'Actually, there are a few more matters I wish to discuss.' He held out a hand and Pollux placed a sealed letter into it. He glanced at it before placing it down on the table and sliding it forwards without the effort of actually moving. Zenas signalled for one of his guards to retrieve it. He handed it to Pandarus, who broke the seal and scanned its contents.

'King Jayr is requesting another mentor to assist with the Companions at Onuric,' Pandarus said.

'You already have a mentor,' Tyron said, folding his arms in front of him.

Jayr spoke without meeting his eyes. 'One mentor is adequate for a handful of women. The number of women arriving at Onuric is growing. Their training is taking too long for demand.'

Tyron uncrossed his arms and leaned forwards. 'Their training? Dogs are trained, women are educated.'

'Call it whatever pleases you,' Jayr said, his expression bored.

Tyron sat back in his chair. 'Why not use your own resources? Surely you have women who can assist?'

'We have teachers of the Asigow language,' Pollux said. 'The rest they must learn from a Syrasan mentor. We are not selling them Zoelin Companions.'

Tyron pressed his hands against his thighs. 'No. You would never do that.'

'We will send another mentor,' Pandarus said, shutting the conversation down.

Zenas said nothing, his eyes on the table in front of him.

Pandarus returned to the letter. 'The second item is a request for a permanent binding of our kingdoms.' He lowered the letter and looked at Jayr. 'The trade agreement is legally binding.'

'You will forgive me for not trusting that agreement to stand on its own. You want us to fight your wars based on a trade agreement that you once broke?'

Tyron shook his head. 'We do not want you to fight our wars.'

Zenas crossed his arms in front of him. 'What is it you are actually asking for?'

Jayr signalled for a servant to fill his cup. 'I am prepared to take your daughter, Princess Cora, as my wife. She would become the Queen of Zoelin.'

'No,' Tyron and Zenas said in unison.

'Given recent events, you will understand my reluctance in handing my only daughter over to you,' Zenas continued. 'Trust works both ways.'

Tyron was relieved to hear his father finally speaking up.

Jayr nodded, clearly prepared for the response. 'I see your bond with Galen, and how hard you work at maintaining it. Prince Pandarus's recent nuptials demonstrate your commitment to a future together.'

'Syrasan and Galen ties have always been strong and mutually beneficial,' Zenas said.

Jayr gave a small shrug as he leaned back in his chair. 'Perhaps they should fight your wars, then.'

Tyron was about to speak up again but Pandarus beat him to it.

'They are a kingdom of peace. Our war with Corneo is not their fight.'

'Nor ours,' Pollux said. 'Yet we are pledging to defend your borders if there is a need.'

Tyron looked across at Pandarus, but his brother said nothing. 'We have asked nothing of you as far as I am aware. Right now, we expect you to stay on your side of the border and not terrorise our people. I think we can all agree that is progress enough.'

All eyes were on him.

'You can see why I manage relations,' Pandarus said, attempting to dissolve the building tension.

'Yes, while Prince Tyron wins your wars,' Jayr said, looking at Tyron. 'I wonder at your rumoured abilities given your incapability to separate heart and head.'

Now it was Tyron's turn to shrug. 'It is a shame you cannot ask your men, whom I slaughtered in Lirald.'

The air in the room seemed to thicken.

Zenas leaned away from the table. 'We will need time to process and discuss these new requests.'

Jayr's mouth stretched into a smile. 'Of course. You have to do what is in the best interest of your kingdom.' His tone was high and insincere.

Tyron glanced at Pandarus a final time. 'Is that all?' he asked, signalling to the letter.

Pandarus folded the paper and nodded. 'That is all.' He found a smile for the faces across from him. 'May I suggest we all rest in preparation for tonight's feast in your honour?'

Pollux nodded and removed his hands from the table, covering the arms of his chair with them. 'We are looking forward to it. You have proven yourselves to be generous hosts.'

There was something suggestive in his tone. Tyron stood and bowed. He did not wait for the meeting to conclude because he did not trust himself to remain opposite those men with his sword in reach. He scooped the weapon up from the table, making a loud screeching noise as he did so, and left with King Jayr's eyes marking his back.

CHAPTER 6

*T*yron's resolve to keep Aldara confined to her quarters lasted until he left the meeting with King Jayr and Grandor Pollux. He realised in his heightened state that the only person he wanted to see that afternoon was her. He would take her for a walk outdoors to save both their sanity and then ensure she was tucked away in her quarters before any Zoelin guests emerged for the feast. Normally Pero would have gone to fetch her, but he went himself, waiting outside the door while Fedora no doubt forced her to change her dress and pin her hair.

She emerged exactly as he had predicted: a dress too cold for the temperature, her hair smoothed into a knot, and painted lips which would unfortunately remain intact that day. She looked happy though, her eyes shining as she rose from her curtsy.

'Good afternoon, my lord.' She was aware of Fedora's proximity.

'Get a cloak. We are going outdoors.'

She smiled at him then. 'Riding?'

He was tempted to say yes just to see her smile grow. 'No, just a walk.'

They stepped outside into the courtyard where the maids were washing clothes and shooing away the chickens that threatened to soil their efforts. All conversations stopped when they spotted Tyron strolling between the wooden tubs.

'Are you trying to avoid your guests?' Aldara asked. They rarely took walks amid the laundry.

'Yes, actually.'

Aldara turned her face to the sky, but there was no sun to warm her that day. Tyron watched her for a moment before facing forwards.

'I suppose it would be inappropriate for me to ask how the meeting went,' she said, not looking at him.

'I'm still trying to process it.'

Aldara glanced down at her feet. 'Did they mention Hali?'

They had mentioned *the mentor*, but not by name. He was not sure what to tell her.

'It's all right,' she said. 'I should not have asked.'

He glanced across at her. 'You can ask me, there is just little to report.' He looked at her properly then. 'Actually, there is one thing to report. One confidential thing.'

She slowed her pace. 'You know nothing you say goes further than me.'

He stopped walking and faced her. 'Pandarus has agreed to send another mentor to assist Hali.'

Aldara was quiet as she thought this through. 'Part of me wants to object, and the other part of me feels grateful that she will not be alone in that place. Who will he send?'

They walked again.

'One of the noble Companions, I imagine. I cannot see

him handing Astra over. Who is your least favourite? I'll put in a good word.'

Aldara smiled and looked across at him. 'Was that a joke? Has the outdoors improved your mood enough to make jokes?'

'A rather tasteless joke, I suppose. I'm guessing none of them will volunteer for the role.'

Aldara thought for a moment. 'Becoming a mentor is what they hope for. Mentors are Companion royalty.'

He laughed at this. 'Are *you* making jokes now?'

'No. It's what Idalia wanted.'

The smile left Tyron's face. When he looked up, he stopped walking, reaching out a hand in front of Aldara to stop her. Grandor Pollux was striding towards them, flanked by a guard. Aldara followed his gaze, and then he heard her sharp intake of breath.

'Go,' Tyron whispered, taking his hand away. But it was too late. Pollux's figure cast a shadow across them.

Aldara lowered into a curtsy. When she returned upright, Pollux's eyes were on her face, studying her.

'I remember you,' he said. 'The first woman to win the flag tournament.' His head swung to the guard behind him. 'Not the first to flee my bed.'

The guard glanced at her, a hint of a smile on his face. Tyron stiffened next to her.

'Welcome back to Archdale, Grandor Pollux. Your memory serves you well.' She was surprised at how poised she remained with her insides screaming.

'You should get back,' Tyron said to her. 'I have kept you from your lessons long enough.'

She glanced at Tyron and then curtsied again. 'Enjoy your stay, Grandor Pollux.'

His eyes travelled down her. 'Will I see you at the feast this evening?'

'No.' Tyron stepped in front of her. 'You will not be seeing her at the feast tonight, or any other night.'

Pollux's gaze shifted to Tyron, remaining there as he comprehended the message. 'What a shame. She was *very* accommodating during my last visit.'

Tyron was still, as though trying to decide his next move. At some point in the conversation, his hand had moved to his sword. It was not a loose grip.

Aldara realised she had stopped breathing. When she tried to force a breath, she struggled with it. She tried again, but her lungs seemed to have closed. 'Excuse me,' she said, curtsying. Without waiting for a reply, she turned and walked towards the castle, stepping around the tubs of lye and cold water, startling the maids as she rushed past them. She stepped inside the empty laundry room and tried to take in a lungful of air. Panic hit her. She could not breathe. She placed a hand against the cold stone wall to steady herself, gasping as she tried to draw breath. The noise coming from her reminded her of the nights that Tyron had woken from sleep claiming the room was filled with smoke. It had all been in his mind as it was in hers now.

She pulled at the neck of her dress and sank to the floor. She looked about for help and Tyron stepped into view. Tears of relief fell when she saw him.

'What's wrong?' he asked, crouching in front of her.

'I can't breathe.' Her voice came out as a hoarse whisper. She pulled at the neck of her dress again.

Tyron reached out and tore the neck of her dress, sending buttons flying in all directions. 'You need to slow your breathing,' he said, speaking firmly but remaining calm. 'Slower.'

Aldara's eyes locked onto his as she tried to follow his instructions.

'That's it.' He breathed slowly, encouraging her to keep time with him. 'Through your nose.'

More tears fell down her face as small amounts of air reached her lungs. 'I'm sorry,' she said between breaths. 'I don't know what happened.'

He sat next to her and rested his back against the wall. 'Are you all right?'

She nodded as she continued to breathe deeply. Everything inside of her slowed, and her vision began to return to normal. Tyron put his arm around her and pulled her across to rest against him. They sat in silence, staring in different directions, trapped in separate thoughts. Two maids walked in, each holding one end of a tub. When they noticed Tyron and Aldara slumped on the floor, surrounded by burst buttons, they backed out through the door.

Tyron stretched his legs out and guided Aldara's head onto his lap. She turned so she could look up at him. He was a mirrored reflection of how miserable she felt in that moment.

'Where is Grandor Pollux?' she asked.

'He's alive, if that's what you're asking.' He brushed a few stray tears from her face and let out a noisy breath. 'This is no way for you to live.'

Her eyes searched his face, trying to read his thoughts instead of having to interpret the few words he offered. 'I panicked. I'm sorry.'

'Stop apologising as though it were a choice.' He removed his hand but his eyes remained on her. 'I understand better than anyone.' He hesitated. 'Why did you panic? He will never touch you again.'

She blinked and the remaining tears ran into her hair. 'I know. It was just a lot of thoughts and feelings all at once. And the last thing I want is to cause problems for you.'

His hand returned to her cheek. 'Let me worry about my problems.'

'It doesn't work that way between us. It never has.'

He combed her hair with his fingers. 'No, it hasn't.'

She reached up and put her hand inside his. 'When he leaves, everything will be as it was.'

He shook his head. 'Until the next thing. There will always be something for you to fear.'

She pushed herself up into a sitting position and took hold of his face. 'There is something to fear in every life. At least here I have you.'

'Do you?'

Her hands fell away. 'Don't shut me out again. I see the workings of your mind. You think by separating yourself it somehow protects me, but it only isolates me. Promise me you will not shut me out because of one moment of panic.'

His mouth was tight, eyes shiny. He looked at her for the longest time before speaking. 'There is no shutting you out, even if I wanted to.' He picked up her hands and returned them to his face. 'Though it kills me to see you gasping for breath because you are afraid. I should have cut his throat when it happened.'

She shook her head. 'You do something that requires far more strength. You put the needs of your kingdom ahead of your own impulses. And you must continue to do so.'

'And what will you do?'

She blinked. 'Whatever I am told.'

'Liar.' He watched her face for a moment. 'Even if you did as you are told, is that how you want to live?'

Another maid walked in, humming to herself as she hung a pair of wooden tongs on the wall. She turned around and wiped her hands on her apron. When she saw them, the tune stopped, she curtsied, mumbled an apology, and fled.

'Let's get you to your quarters.' Tyron said the words, but still he did not move.

Aldara did not move either. She did not want to return to the Companions' quarters and spend another night alone while the rest of the castle attended the feast. 'Perhaps I should just come tonight. It feels ridiculous to hide away.'

Tyron shook his head. 'Absolutely not. I cannot spend the entire night watching you.'

'You once admitted to spending the entire night watching me.'

Finally, a hint of a smile from him.

'Actually, I need to spend more nights in my own bed,' she said, putting some distance between them.

'Why is that?' he asked, pulling her close again.

'The others have started making jokes about the fact that I'm never there. Sapphira told me a few days back that the king has a new Companion who sleeps in my bed, and that I should come by and meet her some time.'

Tyron laughed. 'She is like the female version of Stamitos. A troublemaker. That's why he is so besotted.'

The sound of his rare laughter relaxed her. 'Do you like her?'

He leaned forwards and kissed her. 'It does not matter if I like her. I can see you like her, and that is enough.'

Aldara's eyes were on his lips. 'She is refreshingly honest.' Her gaze went up to meet his. 'Hali liked her.'

Tyron nodded and threaded his hand through hers. 'I hate seeing that pained expression on your face every time you say her name. I wish I could bring her back for you.'

Her expression softened because she knew he meant it. He would do anything within his power if he thought it would bring her some comfort or happiness. 'I know you do. It's one of the many reasons I... think so highly of you.'

They watched one another for a moment.

'I hope you know I think highly of you also,' he said, amusement in his eyes.

She leaned forwards so her face was in front of his. 'So much... mutual regard.'

He cupped her face and kissed her again. 'Yes. So much.'

CHAPTER 7

*E*ldoris was nervous from the moment Stamitos asked to speak with them alone. As she stood waiting inside Zenas's bedchamber, feeling lost in the large space, there was a tightness in her hands and jaw. When her husband's personal esquire finished the buttons on his tunic, Zenas waved him out of the room and turned to face her. Nowadays they spoke in the solar or the throne room. The presence of the bed unsettled them both. She tried to remember how long it had been since she had visited it.

'I thought you would be preparing for the feast,' Zenas said, breaking the silence.

She glanced down at his red tunic. It was the second time the seamstress had let it out that season. 'Stamitos insisted it could not wait.'

Zenas brushed non-existent lint off his sleeve. 'It never can with him.'

She could not argue with that. Whenever Stamitos wanted to discuss something in private, they usually finished the meeting with their heads in a spin. It had been that way since Stamitos's infancy, stemming from his

48

desperate need to come of age, to have the same freedoms as his older brothers. But he still had an adolescent mind, and his actions showed a lack of maturity for a man in his twentieth year.

The door swung open, relieving them of each other's company.

A guard stepped into the room and bowed. 'Prince Stamitos, Your Majesty.'

'Send him in,' Zenas said. He glanced at his wife and gestured towards the chair by the wall.

'I shall stand,' she replied.

Stamitos bounded into the room like an excited hound. Eldoris glanced at her husband before kissing her son. She was still not used to the fact that he had to bend slightly so she could reach him. It seemed just a few years before that she had gathered him on her lap to read him tales.

He clapped his hands together and looked between them. She tried to guess what he was about to say. His carefree eyes gazed at her, a smile always lingering beneath them.

'All right,' Zenas said. 'What was so urgent that it could not wait until tomorrow?'

A full smile broke across Stamitos's face. 'You needn't appear so terrified, Mother.'

She tried to mirror the expression. 'Forgive me, but the last time we spoke like this, you wanted to go north and fight alongside your brother.'

'And Father sent me south.'

'To protect Syrasan's borders,' Zenas said.

'From whom?' His smile was fading. 'I'm not entirely convinced the king of Braul even has an army.'

Eldoris's eyebrows came together. 'You are not experienced enough to fight Zoelin men.'

'I will never be experienced enough if you do not let me

gain experience.' His eyes remained warm despite his complaint.

'What do you want to discuss?' Zenas asked, moving the conversation along.

The smile returned to Stamitos's face. 'Marriage.'

Eldoris felt as though her insides were falling. 'What about marriage?'

'I would like to marry.' He looked at Zenas. 'I want you to hear me out before you object to my choice of wife.'

Eldoris glanced at her husband before asking the next question, the one she already knew the answer to. 'Who is it you are wanting to marry?'

He laughed. 'Who do you think? Sapphira.'

The realisation that she would be partly responsible for the breaking of his heart was almost too much.

'Stamitos, you cannot marry the girl,' Zenas said.

He nodded, but it was not in agreement. 'Because she is not of noble blood?'

'That is one reason. Your older siblings are yet to marry.'

Stamitos shook his head. 'So, I cannot marry until my siblings are married? Did you just make that rule up?'

Eldoris swallowed. 'Stamitos, she is a Companion. You know how marriage works for members of the royal family. Unions need to benefit the kingdom, not individuals.'

He turned and looked at her, his head still shaking. 'I am furthest from the throne. I will never be king. My choice of wife is irrelevant.'

'It is most certainly not irrelevant,' Zenas said.

Stamitos was not finished. 'Even if by some miracle I became king, Sapphira would be the fiercest queen this kingdom has ever known.'

Eldoris raised an eyebrow. 'I do not doubt that. The girl

is… spirited. However, she would never be accepted as queen because she is common.'

They were all silent for a moment.

'I love her,' Stamitos said. 'More than I could have thought possible.

Something pulled in her chest at hearing her son speak those words. 'I know.'

'I don't think you do. It has been that way from the first time I saw her.'

'I believe you.'

He stared at her for a moment. 'Then how could I ever marry another?'

Zenas answered for her. 'Your loyalty to Syrasan and your king will aid you. Sapphira does not expect to marry you. She knows how it is,' he added. 'I am guessing she is not aware this conversation is taking place, or she would have talked you out of it.'

Stamitos looked down at his feet.

Eldoris stepped forwards and placed a hand on his arm. 'I am sorry we cannot give the answer you seek. There are traditions we are obliged to uphold.'

He withdrew from her touch. 'Thank you both for your time.'

'Stamitos, let us finish the conversation before you storm off,' Zenas said.

He shook his head again. 'I am not storming off. You have answered my question. I shall see you at the feast this evening.' He gave a small bow.

'Stamitos,' Eldoris called to his back.

He was already opening the door, and a few moments later it closed behind him. Eldoris and Zenas looked at one another, joined in their son's pain.

'They cannot marry,' Zenas said.

She nodded, and her husband turned away and picked

up his sword, a ridiculous display of craftsmanship that would hinder him if it were ever needed.

'He is not the only one who has developed feelings for his Companion, but I imagine you know that,' he said.

She wished he would meet her eyes when they were discussing their children. 'Yes, I know. But Tyron will do the right thing in the end. Stamitos has never been one for following the rules. How many times did we send men out to search for him as a child?'

'He is thirsty for experience. Always has been.'

'Unfortunately, that makes him reckless.'

Zenas was silent while he thought. 'I have an idea,' he said, looking at her now. 'But he will not like it.'

She had known there was no easy fix for the situation. 'If you send her away, he will go after her.'

'Let it be temporary, then. Some distance will clear his head.'

She watched him with scepticism. 'I am not convinced that it will.'

'I was a young boy once. He cannot see clearly with her in his vision.'

'Stamitos is a different boy to you. He feels a sense of loyalty to her.'

They looked at one another for a long moment. She had not been trying to point out his indiscretions, but there they were, lingering in the wide space between them.

'His feelings may change,' she continued, graciously trying to spare him the shame. 'You cannot imagine feeling any other way when you are that age.'

He nodded, eyes returning to his sword. 'A temporary relocation of the girl and he will see sense again.'

'Are you prepared for his reaction when you tell him?'

He looked at her. 'We will tell him after it is done.'

A sadness came over her. 'And are you prepared for how much he will resent us?'

His lips pressed together beneath his beard. 'I have grown immune to resentment.'

She was unsure if the comment was directed at her but chose to ignore it regardless. 'I suggest you tell no one of your plans other than Pandarus. Stamitos has many who are loyal to him.'

Zenas nodded. 'The sooner Pandarus produces an heir, the safer the throne will be.'

Eldoris tried not to wince at his words. That was what her family had been reduced to—talking about "heirs" instead of grandchildren. 'I shall see you at the feast,' she said, turning away.

He nodded and said nothing. By the time she left his chambers, nausea had gripped her. She knew her husband's plan would not end well for their son, or the woman he wanted to marry.

CHAPTER 8

Tyron could barely keep up with the lies during his father's speech. They sounded rehearsed and strange coming from a man who had raised him on principles of honesty. King Jayr stood alongside him, his guards hidden in the shadows so they would not raise suspicion among the noblemen and the wives who had attended to get a glimpse of the Zoelin king. Tyron looked about, trying to read the expressions of the men who had pledged their lives to Syrasan and its king. He wondered if their thoughts matched their faces, if they bought the deception being sold to them.

'I hope you will all join me in thanking King Jayr, not only for rescuing Syrasan's children from the hands of violent rebels, but for recognising an opportunity, a way to help Syrasan's poor. Young Syrasan women will now have the opportunities usually only afforded a selected few. Not only does the Companion trade bring with it an ally who will stand alongside us should Corneo rise again, but it also ensures that Syrasan families have options other than starvation during periods of famine.'

Tyron glanced at Leksi, who stood next to him. Leksi knew better than to look back at him.

'To King Jayr of Zoelin,' Pandarus shouted from behind the high table, raising his cup.

'To King Jayr,' Leksi said, lifting his with the rest of the guests.

Tyron raised his cup to his mouth and said nothing. As he drank, his eyes met Jayr's, who had been watching him throughout the toast.

'I don't know how you do it,' Tyron said, turning back at Leksi.

'Do what?'

'Play along.'

'We are all playing along. Every man here.'

Tyron turned his back to the high table so Jayr could not lip-read their conversation. 'I cannot play along with this.'

Leksi took a large drink before looking at him. 'The fight is over. The children have been returned, and the trade agreement is already in action. What other outcome are you hoping for at this point?'

Tyron shook his head. 'One where King Jayr remains in his kingdom and Syrasan women remain here.'

Leksi picked up a jar of wine, smelled it, and then filled his cup. 'You are forgetting about the families who are starving to death. Your father said one honest thing in his speech—this gives the poor more options.'

'Why do you smell the wine? You know nothing of its quality from taste, let alone scent.'

'I was making sure it was not water. The servants like to trick you, leaving you with a cup full of wine-flavoured water that you must either drink or abandon as you try to locate the wine.'

Tyron took the jar from him and filled his own cup.

'The families selling their daughters have no idea where they will end up. Once the coin is handed over, it is out of their control.'

Leksi placed a hand on Tyron's shoulder. 'I agree. But at the very least, they know their daughters will be fed.'

Pandarus had stepped down from his podium, walking past his wife, who remained seated. She did not want to walk the room, socialising alongside her husband. Tyron did not blame her.

'An excellent speech,' Pandarus said, joining them.

Tyron's cup went to his mouth so he would not have to comment. He noticed his mother heading for the door. She enjoyed these occasions about as much as he did. Stamitos and Sapphira had slipped from the room at the beginning of the speech, his father's disapproving gaze following them across the room until they were out of sight.

Tyron's eyes rested on Pollux, who was standing with Cora. Pollux bent down to her when he spoke, at one point getting so close that his lips brushed her hair. Her feet remained still, her face poised. Only her rigid posture gave any sign that she was uncomfortable.

Leksi gestured to her. 'I think your sister needs saving.'

Pandarus looked over to where the two of them stood. Pollux had taken hold of her hand and was studying her palm. She glanced across at them, her face slack from too much wine.

'Cora is a smart girl. She can handle herself with any man.'

Tyron went still and stared at his brother. 'This man is different and you know it.'

'I have to agree,' Leksi said.

Pandarus waved a hand at him. 'You agree with everything he says, no matter the subject. And do not think it is lost on me that you have desired her since you were ten years old.'

'Actually, I was nine,' Leksi replied, feigning offence. 'An early bloomer.'

Pandarus ignored him and looked back at Tyron. 'You need to stop fussing over the women in this castle and allow them to perform their roles. Pollux is important enough to have his pick of anyone here.'

'She is our sister,' Tyron said, still not moving. 'You can go and put an end to it, or I can.'

Pandarus smiled, playing it down. 'What are you talking about? She is having a conversation and is free to walk away at any time.'

Tyron's hand went to his sword, and he turned as though to walk over there. Leksi placed a firm hand on his shoulder. Pandarus looked between them, bewildered.

'Clearly my brother has had too much to drink,' Pandarus said. 'Get him out of here before he makes a scene.'

Tyron swallowed and put his cup on the table, the noise making those nearby stop their conversations and glance in his direction. He pulled himself free from Leksi's grip and looked once again at Pollux. The man did not even glance in his direction, yet Jayr's eyes seemed to never leave him. It was almost as if he were waiting for an incident.

'No Syrasan woman, Companion or otherwise, leaves this room with that man. If I find out that anyone other than his king has visited his chambers, I will kill him. Do you understand?' He waited for his brother to answer.

Pandarus's gaze shifted between him and Leksi before giving a small nod. Only then did Tyron head out of the room, walking straight past the guests without so much as a polite smile in their direction. He passed the guards in the doorway and kept walking. Leksi followed.

'Tyron, stop,' Leksi called after him. 'Where are you going?'

'She remains with me until they leave the castle,' he called over his shoulder.

The fact that Pandarus was happy to offer up their sister as a muse did not sit well with Tyron. His boots clicked against the stone floor as he strode down the corridor of the north wing, sword swinging at his hip. He walked straight into the Companions' quarters, startling a maid who was tending to the fire.

'My lord,' said the maid, scurrying to her feet and falling into a curtsy.

Tyron walked straight past her, through the other door and down the small passage to the bedchamber. When he got there, he found Aldara asleep in her bed and Fedora seated at a small table at the far end of the room. She looked up from the letter she was writing and stood. Placing a finger over her lips, she gestured for him to step out of the room. His gaze went to Aldara, curled up like a child with her hair sprawled about her, as he followed Fedora out into the passageway.

'My lord,' Fedora said. 'What are you doing here?'

He glanced across at Aldara. 'I would like Aldara to come to my chambers. I would feel better if she is with me until they leave.'

Fedora's face remained impassive. 'If that is your wish.'

'You disagree?' he asked, doubting his ability to make rational decisions.

Fedora smiled at him. 'I understand that it would make you feel more comfortable. However, she is already asleep, and I am not going anywhere.'

He nodded. He had not considered the fact that Aldara

might be alarmed if she were woken in the middle of the night. 'She could not breathe today. We ran into Grandor Pollux on our walk and... she literally could not breathe.'

Fedora was silent for a moment. 'She panicked.'

'Did she tell you?'

'Of course not. She would never want to appear weak in my eyes. However, it is understandable given everything that took place between them.' She gave a tight smile. 'I suppose that explains the ruined dress I had to send off to the seamstress.'

He raised his eyebrows. 'I am surprised you did not ask her what happened to it.'

'As you can imagine, she is not the first girl to return here with buttons missing from her gown.'

His eyes went to his feet. 'I see.' He pushed his toes into the floor before looking up again. 'Do you ever sleep?'

She smiled, a hint of fatigue showing on her unpainted face. 'Not this night, my lord.'

His eyes returned to Aldara. 'That makes two of us.'

CHAPTER 9

The morning after the feast, Aldara woke early to the creak of beds around her. She opened her eyes. It was still dark. Across from her she could see Violeta and Panthea, faces scrubbed clean and lit by candlelight. They had stripped to their undergarments, not bothering with nightdresses. Panthea blew out the candle and slipped into her bed.

Aldara sat up. 'Where is Rhea?' she whispered, gazing at the empty beds around her.

Violeta struggled to comprehend the question under the fog of wine. 'With King Jayr,' she mumbled before falling onto her pillow and pulling the blankets up over her head. The conversation was over.

Aldara tried to gauge the time. Fedora's curtain was still pulled across, so she knew it was before dawn. Her mentor never slept in. Knowing she would not be able to go back to sleep, Aldara got out of bed and pulled her robe around her. She was careful not to disturb the others, though she suspected she would not have been able to even if she tried. She wandered to the bathing room where she washed her face and cleaned her teeth. Waiting for the water to boil took too long, so she used cold water, enjoying how awake she felt afterwards.

Once dressed, she crept back past the bedchamber and went to the main room where she added a few small logs to the fire. She sat on the floor in front of it, watching the flames grow hungry. When the cold from the floor seeped through her dress, she stood up and glanced at the doorway that opened to the corridor. She wandered over and peered outside, expecting to see nothing but grey light and shadows. Instead, a guard stood at the door. He glanced at her before resuming his position. She backed away, colliding with Fedora. She spun around to face her.

'Sorry, my lady. Why is there a guard at the door?'

'Prince Tyron's request,' Fedora replied, folding her hands in front of her.

Aldara was about to ask why when she realised she knew the answer. Tyron would not take risks when it came to her safety. If he could not be with her overnight, he would take whatever precautions in his means to ensure she was protected by someone in his absence.

A messenger arrived at the door and the guard stepped in front of him.

'It is all right,' Fedora called to the guard. 'He is one of the king's messengers.'

The guard did not move. 'My orders were that no one enters these rooms who is not a Companion,' he said.

If Fedora was annoyed, she did not show it as she stepped past him into the corridor to collect the message from the boy. He handed her a sealed letter.

'A message from His Majesty the King, requiring your urgent attention,' said the boy. He bowed and then left without saying another word.

Fedora stepped back into the room and broke the seal

with her thumb before unfolding the paper. Whatever its contents, it had her full attention. Aldara could not tell whether it was a long note or if she was rereading the same words over and over.

'Is everything all right, my lady?'

Fedora looked up and closed the letter. 'Yes. I am to meet with the king.'

Aldara glanced down at the letter pressed against Fedora's stomach. 'Does the letter say why?' She guessed by Fedora's whitening fingers that it was not a social visit. The information Tyron had shared in private came to mind. One of the noble Companions would be going to Onuric, and there was every chance that when she woke the following morning, they would be one down. She reminded herself that it meant Hali would have someone with her, and then she immediately felt guilty. Being a Companion under King Jayr's rule would be a harsh existence for any woman.

'Never mind,' Fedora said. 'Prince Tyron will be by this morning to collect you for a ride.'

'You spoke with him?'

'Yes, he came by last night.'

Her eyes widened. 'He did? What did he say?'

Fedora's expression did not change. 'That he would take you riding in the morning. Make sure you are ready. And help the other women as they return from their evenings.'

Aldara nodded. 'Of course.'

After Fedora had disappeared through the doorway, on her way to carry out King Zenas's wishes, Aldara stared out into the empty corridor, pushing down the nausea rising in her throat.

~

'Why are you chewing on your lip?' Tyron asked. He could see her mind in action. They had dismounted and were letting the horses drink from the river. It was not really a river though, more of a stream with moss-covered rocks and a collection of forest debris, designed to carry the melting snow away before disappearing with the warmer weather.

She released her lip. 'Lost in my thoughts. Sorry.' She leaned against Loda and looked at him. 'You have said little about the feast. Was it bearable?'

His eyes shifted to the water. 'Are any of them bearable?'

She smiled. 'Did Lord Yuri attend?'

He could barely remember who had attended outside of the Zoelin guests. 'I wasn't taking much notice, if I'm honest. You are rather fond of him, aren't you?'

She pulled Loda's head up from the stream to prevent her from drinking too much. 'Yes. He's one of the kinder ones.'

'He is a dying breed,' he said, squinting against the glare.

Aldara studied him. 'Did you sleep last night?'

'A little.'

'A little?'

'A little.' He could feel her eyes on him, searching beneath the surface.

'Do you need more, perhaps?'

She adjusted a strap on Loda's bridle before planting a kiss on the mare's face. Her braid had come undone. He watched as she tucked the loose strands behind her ears.

'I've told you before, I don't sleep well without you.'

She glanced at him, trying not to appear too pleased. 'Don't resent me, but I had one of the best sleeps I have had in a long time.'

'Ouch. Would it kill you to just to say, "I missed you too"?'

She gave Loda's reins a tug and led the mare closer to him. Otus almost knocked her sideways with his muzzle while attempting to gain her affections. She laughed and rubbed his head. 'I don't want to lie.' She pressed her lips together to stop from smiling. 'What I do miss though are our rides to the meadow in the warm season.'

He had vivid memories of her lying in the long grass, her dress undone, his hands roaming beneath it. 'Yes. Winter rides seem rather dull in comparison.'

She stepped closer to Loda's saddle and looked at him. 'Aren't you going to help me mount?'

He remained still, watching her. 'You don't need help.'

She turned to face the mare. 'I might today.'

He let go of his horse and stepped behind her. She shifted her weight so her back brushed against him. The breeze carried her scent. He moved closer, placing his hands on her waist. She pushed back a little so she was pressed against him. They stood still. He felt primal in that moment, teetering on the edge of his self-control, her breath steady, his catching a little. She tilted her head and his eyes moved to her exposed neck. He lowered his mouth to it. The moment his lips made contact, her eyes closed and her head rolled back against him. She reached a hand up and threaded it through his hair. His hands responded by sliding upwards, and he felt her body soften beneath them. Before she had a chance to completely undo him, he slid his hands down and gripped her hips, lifting her into the air. She opened her eyes and grabbed hold of the saddle as he placed her into it, then collected the reins and offered them to her. Her eyes went to his hands, no longer on her.

'What are you doing?' she asked.

He placed the reins in her hands. 'Taking you back to

my bed.' He turned from her, walked over to his horse, and mounted.

Her eyes followed him, her head shaking. 'Why the big wait?'

A large breath of pent-up tension came from him. 'Because the things I want to do to you cannot be done here. You will freeze.'

'I was feeling rather warm.'

He studied her expression. She had almost driven him to a point where he was prepared to pull her from her horse and have her in the mud. 'Just to be clear, we are returning to the castle and going straight to my chambers. You will not wash or change your dress, or do any of the other unnecessary things that Fedora makes you do. Do you understand?'

She suppressed a smile. 'Yes, my lord.'

He looked away and pushed his horse into a walk. Aldara rode alongside him.

'Can I send a message to Sapphira when we arrive at Archdale? I told her yesterday that I would accompany her to the butts this afternoon for archery practice, once you had released me from confinement,' she teased.

He glanced at her before nodding. 'Of course. But I think you will find that Stamitos is eager to spend time with her this afternoon once Fedora releases *her* from confinement.'

The playful expression fell from Aldara's face as she looked across at him. 'What do you mean? Sapphira was still with Stamitos when we left for our ride.'

He shook his head. 'No, I ate with Stamitos this morning. Sapphira was collected from his bed just after dawn.'

'Collected from his bed? By whom?'

'Fedora.'

Aldara stopped her horse.

When Tyron noticed, he stopped his also and turned in the saddle to look at her. 'What is it?' He could see her thinking.

'Fedora went to meet with the king this morning.'

He waited. 'And?'

'And then Fedora went to collect Sapphira from Stamitos's bed. Neither of them returned to the Companions' quarters.'

He blinked at her. 'What are you worried about?'

'You told me that Pandarus agreed to send another mentor to Onuric. Is it possible that they are sending Sapphira?'

'No,' Tyron said, shaking his head. But even as he said the word, he could see why they would do exactly that.

'Fedora does not pull Companions from the beds of the men who own them,' Aldara said, her tone almost pleading.

He realised that Stamitos had not been given a good reason for the separation that morning. His brother had seemed put out by the lack of explanation. 'How fast can you ride?'

She tilted her head. 'Faster than you if the flag tournament is anything to go by.'

He dug his heels into his horse and Otus lurched into a canter. Aldara followed close behind. He had a sinking realisation that he was being kept in the dark once again. But this time, the fallout would be closer to home.

CHAPTER 10

yron walked into the throne room without waiting to be announced. The guard at the door ran after him, but seeing King Zenas's resigned expression, he stepped outside and closed the door. Zenas and Pandarus were seated at one end of the large table, a foot resting upon a leg in a casual manner reserved for family. Tyron knew he had to be careful in how this played out, as he had Aldara to consider. If his father was sending away his sons' Companions without their knowledge, that left her vulnerable.

'What is it?' Pandarus said, not moving.

Tyron took a seat next to him to demonstrate a calm state of mind. 'Has Stamitos's Companion been sent to Onuric?'

'Why do you ask?'

That was all Tyron needed to hear to know it was true. He had already been to the Companions' quarters to see if Sapphira had returned there since their departure. Fedora had explained that she was not permitted to answer questions on the matter. He had seen out of the corner of his eye the change in Aldara's posture at hearing those words. The slight bend of her shoulders as her insides fell. How much more would she lose to the life he had inflicted on her?

Zenas looked at Tyron, saying nothing.

'More secrets, more silence. When will it end? What mess am I to clean up this time?'

'Stop being dramatic,' Pandarus said. 'We could not very well tell you and not Stamitos. You have made it clear where your loyalties lie.'

'With my kingdom. That is why I am here with you and not knocking down the door of Stamitos's chamber. One of you had better explain what is going on.'

'Careful when addressing your king, brother. We would not want to see that temper of yours getting you into trouble.'

Zenas cleared his throat. 'That is quite enough, Pandarus.' He exhaled and looked at Tyron. 'Does it really need explaining? The boy was attached. I saw an opportunity to salvage the situation.'

'Attached? You object to them seeming attached?'

Zenas pulled a handkerchief from his pocket and pressed it to his brow. 'He wanted to marry the girl.'

Tyron leaned back in his chair and crossed his arms. 'That is ridiculous. Who told you that?'

'Stamitos,' Pandarus said. 'He asked permission himself.'

Tyron said nothing. It was one thing to want it, but quite another to ask for it. 'He said nothing to me of marriage.'

'He said nothing to me either, but that doesn't mean I did not know. You have seen them together. They are hardly discreet.'

Tyron looked at his father. 'So, you just sent her away, problem solved?'

'Hardly,' Zenas replied. 'The arrangement may be temporary. We can discuss her return when Stamitos begins to see sense again. I had to act in his best interests.'

'Which translates to Syrasan's best interests,' Pandarus added.

'Yes, thank you for explaining the workings of a monarch.'

Pandarus shrugged. 'Well, sometimes I wonder at your understanding.'

Zenas put up a hand to silence them both. 'God help this kingdom when I am in my early grave thanks to the two of you.'

Tyron leaned forwards. 'He will go after her. As soon as he finds out, he will go after her.'

'He will not get past the gate,' Pandarus said. 'The guards have been informed.'

Tyron sat up and looked at his brother. 'A gate and a few guards will not keep him in. I hope you have a backup plan.'

'The girl is halfway to the border by now. We will speak to Stamitos once she has crossed into Zoelin.'

Tyron shook his head. 'Stamitos will not care about borders. He will cross into Zoelin if he is forced to.'

'And how do you know all of this?' Pandarus said, appearing amused.

Tyron's eyes remained on his father. 'Because it's what I would do.'

The room went quiet. Tyron realised that his admittance had probably only pushed Aldara further into their sights.

A knock came on the door and a guard entered. 'Her Majesty the Queen.'

Eldoris rushed into the room before Zenas had a chance to accept her. She was flushed and out of breath.

'What is it?' Zenas said, moving around the table towards her.

She took a few breaths before speaking. 'It is Stamitos. He knows.'

'Get more men on the gate,' Pandarus shouted at the guard.

'It is too late for that,' Eldoris said. 'He is already through, and he is going to get himself killed.'

Zenas looked at Pandarus. 'Go after him. Make sure you find him before he finds the girl.' His gaze shifted to Tyron. 'Let Pandarus do the talking. You get everyone back to Archdale in one piece.'

Tyron was already running from the room.

Tyron asked for the fastest horse. He did not care who it belonged to. It turned out to be the second fastest horse, as Stamitos had made the same request minutes earlier and was now galloping towards trouble. Tyron sent Pero to find Leksi, requesting that his friend join them on the road as soon as he was able. He would have preferred to wait for him given what they potentially faced, but every moment they lost put them another moment behind.

The portcullis went up and the horses galloped through it. The guards stepped back, ensuring they were clear of the charging horses. Tyron went a little faster, hoping to make up the lost time, but there was no way they could maintain that speed over a long distance. He suspected that Stamitos would ride his horse to its death in his attempt to catch Sapphira before she reached the border. He also knew that Stamitos would cross the river if he made it that far. What power did a body of water hold when you were no longer playing by the rules? The bridge was unguarded, a statement of trust between the kingdoms. It left both kingdoms vulnerable.

'Tyron!'

Tyron glanced over his shoulder at the sound of Leksi's voice. He slowed his horse to a canter so Leksi could catch up. Pandarus's tiring gelding slowed as well.

'Stamitos has a much bigger problem now that I know who took my horse,' Leksi shouted over the clap of hooves. 'If my mare pulls up lame, I will beat your brother with the expensive bridle he also stole.'

They dug their heels into the horses, speeding up again, their eyes forwards, searching round each bend. They stuck to the main road as it was the most direct route, the route King Jayr and his men would take and therefore the route Stamitos would follow. They rode side by side, saying nothing of their tiring horses and growing thirst. Tyron glanced across at Pandarus who sat tilted forwards in his saddle, no doubt calculating every possible outcome. The king had sent him to act in the best interests of Syrasan, and sent Tyron to act in the best interests of his son. The two were not compatible.

'What exactly is the plan?' Leksi shouted.

Tyron turned his head towards him. 'The Zoelin men leave with Sapphira, we leave with Stamitos. Everyone remains alive.'

'Sounds simple enough,' Leksi said, humour in his tone. 'How many in the party?'

'Grandor Pollux and a guard,' Pandarus said.

Leksi looked at Tyron. 'You should have brought more men.'

Tyron was about to agree with him when a group of horses came into view. They were stopped in the middle of the road. Pandarus raised a hand and the three of them slowed to a walk. Tyron recognised Stamitos upon Leksi's prize mare, sword in hand, face contorted as he shouted his demands at the men. Lord Pollux sat relaxed in the saddle, calmly observing him. Sapphira sat on horseback a short distance away, blocked by the Zoelin guard who accompanied them.

Leksi glanced once more at Tyron. 'Pollux leaves with the girl, we leave with Stamitos. Right?'

'And I do the talking,' Pandarus said. 'Bind Stamitos if you have to.'

Tyron could only nod. He was imagining Aldara seated on that horse, blocked by that guard. He knew the lengths he would go to for her.

Their plan was hopeless.

CHAPTER 11

'Stamitos! Put your sword away. You are scaring our friends,' Pandarus said as the three of them approached. He kept his tone light.

Stamitos did not look away from Pollux. He was too well-trained. The three men stopped their horses a short distance from the group.

'I must apologise,' Pandarus continued. 'My brother was not informed of the arrangement. As you are aware, the girl is his Companion.'

Pollux glanced at Pandarus and then let his eyes settle back on Stamitos. One inked hand held the reins, the other resting on the top of his leg, near his sword. He did not appear alarmed by the confrontation, but he was ready. Tyron looked at Sapphira, whose chest was rising and falling at a fast speed. She glanced at him, a helpless expression on her face, and then returned her attention to Stamitos. She had the sense to remain quiet.

'I think it is time you shared your plans with your brother before I get *my* sword out,' Pollux said.

Pandarus moved his horse forwards a few paces. 'Stamitos, put your sword away so I can talk to you.'

Stamitos shook his head. 'There is nothing to talk about. It was a misunderstanding. Sapphira returns with me.'

Pollux inhaled and glanced at the guard who was watching Stamitos with the same bored expression. 'I follow the orders of my king. When he tells me to return the girl to you, I will return the girl to you. For now, my orders are to escort the girl to Onuric Castle. And you are delaying me.'

'You are not listening,' Stamitos said. 'The girl is returning with me to Archdale.'

'Stamitos,' Tyron said, his voice soft. 'You need to put the sword away.'

Stamitos looked away from Pollux for the first time, a fleeting glance in Tyron's direction. The first indication that someone was getting through to him. 'Tyron, you know I will not leave here without her. Tell him.'

Sapphira tried to move her horse around the guard and he immediately blocked her with his own. 'It's all right,' she called to Stamitos. 'It's a temporary arrangement. Let me go with them.'

Stamitos laughed. 'Who told you that? Fedora? If you leave with these men, we will never see each other again.'

She swallowed and looked to Tyron for help. He was trying to think of a way to get through to his brother, but before he had a chance to speak, Pollux said, 'You have had your moment to make an embarrassing display of your affections. Now we are leaving.'

'Not without Sapphira,' Stamitos replied, walking his horse a few paces closer.

'Stamitos, stop,' Tyron called out, pushing his horse forwards.

Pandarus and Leksi followed closely. The guard drew his sword then. Stamitos's blade remained pointed at Pollux, who held all the power in that moment. Everyone was still. Leksi's and Tyron's swords remained tucked in their sheaths. They both knew that any more weapons in the equation would only panic everyone.

'Let's all calm down before someone accidentally gets hurt,' Pandarus said, raising his hands.

'I am calm,' Stamitos replied, looking down his sword at Pollux.

'Go ahead with the girl,' Pollux said to the guard. 'I will catch up in a moment.'

'You do not want to do that,' said Stamitos. 'I am not playing here.'

The guard swung his horse around and hustled Sapphira along in the other direction.

'Tell your brother to put his sword away before I take matters into hand,' Pollux said.

Before another word could be spoken, Stamitos kicked his horse hard in its sides and it lurched forwards. The tip of his blade moved towards Pollux's chest. Pollux drew his own sword, and in one fast sweep, he cut off Stamitos's hand.

Everything slowed in that moment. Tyron watched as the sword, and the hand holding it, fell by the hooves of Pollux's horse. He heard Sapphira scream as her horse was pulled away from the group by the guard. Stamitos's horse came to a stop beside Pollux so they were facing one another. Stamitos turned his white face down to look at the limb where blood now spurted.

Within moments, Leksi had a blade pressed against Pollux's throat, waiting for instructions. He would take his head off at Tyron's word. Stamitos tipped to one side as the shock paralysed him. Tyron's horse was beside him in moments, catching the weight of him as he fell. Tyron dismounted and pulled Stamitos from the saddle, covering the wound with his hand to stop the bleeding as he carried him behind Pandarus's horse out of harm's way.

Sapphira's angry screams faded with the growing distance while Pollux wiped his sword and returned it to its sheath.

'That's brave of you,' Leksi said, his hand steady. The slightest change in pressure would pierce the skin.

Pollux glanced at him. 'Normally, if a man comes at me with a sword, that man is dead. I have spared his life out of respect to your family and to uphold the wishes of my king. Next time I will take off his head. Are we clear?'

Leksi's sword remained against his throat. Tyron had removed his tunic and shirt and was pressing the shirt against the amputated limb. He had seen men bleed out within minutes.

'Give me your belt,' he said to Pandarus.

Pandarus removed his belt and tossed it to him. Tyron secured it above the elbow. It was a sight he had seen many times, but those men had not been his brother. Panic rolled over him as he worked. Pandarus's eyes returned to the pale and bloodied hand on the ground, which still wrapped the sword.

'What are we doing?' Leksi said, eyes remaining on Pollux. 'Someone talk to me.'

Pandarus looked across at him, face pale and hands trembling. 'Let him go,' he said. His voice was almost a whisper.

Leksi turned his head to Tyron for confirmation. Tyron stopped what he was doing and looked up at Pollux. There was a long, still silence before he finally nodded.

'Are you sure?' Leksi said.

Tyron found his voice. 'Yes.' His eyes returned to

Stamitos as he tied the ends of the shirt to secure it around the limb.

Leksi reluctantly removed his sword. Pollux watched him return it to its sheath and then looked at Pandarus. 'Am I to expect any more visitors on my journey?'

Pandarus shook his head and tried to hide his light-headed state. 'No.'

Pollux swung his horse around and trotted off after the others. Sapphira's screams had reduced to long wails. They echoed along the road, filling the space where she had been.

Pandarus remained on his horse, holding his saddle. 'Should we bring the hand?'

Leksi dismounted and took off his own tunic. He picked up the hand as though it were a glove and pulled the sword free of it, then wrapped the hand and returned the sword to Stamitos.

'We probably shouldn't leave it lying in the middle of the road,' he said by way of explanation.

Pandarus looked at Stamitos for the first time. 'Will he live?'

'Thieves lose hands all the time. A few weeks later and they are back stealing,' Leksi said, bending down to help Tyron.

Stamitos had gone silent from the shock.

'He needs a physician though,' Tyron said. 'The wound needs tending to now to reduce the chances of infection.'

Stamitos's eyes were on Tyron.

'We're close to Nuwien,' Leksi said, helping Tyron lift him from the ground. 'Let's take him there.'

～

The physician's name was Hesper. He opened his small home to the men, asking questions related to the injury and nothing more. His wife and three daughters made up a cot in the kitchen by the stove. Tyron and Leksi laid Stamitos down and stepped back so the physician could get to work. Hesper whispered instructions to his wife and daughters, who dashed about the house fetching water, vinegar, clean bandages, and an iron cautery. They moved in a way that suggested they had done it many times before. It was like a dance as they passed one another. Stamitos remained conscious, his eyes following them about the room, his mouth mute.

'The bleeding has slowed,' Hesper said as he examined the limb. 'We will need to cauterise it.'

Tyron glanced at Leksi. They had seen the procedure carried out enough times to know it was going to be painful for everyone involved.

'I will fetch something for him to bite down on,' said Hesper's wife, disappearing from the room. She returned with a smooth piece of wood.

Pandarus stood next to the stove, looking everywhere but at Stamitos. Leksi and Tyron positioned themselves on either side of Stamitos as the iron in the stove glowed orange. Hesper finished cleaning the wound and then nodded at his wife, who carefully removed the iron and handed it to him.

'Bite down on this,' Tyron said, holding the piece of wood to Stamitos's mouth. Stamitos opened his mouth and bit down, his wide eyes on Tyron's because he knew what was next. There was a hiss as the iron made contact with the limb, the smell of burning flesh filling the small room. Pandarus covered his mouth with his hand and his eyes went to his feet.

'Eeeeerrrrhhhhgggg.' A few tears ran down Stamitos's face before he lost consciousness.

The eldest daughter rushed forwards to take the iron from her father. Hesper kneeled on the floor, gesturing for items held by members of his family. When he was done, he rested on his heels for a moment before pushing himself up to a standing position.

'I cut the wound in a way that let me use the healthy skin to cover it. It's been cleaned with vinegar and I have applied myrrh oil, but we will need to change the bandages frequently to prevent infection.'

Tyron nodded.

Hesper smiled and his entire face creased with the gesture. 'You are welcome here for as long as you need.' He looked down at Stamitos, who was wavering between awake and unconscious. 'You did well to minimise the blood loss. We'll let him sleep now, but we'll need to wake him to get fluids into him. If you want to get some air, my wife will stay with him while I clean up.'

'Thank you,' said Tyron, glancing down at Stamitos.

Leksi, Pandarus and Tyron stepped outside and let the icy breeze carry away the smell of burning flesh. The road through the village was lined with quaint houses. A few houses down, there was a large stone well with two young boys leaning either side of it. They were dropping rocks down into the water and making guesses at its depth. A woman arrived to reprimand them, then dragged them away by their arms, ignoring their objections. It was helpful to watch the small happenings of a village and become lost in the mundane. Tyron had always imagined he would be well-suited to such a life. A quiet life in a village where everyone contributed in a meaningful way.

'I will return to Archdale,' Pandarus said. 'Update the king and make transportation arrangements for Stamitos.'

'I'll accompany you. Unless you need me here,' Leksi said, looking at Tyron.

Tyron shook his head. 'There is barely enough room here for me. Go with Pandarus.'

They fell silent again, still processing the events of the afternoon.

'If only he had put the sword away,' Pandarus said. 'He is lucky to have only lost a hand. He could have lost his life.'

A young boy was waiting close by with the horses. Tyron watched as Pandarus walked over to him and took the reins without saying a word. Leksi gave Tyron's arm an affectionate slap before following Pandarus. When he reached the boy, he bent down to him.

'Did you water these horses?' he said, his tone serious.

'Yes, my lord,' the boy replied, nodding furiously.

Leksi pulled a coin from his pocket and handed it to the boy. 'This one needs some grain and a brush,' he said, gesturing to Tyron's horse. 'Do you think you can do that for your prince?'

The boy's eyes went wide as he stared at the silver coin in his hand. 'Yes, my lord. Thank you, my lord.'

Leksi ruffled the boy's hair as he took the horse that Stamitos had taken from the stable. 'I'm not letting the theft go just because he lost a hand,' Leksi called over to Tyron.

Tyron wanted to smile at his friend, but it did not come.

Leksi mounted and looked at Tyron once more. 'Do you want me to deliver any messages?'

Tyron blinked. Aldara would be going out of her mind cooped up in the Companions' quarters with no word from him. He glanced at Pandarus, whose gaze was fixed on the road ahead. 'Send Pero on horseback along with the royal wagon in two days. Inform Fedora that Sapphira is on her way to Onuric as planned.'

'That's it?'

'That's it.'

Pandarus looked at Tyron and gave a brief nod before swinging his horse around and starting down the road. 'Let's go,' he called to Leksi over his shoulder. 'We will be travelling in the dark soon.'

Leksi's eyes shone with amusement. 'See you in a few days,' he said to Tyron.

'Mind the dark,' Tyron replied, a hint of a smile forming. He watched the men ride off, small chunks of mud flicking up from the horses' hooves.

'He's awake, my lord,' came a soft voice behind him.

Tyron turned to find the eldest daughter standing in the doorway. He glanced back once at the road where the horses were now disappearing behind the houses that lined the bending road, then went inside to share his brother's pain.

CHAPTER 12

*I*t became clear to Aldara that Fedora did not agree with the king's decision to send Sapphira to Onuric. It showed in Fedora's restless, agitated state, and her shortness with the women. Or rather, shorter than usual. She had carried out his instructions because it was her role as mentor, and because, while she no longer shared his bed, she remained his possession. Aldara, aware of the havoc her actions had caused after Hali's departure, did as she was instructed by Fedora. She owed it to her mentor, who was struggling with inner conflict.

Fedora showed her gratitude by sharing with Aldara the small amount of information she knew. Stamitos had gone after Sapphira. But she already knew that, because he had come to the Companions' quarters looking for her, and when Fedora has suggested that he speak with the king, he had turned to Aldara for answers. All she could offer was silence on the matter and a mournful expression stemming from the feeling in her gut. He had taken his questions to the queen, knowing his mother would not be able to lie to his face. He went after her, and the princes followed.

That evening Leksi had shown up at the door, dishevelled and visibly exhausted. Aldara was seated in an armchair, reading. He glanced past the guard at her when he arrived and nodded in her direction before moving out into the corridor to speak with Fedora. Muffled words reached Aldara through the open door, but none of them were for her. He spoke only of Sapphira, confirming she was on her way to Onuric as planned. When Fedora had stepped back into the room, she had looked over at Aldara and said, 'Say nothing to the other women other than the fact that Sapphira has been moved on.'

Aldara had nodded, unable to find words that would not spill into questions.

The following morning, she sat pretending to listen to the lesson on Asigow's history. Lessons related to Asigow were becoming more frequent. Due to the Companion trade, a kingdom that had once felt worlds away was creeping closer. The women listened as Fedora described the marriage customs of these obscure people. People who worshipped the sun and pierced their skin with silver. People who painted their doors with the blood of the dead to keep evil out of their homes. The women tried to take it in, but they were distracted by their fear. Fear is contagious in confined spaces. The news of Sapphira had rocked every one of them.

Aldara tried to take comfort in the fact that Sapphira and Hali would have each other and tried not to dwell on losing them both. After the lesson, she hid in the dressing room, her mind overwhelmed, imagining possible outcomes. She lay down on the floor with a book she had no intention of reading, waiting for Tyron to come back and tell her they would be all right.

Aldara woke up on the dressing room floor with Astra kneeling in front of her, violently shaking her shoulder. She sat upright and the book tumbled from the skirt of her dress onto the floor between them.

'What is going on?' Astra said, annoyed.

Aldara was trying to gauge the time. 'What do you mean?'

'You know exactly what I mean. Why was Sapphira sent to Onuric?'

Aldara blinked as she processed the question. 'I know as much as you do.'

Astra sat back on her heels and gave her a scalding look. 'I just heard from a maid that Pero will be going to Nuwien tomorrow to join Prince Tyron.'

'Tyron is in Nuwien?'

Astra shrugged. 'I will tell you everything I know after you tell me why Sapphira was sent to Onuric.'

Aldara's eyes remained on her. 'I am not permitted to talk about it.'

'Sapphira is gone. You are going to need one friend around here. I am capable of keeping my mouth closed on the subject.'

Aldara was torn between her loyalty to Fedora and her need to know why Tyron was in Nuwien. 'The king wanted them separated.'

'I knew it was not because anyone thought she would make a good mentor.'

'She will be a terrible mentor.'

'She was a terrible Companion.'

'Not to Stamitos,' Aldara said, feeling defensive of her friend.

Astra thought for a moment. 'They became too close.

That is what happens when you are careless with your feelings. If they had not been so blatant in their affections, she would still be here.'

When Aldara could wait no longer, she said, 'Now tell me why Prince Tyron is in Nuwien.'

Astra stood up. 'I have no idea.'

Aldara narrowed her eyes. 'You said you would tell me everything you knew after I told you what was going on.'

'Yes, and that is all I know. Pero will join the prince in Nuwien.'

Aldara exhaled and looked at her. 'You manipulated me.'

'Do not let yourself be wounded by it. We are trained in the art of manipulation.'

'Not to use on one another.'

Astra waved a hand. 'I have been doing this for a lot longer than you.'

'Careful, you are showing your age.'

Astra suppressed a smile. 'All the more reason I need to hone my skills.' She went to leave but stopped in the doorway. 'Do not worry, I will not let on that I know a thing.'

Aldara pulled her knees up and pressed her face against them.

She felt as though she might lose her mind being trapped in the Companions' quarters. Tyron had told her to remain there, but that was two days earlier, before he disappeared from the castle. No one seemed to know when he might return. No one seemed to know anything. Aldara learned from Edelpha, one of the chambermaids, that the king was leaving for Nuwien that morning. The royal wagon sat waiting to collect him at the entrance. Her mind ran wild with possible explanations.

After their morning lesson, she tried the only tactic she could think of to be released from her comfortable prison.

'You want to go where?' Fedora asked, despite hearing the first time. They were standing in the dressing room hanging the dresses that had been dropped off.

'To church, my lady.'

'For what purpose?'

She paused to think. A mistake. 'To pray for the welfare of the princes. Light a candle for them.'

Fedora did not seem convinced. 'To pray for the princes?'

'And to pray for forgiveness… for my sins.'

'Such as lying?'

Aldara pressed her lips together. 'I will return immediately after the sermon.'

'I can accompany her,' Astra said, walking in and snatching the dress Aldara was holding. She held it up to look at it. 'I was planning to attend anyway to pray for Aldara's soul,' she added, studying the garment.

'Very well,' Fedora said. 'I should warn you though, I have no tolerance for games at the moment. If I find out you took any detours, I will confine you to your bed.'

Aldara glanced at Astra, who was now watching her. 'Yes, my lady.'

The two women dressed in conservative garments that wrapped their necks and covered their arms, then walked along the south wing corridor towards the church. It was no coincidence that the Companions' quarters were tucked away in the north wing at the opposite end of the castle.

'Why are you really attending church?' Astra asked. She kept her eyes forwards and chin raised.

'I enjoy the way the priest focuses on us every time he mentions the burning fires of Hell. I have missed it.'

Astra glanced at her, a smile flickering. 'Do not be intimidated by him. He is just a man.'

'A man of God.'

'But still a man. Just ask Violeta.'

Aldara looked across to see if she was joking. 'No.' She was about to question her further when a body slumped against the corridor wall in front of them caught her eye. She stopped walking and grabbed hold of Astra's arm. Princess Cora's head swung in their direction. Her drunken eyes took them in before her head rolled forwards again.

'Dear God,' Astra whispered. 'This is all we need.'

'I will go find one of her ladies.'

'No,' Astra said. 'You heard Fedora. If she finds you wandering about the castle you will be in trouble. Wait here and I will find someone to help.'

'We could help her,' Aldara whispered.

Astra tilted her head. 'If you try to touch her, she will have you beheaded. Keep your distance.'

Aldara nodded and watched her walk off down the corridor, straight past Cora, who raised her eyes to watch. Cora turned her head then and fixed her gaze on Aldara.

'What are you staring at?' she asked, her speech slurred.

Aldara took a few small steps towards her so she would not have to raise her voice to reply.

'That is far enough,' Cora said.

Aldara stopped walking. 'Astra has gone to find someone to accompany you to your chambers.'

'You mean help me.' Cora stared at her. 'I see what you are doing.'

'What is that?'

'You are judging me. Do not judge me. I will not have the castle's whores looking down their noses at *me*.'

'I am not judging you, my lady. I would like to help you.'

'Of course you are. You move in here, into my family's home. You and the rest of those women. You tear apart the lives of the very men who handed you privilege, my brothers, and then you have the audacity to act surprised when I am driven to drink.'

Aldara said nothing. Her eyes returned to the corridor, hoping Astra would hurry.

'What sort of life do you think he will have now with one hand?' Cora said, watching her through blinking lashes.

Aldara's eyes returned to her. 'Who?' Her heart was slowing. 'My lady, who are you referring to?'

'Stamitos.'

Aldara went cold. 'What happened to Stamitos's hand?'

Cora leaned her head against the wall and closed her eyes. 'He sliced it off. Grandor Pollux cut it off when Stamitos tried to recover his whore.'

Aldara stepped sideways and put her hand out to grab hold of the wall for balance. 'He chopped off his hand?' Her voice was almost a whisper.

Cora opened her eyes and looked at her. 'What do you care? You do not have to share a bed with him.'

Aldara was no longer listening. 'He just wanted to be with the girl he loves. Why is that such a sin? Why is that so frightening to people?'

Cora blinked and a few tears ran down her cheeks. She did not bother to wipe them. 'He was always so kind as a child. He never saw the faults in others like I did.'

'He is still kind.'

Cora blinked again. 'I used to think he was just naive.

Now I see that he is a better person than me. I cannot see past people's faults.'

'That must be exhausting, as we all have faults.'

Cora narrowed her eyes on Aldara. 'And what are my faults?'

She thought for a moment. 'Your inability to see past people's faults?'

Cora's face softened. 'You will be next, you know.'

Aldara swallowed. 'Next?'

'They will send you away when they realise Tyron loves you. And what will Tyron do? He will go after you, just as Stamitos did. Except Tyron is a soldier who will kill the men who stand in his way. He will go against his king and likely die as a result. He will do all that for you. His blood will be on your hands.'

The sound of footsteps coming towards them made them both look up. It was Astra, with one of Cora's ladies in tow. The girl rushed ahead of Astra when she caught sight of Cora sitting against the wall. She glared at Aldara as she pulled the princess to her feet, wrapping an arm about her.

'I am fine,' Cora said, almost collapsing to the floor. 'I just need to rest for a moment.'

'You can rest in your chamber,' whispered the girl.

'Would you like me to help?' Aldara offered.

The girl shook her head. 'You can help by keeping your unsanitary hands to yourself.'

'Come, Aldara,' Astra called.

Cora looked at Aldara. The hate in her eyes had faded to something resembling distrust. Her lady moved her along in the other direction, holding her up as best she could.

'Let's go,' Astra said again. Her voice was quieter that time.

Aldara watched them for a moment. Cora's steps were uneven, creating more work for the girl propping her up. Her hair had come loose at the back where it had rested against the wall. Not a crown in sight. She turned and followed Astra down the corridor towards the church, where the priest could cleanse them of their sins.

CHAPTER 13

*T*yron slept on a straw mattress by Stamitos's cot, despite the offer of private sleeping quarters. He wanted to remain close to his brother, who had barely spoken since the incident. As he lay with his legs bent to prevent his feet from hanging off the end, he listened to the wood shift and groan within the small stove. It was their second night in the small house, and he could not tell whether Stamitos was sleeping or just keeping his eyes closed so Tyron would leave him be.

'I suppose you think me a fool,' Stamitos said, answering Tyron's question.

Tyron was silent for a moment. He was relieved to hear his brother talk. 'You wanted to protect her. I understand.'

Stamitos blinked away tears. 'I wanted to marry her.'

Tyron stared at the roof. It was low, and he had to remember to duck each time he entered the house. 'They will never let you marry her. Not then, not now.'

'No one will marry me now.'

Tyron turned his head. All he could see was his brother's elbow as he wiped at his eyes. The other arm remained elevated against his chest. 'You are still a prince of Syrasan. They have not taken that from you.'

'Sapphira did not care that I was a prince. She cared that I could shoot straight.'

Tyron looked back at the roof. 'I am sorry that I did not protect you. In showing restraint, I failed you.'

'This is not on you. I should have been ready for him. I underestimated his skill.'

Tyron closed his eyes for a moment. 'We are all guilty of underestimating them.'

'He could have killed me. He *should* have killed me. When I moved towards him, I had meant to drive my sword through his chest.'

Tyron's eyes opened. 'The man has enough sense not to kill a prince of Syrasan. It was self-preservation. He would have been dead within moments.'

Silence.

'I can still hear Sapphira's screams. I had never seen her afraid until that moment. I keep imagining how I would feel if they had cut off *her* hand and then forced me to leave with them. She may think me dead.'

'We were there to care for you. Sapphira knows you are in good hands.'

'Interesting word choice.'

Tyron mentally cursed. 'Sorry.'

More silence.

'How will I fight?' Stamitos asked. His good hand returned to his face again.

'You won't.'

'Then what will I do? What purpose can a cripple have?'

'You have lost a hand, not a leg. It will be all right.'

'I'm not like Pandarus. I will make a terrible advisor.'

Tyron thought Pandarus was a terrible advisor but did not say as much. 'We will figure it out later. You need not have your future planned out tonight.' The pile of wood collapsed in the stove and a surge of heat filled the room. 'I want you to promise me that you will leave Sapphira be for now. I will not let you die for the girl. Her life is not under threat.'

'If you think that, then you don't know her very well. She does not like to be ordered around.'

'She will have to get used to it.'

Stamitos's good arm returned to his side. 'You sound like Father. Everyone has a role they must fulfil.'

Tyron swallowed. Stamitos was silent for such a long time that Tyron assumed he had fallen asleep.

'Everything is changing.' Stamitos said. 'Those women should be afraid. Aldara should be afraid.'

Tyron's wide eyes studied the detail of the roof.

'You can't protect her,' Stamitos said.

Tyron rolled onto his side so his back was to his brother. 'Get some sleep.'

The royal wagon arrived late in the morning. Tyron was surprised when his father stepped out onto the muddy road, panting with the effort. Zenas rarely left Archdale anymore except for the flag tournament and the occasional meeting in Veanor. Tyron waited outside the front door, bowing as his father approached.

'He is up and eating,' Tyron said. 'I hope Mother is not running about Archdale in a panic.'

Zenas paused in the doorway next to him. 'It could have been much worse.'

Tyron nodded and led Zenas through to the kitchen where Stamitos was seated on his cot, sipping salted broth from a cup. Hesper had rebandaged the arm and made a sling that went about his neck to keep the limb elevated. Zenas stopped and stared at his youngest son. Tyron could see by his face that the sight lit a fire inside of him.

Stamitos placed the cup down and looked up. 'Did Mother send you?'

'Yes, actually. Though I did not need convincing.' Zenas stopped by the stove to warm himself. 'How does it feel?'

'Probably how you would imagine.'

Tyron leaned against the wall, peering out of the small window at the front of the house. Hesper walked into the room and bowed in front of Zenas. The rest of his family stood behind him.

'Your Majesty,' he said. 'I am Hesper, the physician who has been treating Prince Stamitos. This is my wife and my three daughters.' He stepped aside so they could curtsy.

The eldest of the daughters stepped forwards and spoke. 'May I offer you some refreshments, Your Majesty?'

Zenas's gaze moved up and down the girl before answering. 'Yes, thank you.' She curtsied and left them.

It was the first time Tyron had noticed that the young girl was rather pretty. She was tall with a long neck and wore her dark hair braided to one side. He saw her through his father's eyes. She looked eerily like Idalia, the king's Companion who had died from an infection after she had tried to terminate a pregnancy. He glanced at Stamitos to see if he had noticed the moment, but he was staring into his cup.

Hesper and his family left them to talk privately, but the size of the house meant that anything they said could be heard.

'I will be honest,' Zenas said, his gaze returning to Stamitos. 'I did not want to send the girl off to Onuric. However, you forced my hand when you asked to marry her.'

'In doing what was best for your kingdom, you betrayed your son,' Stamitos replied, looking up.

Zenas continued as though he had not spoken. 'It was not an easy decision, but I did what was necessary. It was foolish of you to go after trained Zoelin soldiers, alone and waving your sword about.'

'Rest easy, Father,' Tyron said, watching Stamitos's face harden. 'He lives. Everything is as it should be.'

'Except now he is minus a hand,' Zenas said, his temper flaring.

'How disappointing for you and all your plans,' Stamitos replied.

'He lost the woman he loves and a hand all in one day,' Tyron said, pushing himself upright. 'Perhaps this conversation can wait until he is more recovered.'

Zenas's eyes remained on Stamitos. 'The arrangement could have been a temporary one. We could have brought the girl back at a later time when you were settled. Now that I see her influence, I think it best she remains at Onuric.'

'Once I was settled?'

'I am referring to clarity of mind.'

'Ah, you are referring to love,' Stamitos said, leaning back a little.

Zenas glanced at Tyron, who said nothing.

'You needn't worry now,' Stamitos continued. 'I cannot marry her. If I asked for her hand, it would only prompt laughter at the irony of the question.' He stood and stepped past Zenas. 'I need some air.'

Tyron and Zenas stared down at their feet. The eldest daughter returned to the room, taking her cue from the silence, and laid a steaming bowl of soup on the table. The room smelled of chicken and herbs, much better than the previous day's blood and stale flesh. She disappeared out of the room again, returning moments later with a jar of mead and a cup.

'Apologies, Your Majesty, but I have no bread to offer you.'

Zenas walked over to the table and studied the soup and honey wine. 'Grain is expensive and in short supply. This smells wonderful.' He looked at her. 'What is your name?'

She clasped her hands together in front of her. 'Ella, Your Majesty.'

'Is it short for something?'

'Ellarosa. My sisters could not say it properly when they were young, so we shortened it to Ella.'

Zenas smiled. 'Which do you prefer?'

'Ella, Your Majesty.'

His eyes returned to the soup. 'Thank you, Ella.'

She curtsied and left them once again.

Tyron watched his father take a seat, dwarfing the table in front of him. The chair groaned. 'She looks like Idalia.'

Zenas nodded but his eyes remained on his food. 'Yes. She does.'

It was unthinkable to Tyron that his father could entertain the idea of companionship at such a time. He looked back out the window to where Stamitos stood in the middle of the road, eyes north. His head was stooped, the light gone from his face. It was a stark contrast to the breathless laughter he had witnessed a few days before.

Fear ignited inside Tyron as he watched his brother. He knew if Aldara was given over to King Jayr or his men, he would kill any man who hindered his attempts to recover her. If his hand was sliced off, he would pick up the sword with the other before he let a man like Pollux take her across the border. How powerless he was and how easily it could all go wrong for them now. He could not control the decisions made *in the best interests of Syrasan*. He wondered if a safe place even existed for her anymore, and where that might be. She had grown happy with the life they had forged together, but that life was changing, and she would keep losing. She was no longer safe at Archdale, even with him beside her.

He realised at that moment that he was not reflecting on his fears—he was making plans. Plans that would hurt her. Plans that would break him.

CHAPTER 14

When Tyron arrived at Archdale, he felt a mood within its walls that resembled grief. He was unsure whether it stemmed from Stamitos's injury or the events that would take place that afternoon. He helped Stamitos get settled into his quarters, waving away his brother's squire who was trying hard not to look at his mentor's missing hand.

'Why don't you take a walk outdoors?' Tyron suggested.

Stamitos sat on the bed and shook his head. 'I think I'll wait for the news to spread and the gossip to run its course before I go parading about the castle grounds.'

Tyron checked once again if he needed anything. The answer did not change—he wanted to be alone. Tyron nodded and left the room before his mother and sister arrived to mourn the lost hand, heading to his quarters, where he had asked a servant to fill a tub with boiled water. He wanted to wash away all traces of the past few days.

Pero wandered in and frowned at the steam rising from the water. 'Shall I add some cold water, my lord?'

'No.' There was a part of him that enjoyed the burn.

When the heat overcame him, he got out and dressed. He sat by the window in his bedchamber, forcing down the boiled chicken and vegetables Pero had brought him. The food refused to break down inside his mouth. It was painful to swallow.

Pero knocked on the door and entered. 'Leksi is here to see you, my lord.'

The food threatened to return to his mouth. Once he spoke the words aloud to Leksi, they would become more than just plans in his head. 'Send him in.'

Pero disappeared and moments later Leksi stepped through the door, appearing fresh and well-slept. He always presented that way.

'I've already checked in with the patient,' he said, leaning against the bedpost. 'Aside from his wounded pride, battered heart, and a missing hand, I thought he seemed rather well.' He looked at Tyron. 'I can't say the same about you. What is the matter?'

Tyron's body was heavy with the words. 'I am going to send Aldara to live with her family.'

Leksi exhaled and nodded. 'I see. Why?'

Tyron just stared at him.

'Afraid of losing a hand?'

If only that were the reason. 'Afraid for her, and afraid of the person I will become if the king sends her over that border.'

'You mean afraid for the Zoelin men who stand in your way?'

'Something like that.'

Leksi thought for a moment. 'What will happen to her if you send her to live with her family?'

'She will be away from all of this. Safe from the uncertainty.'

Leksi shifted his weight onto his heels. 'She will also be shunned and labelled a whore.'

Tyron flinched. 'Don't.'

'It's the truth and you know it.'

Tyron shook his head as he thought. 'What would you do?'

'No idea. I have never felt that way about a woman.'

'What if it were your sister?'

'There are laws against that sort of thing.'

Tyron's eyes rolled in his head. 'No, what if it were your sister in that situation?'

'I'd castrate the bastard who had ruined her,' he replied, smiling.

Tyron did not smile. 'I thought I might give her some land. Improve her prospects.'

'Her prospects?'

'Yes. She will be an appealing prospect with land.'

Leksi laughed. 'I might not know anything about love, but I know women. Give her the land if it pleases you, but don't give her that explanation.' He glanced down at his feet. 'Will you tell her yourself?'

Tyron rested his elbows on his knees and nodded at the floor. 'Yes. She would not accept it from Fedora. Nor should she.'

Another knock came from the door and Pero appeared again. 'Her Majesty the Queen is waiting to see you.'

'Good luck with that conversation,' Leksi said.

Tyron forced his gaze up. 'I will be out in a moment.' Once Pero was gone, Tyron looked at Leksi. 'Will you take her tomorrow?'

Leksi nodded and bowed because he knew Tyron hated it. 'I'll await your instructions.'

$\sim$

They stood on the open grass in the centre of the bailey. It was such an odd meeting place; there was not even a tree to shield them from prying eyes. Aldara had thought something was wrong when Fedora relayed Tyron's message. Whatever he had to say, he did not trust himself to say it in private.

'How is Stamitos?' Aldara asked. Tyron was having difficulty looking at her, and it was making her nervous.

'About as well as you can imagine.'

She nodded. 'How are you?'

He looked at her then, but his gaze did not stick. It wandered to the walls and then settled on his feet. 'To be honest, I have been better.'

She swallowed. 'Do you want to tell me what we are doing out here? I feel as though I am about to be publicly beheaded.'

He smiled, but it faded as quickly as it came.

'Tyron, please tell me why you cannot meet my eyes.' He forced his eyes up to meet hers, but his tortured expression only frightened her. She took a step back from him. 'Say it.'

He nodded, finding the right words. 'More than anything else, I need you safe. The events of the past few days threaten that.'

She blinked and waited for the rest.

'It is an uncertain time for all the Companions. And I cannot protect you from it.'

She felt her chest restrict because she knew what was next.

'I cannot protect you here,' he continued. 'Not in the way I had hoped.'

She stood still as the words washed over her, unsure why she was surprised by them. She knew the makings of his mind and the way he felt about her.

'Tomorrow, Leksi will take you home to your family.'

'Stop,' she said, shaking her head. 'I am not ready to hear it.' He nodded and looked away. Her arms felt heavy suddenly. 'If you are concerned for my safety, I am safest here with you.'

'And when the king sends you away?'

'Stamitos asked to *marry* Sapphira. We would never be that careless.'

He linked his hands on top of his head. 'I do not need to announce my feelings aloud for people to see what is between us.'

She glanced back at the castle, wanting to reject his words but realising the truth in them. Some maids had wandered out and were so lost in their conversation they did not notice the prince and his Companion standing like strangers.

Tyron took a step towards her. 'I would die before I handed you over to King Jayr. That is dangerous for both of us. You are safest in the South with your family, away from this life.'

What could she say to that? Even before Cora had pointed it out, she had come to that realisation. The difference was she did not have the strength to engage with the facts. 'I… I don't want to go.'

His hands ran down his face. He was coming to the end of his calm. 'I don't want you to go. Do you think I am doing this because I want you to go?'

She watched him compose himself. 'Let's think this through,' she said, her voice soft. 'Perhaps there is another way we have not thought of.'

'We?' he said, eyebrows raised. 'You knew this was coming, didn't you? You hold the same fears I do.'

She glanced at the castle. 'Not for myself, for you. I know you, how you would react…'

'Then you know this is best for us.'

She shook her head. 'There must be another way, one that does not take me away from you.'

'There is no other way!' he said, pacing in front of her. 'I need you safe! Are you even listening? You have always had your own version of listening, and it's painfully selective.'

'I would listen much better if I could keep up with your wishes and moods.' She was losing patience also. 'A few days ago, you would not release me from your bed. Now you are sending me away. I'm just asking you to slow down for a moment instead of banishing me. I hardly think the king is going to cart me off to Onuric given recent events.'

'And when Pandarus takes the throne?'

She looked around and lowered her voice. 'Now you are being ridiculous. We cannot plan our future based on events that may not take place for years.'

'We cannot plan a future at all!'

She reached out to touch him and he pulled back from her. She took a few deep breaths and tried again. 'We could distance ourselves for a while.'

'Last time I tried that tactic, you were attacked by Zoelin men.'

'You could marry,' she said. 'No one will care about us once you are wed.'

He stilled and looked at her. 'Can you hear yourself? You think me marrying will help us?'

She knew it was not her best suggestion, but the alternative was unthinkable. 'I don't know…'

'Do you want to attend my wedding and listen to my nuptials? Do you want to wonder every night I am not with you if I am in bed with my wife?' Her hands covered her face, but he was not done making his point. 'Do you want to see my wife pregnant with my children? Watch me play with them from an appropriate distance? Will that make you happy?'

Her hands went over her ears. 'All right, you have made your point.' Her eyes heated with tears.

'That is why I am forced to make the grown-up decisions, because you think like a child.'

She stepped closer to him. 'All right, I get it. You want me to hate you. Then it will be easier for you to send me away on a nervous whim.' Her eyes burned but she refused to cry.

He closed the distance between them and towered over her. 'You seem to have forgotten that your entire purpose for being here is to serve my whims.'

She pushed his chest, but only she moved. 'You sound like Pandarus.'

'And you sound like you have forgotten your place. *I* make the decisions, and you curtsy and say "Yes, my lord".'

She went silent, barely recognising him. Fear had that effect on him. It drove him to insanity. She forced her trembling hands to still and dropped into a curtsy. When she rose, she looked up at him, eyes blazing. 'Yes, my lord.'

He slowed his breathing and collected his words. 'Return home where you will be safe. Where there are people who love you and will look out for you the way I would in another life.'

She fought the urge to be sick on the grass. 'You don't get to change your mind later on. If you send me away, you better mean it.'

He nodded, his hands at his sides. 'You have a chance at a real life. I am organising land for you.'

She blinked and a tear betrayed her. 'Women cannot own land.'

He took a sharp breath in. 'I am aware of the laws. The land will be in your father's name. Until you marry.'

She stared at him, watching him trip over the words. 'Am I supposed to be thankful for a piece of land, given to me in hope that some man with no wealth will see past the whore he is marrying? Keep your land.' She felt as though she were bleeding out in front of him.

He glanced down at her hands, which were now pressed against her chest like a shield. 'I do this for you.'

She already knew that. He had the maturity to act in her best interests while she wanted to pretend none of it was happening. Her breaking insides were exhibiting as something else, something resembling hate. 'It is your decision to make, *my lord*. I will obey you. As you pointed out, that is what I have been *trained* to do.'

He looked at her, his mind and body spent. 'I wish things were different.'

She pushed through the tightening in her throat and kept her eyes on him. 'Keep well, my lord. And stay safe.' She swept into a low curtsy. When she rose, she did not even glance at him before walking towards the castle, the skirt of her dress dragging across the wet grass because she did not care to lift it. Tears blinded her as she willed her legs to keep moving. She did not go to the door she had exited, heading to the laundry door the servants and maids used instead.

When she stepped inside, a sharp, painful noise escaped her and her hands went to her mouth to hold in the cry. She dropped to her knees, her body folding over itself as it heaved with mute tears. Her forehead pressed against the cold floor and her hand remained over her mouth for fear of what might come out of it.

Get up, she told herself. *Get up. You cannot fall apart within these walls.*

CHAPTER 15

*D*ressed in a heavy cloak, Aldara moved her gaze about the mounting yard. A groom stood nearby with a saddled and waiting Loda. The weather was about as pleasant as it got that time of year—still and cool. There was no reason to delay the trip. No reason at all.

She glanced at the path that led to the castle and then down at her boots. He was not coming.

'Miss,' said the groom.

'One moment,' she replied, still not moving. She glanced at the small bag in her hand that contained a few cotton dresses and a piece of paper granting her release from the sale agreement. When Fedora had handed it to her, she had studied the formal language written in Tyron's hand and then let it drop to the floor. Fedora had insisted she take it in case anything should happen to Prince Tyron. It would protect her, she had said.

It had been a different style of departure, one done in daylight, with the other Companions' knowledge. Tyron had not wanted her pulled from her bed in the middle of the night. He had wanted her to travel in daylight, and had assigned more men than was necessary for the simple jour-ney. Fedora did not want a spectacle made, though she need not have worried, the noble Companions appearing indifferent as they said a few words before fleeing the room. Only Astra had remained while Fedora delivered a speech on gratitude in place of a goodbye. Aldara wanted to know if Sapphira's father would be informed of his daughter's transfer, but Fedora had taken a risk in informing Hali's family without Pandarus's consent, and she would not take that risk again given all that was happening. Aldara had grown to love Fedora, despite her hard exterior, but she had no more room for grief.

'I'll take that for you,' Leksi said, appearing in front of her.

She jumped and looked up. He held out his hand to take her bag, so she gave it to him. In her other hand was the longbow and a quiver filled with arrows that Sapphira had not been allowed to take with her.

'I can wear these,' she said, lifting the quiver over her head.

'Can I trust you not to shoot me in the back?' he asked, smiling.

She gave a small smile in return. 'You better travel behind me just to be safe.'

He laughed. 'We had better move. I have clear instruc-tions to transport you during daylight. I wouldn't want to put Prince Tyron in a bad mood.'

'Isn't it a little soon for jokes?'

'You caught that. Good for you.'

Aldara squinted at him. 'How did he seem this morning?'

He tilted his head at her in way that suggested she should know the answer.

'I thought he might come and say goodbye.'

Leksi turned and walked over to Loda, strapping the bag to the back of the saddle. 'He will not be coming. Let's go.'

Aldara stepped up beside him. The groom holding the mare dropped to his knee and bowed his head. Confused by such a grand gesture, Aldara turned to find Queen Eldoris stepping into the mounting yard. She had a guard in tow and appeared at ease in the unfamiliar environment. Leksi bowed, a reminder to Aldara to curtsy. She intended to hold the position until the queen passed, but Eldoris's laced boots came to a stop in front of her. Aldara returned upright and they stood face-to-face.

'I thought I might have a word before you leave,' Eldoris said.

Leksi excused himself, and the groom led Loda away from them. The two women watched the men disperse, listening to the click of horseshoes on the cobblestones. Once the men were out of earshot, they looked at one another.

'How can I help you, Your Majesty?' Aldara was surprised to find Eldoris meeting her eyes. She normally had a way of looking through her.

'I understand that you are leaving Archdale today.'

Aldara swallowed. 'Yes,' she replied, unsettled by the soft gaze.

'It was a very difficult decision for my son to make. I truly believe he has acted in the best interest of both of you.'

Aldara was not sure whether to respond or wait to see if a question followed. She remained silent.

'I suppose you are wondering what I am doing here,' Eldoris said. 'I do not make a habit of liaising with the Companions. You can understand why that is.'

'Yes, I understand.'

Eldoris remained tall and unblinking. 'I could not let you leave without acknowledging your contribution to Prince Tyron's recovery. As you aware, my son is a fierce fighter, but the acts of his body betray his mind. I have never known a fighting man who feels the death of the fallen as he does.'

There was a silence left for Aldara to fill.

'I would imagine all men feel the loss. People find different ways to cope.'

Eldoris studied her for a moment. 'And my son found you.'

'My understanding is that Prince Tyron always heals with time.'

Eldoris gave a gentle smile. 'He has always found a way to exist among the living, but the truth is something in him died during that first battle many years ago. Each battle since has been a small death for him. But you brought him back to life, even if it did not last.'

Aldara said nothing.

'Now you are leaving, and I feel myself bracing against it. What am I to do with two broken-hearted sons?'

Aldara glanced at Leksi, who was now mounting his horse. 'I wish I had answers, Your Majesty, for all of your sakes.'

Eldoris followed her gaze to where Leksi was waiting. 'God bless you, Aldara. I hope you find happiness in this short life and that your own heart heals with time.'

Aldara shook her head. 'I was only his Companion. My heart was closed.'

Eldoris nodded. 'I see. Then I wish you safe travels.'

'Thank you, Your Majesty.' Aldara curtsied low and watched the queen's feet turn and step away.

≈

When Aldara arrived at the farm, her senses were overwhelmed. The site of the barren paddocks was strangely comforting. The familiar smells of the forest drifted across them, bringing memories of a carefree childhood she had suppressed so deeply, she feared they might not have happened. Sheep bleated in the barn and the grazing horses lifted their heads, emitting a low whinny of recognition. Loda raised her head to listen.

Dahlia stood in front of the small house, waiting to greet the king's men. She wore her good dress and no apron, suggesting she had been warned of her daughter's arrival. Aldara could feel her mother's eyes on her as they approached. She would no doubt have plenty of questions once the men had departed.

Aldara came to a halt behind Leksi and the two guards stopped behind her. Before her mother had a chance to speak, Kadmus came bounding out of the house like an excited dog. He pulled her from the saddle and spun her around like she was five years old before dropping her to the ground.

'Good God, you are twice the weight you were when you left here,' he said, face beaming.

'It won't take long for it to disappear.' She wanted him to swing her around again, because for a moment she had forgotten why she was there.

Leksi dismounted behind her and walked over to Dahlia. He handed her a small pouch of coin.

'What is that?' Aldara said, stepping away from Kadmus and walking towards them.

Leksi put his hands up and walked back to his horse.

'A gift from the prince,' Dahlia said.

Aldara heard the clink of coin as her mother shoved it into her pocket. 'Prince Tyron said nothing of this. We don't need his charity.'

'Mind your business and go fetch some boiled water for the men,' Dahlia said, narrowing her eyes.

Aldara glanced at Kadmus. He was not one for conflict. Taking hold of Loda's rein, he began to lead her away. 'I'll put the mare in the barn.'

Aldara shook her head and turned back to Leksi. 'I told Prince Tyron that I wanted nothing from him.'

Leksi mounted his horse and looked at her. 'I do as I am told.'

'Anyone would think I was still his property. I have a piece of paper that says otherwise.' It was a childish comment, but Fedora was not there to reprimand her.

'Aldara, still your tongue,' Dahlia said.

But her mother was there to fill the void.

'Thank you for the offer of water,' Leksi said to Dahlia. 'We have our flasks, and we need to travel while there is still light.' He looked at Aldara. 'Thank you for the pleasant company. And for not shooting me in the back.'

'You have not made it off the farm yet.' The weight of another farewell drained the anger from her. 'Thank you for returning me home. I will never forget your kindness during my time at Archdale. Prince Tyron is lucky to have such a loyal friend.'

He nodded and turned his horse. Aldara watched the men trot past the ageing fence posts and turn onto the narrow road that would lead them back to Archdale. She wondered if she might eventually grow immune to the pain of goodbyes.

The creak of the barn door opening made her turn around. Her father appeared, moving like a much older man than the one she remembered. When he saw her and smiled, the extra years faded away. Aside from the streaks of grey through his hair, he looked as she remembered him. His pace quickened and he held out his arms to her.

She ran to him then, dissolving into a ten-year-old girl dependent on her father's affections. The force with which her body hit him reassured her of his resilience. She buried her face in his chest and his lips pressed down on her head.

'I had almost forgotten how beautiful you are,' he whispered.

'And I had forgotten how cruel old age can be,' she whispered back.

He laughed from his belly and held her at arm's length so he could look at her properly. 'They've fattened you up. Hopefully the extra layer gets you through to harvest,' he said, winking. He walked towards the house with one arm secured tightly around her. 'You are back just in time. The real work will begin soon. You have probably forgotten what hard work is like.'

Kadmus caught up and fell into step beside them. He was carrying Aldara's belongings. 'Unless you count singing songs and reading prose aloud as work.'

'It absolutely is when you have as little talent as me.'

Dahlia stood waiting in the doorway of the small house, arms crossed against the cold. She blended into her bleak surroundings. 'There will be hard labour required of you here. And there will be no one waiting on you.'

'No one waited on me at Archdale.'

'You'll be getting your own food and washing your own clothes,' Dahlia continued.

Aldara squinted at her. 'I know how things work here. I lived here for sixteen years, and I was only gone for two.' She stepped past her mother and went inside, the wooden floors creaking under her feet.

She paused. Nothing had changed within the house. It was the same small space with two beds at the back, a table, and four chairs that were dragged over to the stove in the evenings when the temperature dropped. A wooden ladder connected the loft where her parents slept. The raised space offered little privacy, worries and arguments reaching all corners of the house. Aldara glanced at the small stove that heated the room and the watered-down soup.

'You are not at Archdale anymore,' Dahlia said, passing her.

Aldara watched her back. Kadmus stepped up next to her and looked about. He was still carrying her bag.

'Give the bag to Aldara,' Dahlia said, turning to the stove and stirring the soup. 'She can carry her own things.'

Kadmus glanced between them and then handed it to his sister without saying a word.

'Thank you,' Aldara said. She went to the back of the house where the beds were pressed against the wall and found space for the few items of clothing she had brought with her. They were of high quality and fancy by local standards, despite being the dresses she would have worn while completing chores at Archdale. She knew they would wear and fade, and eventually be replaced by inferior garments. Shaking them out, she then rolled them up to be stored in the chest alongside her longbow and quiver. Removing her cloak, she sat on the thin mattress, running her hand along the coarse wool blanket. When she looked up, she noticed her mother watching her.

'What happened?' Dahlia asked.

Aldara had known this was coming. She exhaled and shook her head. 'I honestly don't know where to begin.'

Dahlia continued to watch her. 'I know how things work at Archdale. Women are not given back. They are sold to noble families.'

Aldara glanced at Isadore and Kadmus who had taken a seat at the table, their eyes on the tools they were holding.

'People will talk of your return,' Dahlia continued. 'I need all the information if I am to defend my family.'

Aldara stood up and joined her mother by the stove. 'I'm sure they talked plenty when I left. Whatever they have to say, I have heard it already. The time for worrying about other's views has long passed.'

'Are you with child?' Her tone was matter-of-fact, surprising given the weight of the question.

'No, Mother. All the women consume herbs that reduce the risk of pregnancy.'

'Those herbs are used by women all across Syrasan. They are not a guarantee.'

She knew that. The memory of Idalia's body being wrapped and carried away was a constant reminder of it. 'They worked for me.'

'Well, they did not work for me,' Dahlia said, glancing briefly at Isadore.

Aldara looked up at her again. 'I guess that explains why you despise me so much. Was I the outcome of the failed remedy?'

'I don't despise you,' Dahlia said. 'I wanted something better for you. Much better than this.'

Aldara was unmoved by the sentiment. 'Is your life so bad? You have a husband who practically serves you, two living children. You also have a farm that produces food on land that is ours.'

Kadmus and Isadore stood up at the same time, their chairs scraping the wooden floor, and walked out of the house. They always preferred the cold outdoors if the alternative was a warm house filled with tension.

Dahlia watched them leave and then turned back to Aldara. 'You have changed,' she said, studying her daughter. 'You are stronger, perhaps.'

'What were you expecting when you thrust me into that

life without so much as a conversation as to what my role would be there?'

'It did not matter what your role was. Anything is better than a life of poverty.'

Aldara swallowed. 'It's not what you imagine. It's not easier than this life.'

Dahlia turned her face to the soup. 'You were spoiled here as a child.'

'I was happy here as a child, despite your best efforts.'

Dahlia picked up her soiled apron and tied it around her waist. 'You come back here with your fine new dresses, forgetting what it is to wear rags.'

Aldara could not continue. 'Stop measuring your wealth in coin. You are missing the things that matter. Have the dresses for yourself if you think they will bring you happiness, but I can assure you they will not.' She walked over to her bed and scooped up her cloak. 'Unless you need my help, I'm going to go find Father and Kadmus. Make myself useful,' she added.

Dahlia gave the soup one more stir and then looked at her. 'Why did he send you back?'

Aldara shrugged, imagining the expression on Fedora's face at seeing the gesture. 'It's not what you think. He thought I would be safer here.'

'Safer from whom?'

'Safe from uncertainty. The Companion trade has changed things.' Aldara was not sure how much her mother knew of the agreement.

Dahlia nodded. 'There has been talk of it in the village.' She put down the spoon. 'But why send you away? What was he afraid of?'

Aldara shook her head again. He was afraid of many things. 'Two Companions were sent to Onuric Castle in Zoelin to mentor the women being traded. One of them was Prince Stamitos's Companion, who was sent without his knowledge. It did not go well.'

Dahlia's eyes were alive now. 'Prince Tyron sent you here to ensure you would be safe.'

'Yes.'

'Why?'

Aldara opened her hands and shook her head. 'You already said it. He wanted me safe.'

'That does not answer the question of why he is so concerned for your safety.'

'He did not want me falling into Zoelin hands.'

'Yes, but why?'

'Mother, tell me what answer you want and I will give it you.'

'An honest one,' she said, crossing her arms in front of her. 'Why did Prince Tyron give you back to your family? If he did not want you sent to Zoelin, he could have sold you to a Syrasan buyer.'

'Because he did not want me traded like stock.'

'Why?'

Aldara looked around, searching for words. 'Because... he has a kind heart.'

'And because he loves you?'

Aldara stepped back from the words.

Satisfied by that reaction, Dahlia turned back to the stove, reached into the barley bag, and threw a handful of it into the soup. It sank to the bottom, clouding the water.

'There is no place for love between a prince and his Companion,' Aldara whispered.

'Another reason you are here,' Dahlia said, not looking at her.

Aldara walked past her mother and out the door.

Outside the air was cooling as the sun began its descent. Aldara wrapped her cloak around her and headed for the barn. She needed to do something physical to distract herself from the raw mental ache. Every mention of him, every thought of him, was followed by the sensation of falling. She wanted to tear out every memory of him so she could at least breathe properly.

She slipped through the small side door, closed it behind her, and leaned against it. The sheep eyed her with suspicion. Loda was tethered outside of her stall, saddle removed, waiting to be groomed. Their other horses had been brought in out of the cold and stood together for warmth. The milking goat walked over to greet Aldara, checking her hands for food. Once it realised there was nothing on offer, it trotted away to cause havoc among the sheep. The lucky remaining hens had settled themselves in secret nooks of the barn. Except for the rooster; he was scratching at the hay in search of food while keeping a watchful eye on Aldara. She was surprised to see a rooster at all; they usually drove Dahlia mad with their crowing and ended up in the pot on the stove as soon as they reached maturity.

She pushed off the door and walked over to where Loda was tethered, running a hand down her neck. 'Don't be expecting any fancy feeds from now on,' she said, picking up a brush and sweeping it over her. After she had put the mare into her stall, she sat on the straw-littered floor next to it and watched Loda pick through the old hay.

Kadmus came through the large door and the sheep dispersed. He shrugged off his cloak and walked over to where she was sitting. 'You're still in one piece.'

'Externally, yes.'

'Look at how lazy you have become. There is tack that needs cleaning, you know?'

She smiled, eyes on Loda, who was circling in preparation for a luxurious roll. Kadmus grabbed a pail of soaked

117

barley and divided it between the feeding pails. 'Do you want to tell me what happened at Archdale?' he asked without stopping.

'No. Not today.'

'All right. Then do you think you can stop moping long enough to help me?'

She glanced at him. 'That I can do.' She stood and brushed the hay off her dress. The smell of the barley reached her as she neared him.

'I am glad you are back,' Kadmus said.

Her gaze returned to him. His tunic had a hole in the sleeve and was fastened with a piece of rope. 'Where is your belt?'

He picked up the last pail and looked down at his waist. 'It's being used as a girth on my saddle. Long story. I can replace it now, thanks to your generous royal lover.'

She reached down and picked up a pail. 'Let's not speak of him. Or make jokes. Not yet, anyway.'

He nodded. 'I wasn't trying to be funny.'

'Because you rarely succeed?'

He scooped up a small handful of barley and threw it at her.

'That's for the horses!' she said, laughing. The sensation was so unusual that she fell silent as soon as she felt it.

Kadmus noticed. 'You are allowed to laugh.'

'I know,' she said, brushing the barley off her dress. 'I am just surprised that I can.'

He picked up the other two pails. 'That's why he sent you here, isn't it?'

He was right. Tyron had sent her not only to a place where she was safe, but a place where she could laugh freely. Nausea rose within her as she recalled their final words to each other, words they could not take back. He had known she could find happiness in her old life. That was why he gave up her up, leaving himself alone inside the cold walls of Archdale. She said the words aloud that she had been unable to say to him. 'He made the right decision.'

But the pain of that decision would follow them.

CHAPTER 16

*E*ldoris looked at the untouched tray of food beside Tyron's bed. When he did not offer her a chair, she dragged the one near the window over to his bedside and sat down, taking in his long beard. It had been almost a month since the girl had departed, and he had not trimmed it once. His long hair hung across his closed eyes. He was not sleeping, just shutting her out.

'There is a man arriving tomorrow,' she told him. 'I believe he may be able to help you.'

He opened his eyes for a moment, but the weight of his lids made them close again. 'Do not waste any more of the physician's time. There is nothing wrong with me.'

She poured some water into a cup and offered it to him. 'There is nothing physically wrong with you, but your mind continues to… prohibit your health. This man is not a physician as such.'

He did not take the water from her. 'Another priest? To rid me of my demons?' He opened his eyes then.

She suppressed a smile. 'I apologised for that. I thought we ought to try God's way first.'

He propped himself up on his elbows and looked at her. 'Who is he?'

'I suppose he is a physician of sorts, one who specialises in healing the mind. My sister recommended him. He is travelling from Galen and will arrive in Veanor tomorrow.'

Tyron frowned at her. 'A healer who does not resort to exorcism or copious amounts of potent herbs?'

Eldoris exhaled. She understood his reservations. He had been alone in the dark for years. 'His approach is scientific. That is all I know, I am afraid.' She glanced down at his body, which had begun to waste. 'Would it help if she were here?'

He pushed himself up into a sitting position, not bothering to cover his bare chest. 'You wanted her gone, now she is gone. Must we keep discussing it?'

Eldoris took a long breath in. 'I want you well more than I want the Companion tradition eradicated.'

'How is Stamitos today?' Tyron said, changing the subject.

Her expression softened. 'His arm continues to heal, but he seems to spend as much time in his chambers as you.' She looked down into her lap. 'He went to pick something up with the missing hand while I was visiting with him yesterday, claims he can still feel it.'

'That is not uncommon.'

'It is heartbreaking to watch. I seem to be running out of ways to help my children,' she said, looking up.

Tyron nodded. 'I'm sorry for it, you know. Perhaps you all blame me.'

Eldoris felt her chest pull. 'Not at all. Why would you say such a thing?'

'Because I am an excellent swordsman and I could have acted before it came to that.'

She felt guilty at having had that exact thought when

she learned what had taken place. 'If any harm had come to Grandor Pollux, it would not have boded well for our alliance.'

Tyron regarded her. 'That is what we all say, but not what we think. Leksi had a sword to the man's throat. I told him to put it away.'

'Because it would not bring back your brother's hand.'

'I had a dagger I could have used any time I pleased. I have killed men at a much greater distance.'

'And then we would have been left with King Jayr's advisor dead on Syrasan soil. That is why you did not act, because it would have been an act of war.'

Tyron let out a loud breath of air. 'What is Father's great plan for him now?'

'He does not have one at this point,' she said, shifting in her chair. 'He cannot fight. And we will struggle to find a partner for him…'

'I know a young woman who would marry him, but she is in Zoelin.'

Eldoris closed her eyes. 'She is currently a *prisoner* in Zoelin.'

Tyron blinked. 'What do you mean?'

'We received word from Drake Castle that there was an incident.'

'What sort of incident?'

Eldoris had planned on keeping the news from Tyron, but he clearly cared for the well-being of the girl. Not only because Stamitos loved her, but due to the friendship she had shared with Aldara. 'Pandarus left for Zoelin this morning to investigate—or rather, smooth things over. King Jayr is eager to satisfy his buyers and wrote requesting that we send another mentor in her place.'

'We are running out of those. Does Stamitos know?'

'No. You cannot say a word. Let us wait until Pandarus

returns, and then we can decide on a course of action.' She stood and bent to kiss Tyron's cheek. 'In the meantime, let's focus on getting you out of this room.'

'I get out most days.'

She returned upright. 'And by the afternoon you are exhausted. Pero tells me you are still waking from dreams during the night.'

'Pero needs to stop telling you things.'

'He is loyal to his queen.'

'Yes, it's a problem.'

There was humour in his tone, which pleased her. 'I would not be doing my job as your mother if I did not watch over your welfare.'

He reached across and picked up the cup of water, emptying it in a few gulps. 'Let's pray this man from Galen can perform miracles,' he said, setting the cup back down.

'I never stop praying,' the queen whispered.

There was no easing back into her old life; there was too much to do. Once the sun had gained strength, they planted seed potatoes outdoors and hoped they would survive the frost, then prepared the soil for barley. Isadore and Kadmus worked long hours with the harrow while Aldara and Dahlia took care of the rest of the chores on their own. They waited for the air to warm so they could shear the sheep and try to sell the wool at market. The profits from the wool would see them through until the lambs arrived. If they sheared too soon, there would be no lambs at all.

'How is the quality of the wool this year?' Aldara asked Dahlia as they were closing the barn door behind the sheep.

'It will do.' Dahlia placed her hands on her hips while she caught her breath. The sheep had been grazing in the far paddock and had not made the journey easy for them. She squinted against the low sun. 'We are surviving on the prince's charity right now.'

Aldara glanced down at her raw hands and picked at a splinter in her finger. Fedora would be horrified to see the state of her hands. It was funny how she continued to have those thoughts.

'They will toughen up,' Dahlia said, walking past her towards the house.

They had been repairing fences all week. Wild boars did more damage to them than the two women could keep up with. The weight of the posts and the labour-intensive task left Aldara's entire body aching at the end of each day.

'I still have to launder the clothes,' Dahlia said, not stopping. 'When you are done feeding the animals, the items will need to be hung.'

Aldara exhaled. She had no idea if her arms would cooperate given how much they were shaking. 'All right.' They too would toughen.

Every evening, Isadore fell asleep in his chair while Aldara weaved as best she could with blistered hands. Dahlia would stand near the stove preparing barley bread for the following day. If there was no grain, she would simmer up the bones from the evening meal to make a broth. She was always on her feet, which showed in her cracked heels.

Kadmus's eyes would follow her about the house. As soon as she was out of earshot, he would ask Aldara to share stories about Princess Cora. He was intrigued by her and, like most men, besotted. Aldara would try to recall small details that might interest him, but she never mentioned the day she found the princess intoxicated in an abandoned corridor. There was something about the encounter that felt private, and a retelling of it felt like a betrayal. To whom, she did not know.

Dahlia would eventually collapse into a chair to mend their clothes and tut at anything she had overheard. When there were no more stories to tell about Cora, Aldara told others. Stories about the Companions, Prince Stamitos, Prince Pandarus, the queen. Occasionally she would exaggerate them just to hear Kadmus laugh because she had missed the sound of it. She never spoke about the king out of respect, and never about Tyron because she could not bear it. And Kadmus never asked.

Nights were the only time she indulged thoughts of him. She replayed their final meeting in her mind, dissecting it, punishing herself for it. The hardest part was when her mind went further back, to days of bare skin and open mouths, of glances and careful distances. Days of shared pain and something else. She would lie awake waiting for sleep to come, her body exhausted and mind racing, long after the stove had stopped offering heat. Then the room would fill with silver light, and a new day would begin.

Whenever Dahlia went into Roysten for supplies, Aldara remained on the farm, wanting to avoid the judgemental stares and frozen smiles from families she had known all her life. People tended to be in better spirits in the warm season, so she held off for optimum weather before venturing into ridicule.

One afternoon, Dahlia returned from the village with a small bag of dried beans and some salted pork. Aldara could tell she was in a bad mood the moment she stepped down from the cart.

'Were there any letters?' Aldara asked.

Letters were distributed via the local priest.

Dahlia stilled, narrowing her eyes on Aldara. 'I have been trying to feed us, not attending church. Who are you expecting will write to you?' She thrust the few goods at her daughter.

'No one,' Aldara replied, looking away.

'Add half of the beans to the pot,' Dahlia said. 'A lot of good Prince Tyron's coin does us when there is barely any food available to buy.'

Aldara flinched.

'You better make it a third,' Dahlia said, walking away. 'God only knows what we will be able to buy next time.'

'We'll have potatoes soon,' Aldara called after her. 'And carrots.'

'We'll be eating them green at this rate.'

'Perhaps you should let Kadmus slaughter a sheep.'

Dahlia stepped into the house without replying.

By evening, there was still no improvement in her mood.

'Those ewes better produce lambs,' she said. Her head shook as her thoughts raged inside of her.

'It is too early to confirm how many, but there will be lambs,' Isadore said. He was not asleep after all, just slouched in his chair with his chin resting on his chest and his eyes closed.

Later that week the barley ran out. There was no more bread. Aldara shook the empty bag above the empty pot and watched the dust settle atop the liquid. She went outside and dug up a few potatoes.

'They're still green,' Kadmus said as he walked past her on his way to the barn.

'Yes, I'm aware of that. When are the chickens going to start laying again?' she said to his back.

'Probably when the lambs arrive,' he called over his shoulder.

That evening Kadmus made a comment about the green potatoes. It was only a joke, but Dahlia stood up and shouted at him across the table.

'Go and find something to put in it or keep your mouth closed!' Because there was nowhere for her to go, she sat down again.

Kadmus stood up and went off to the barn. They heard the creak of the small door as it opened and closed. The distressed bleating of a ewe made them all go still in their chairs. Dahlia later discovered that the ewe he had slaughtered was pregnant. She did not speak to anyone for three days, but each one of those days they sat in content silence, bellies filled with mutton. They used the entire animal, nothing wasted. When all that remained was a carcass, they boiled the bones until they fell apart in the water.

'Tell me again about the food at Archdale,' Kadmus said one evening.

Aldara put the basket down and described the food at some of the feasts she had attended. Details of entire roasted pigs, baked quail, the freshest wheat bread she had ever tasted, the finest wines from Galen where grapes grew like weeds. Dahlia pretended she was not listening, but even the strong feel hunger.

Later that night, Aldara and Kadmus lay awake in their beds, listening to the sounds of those sleeping above them.

'It wasn't all feasting and fun, was it?' Kadmus asked.

Aldara had known he was awake by his breathing. 'No. It wasn't all feasting and fun.'

Kadmus was silent for a moment. 'Did he ever hurt you?'

'Tyron never hurt me.' He had never meant to.

'What about Pandarus? I saw the two of you together at the flag tournament. He was angry at you for some reason.'

Because I saw through him, she thought. 'He never put a hand on me,' was all she said in reply.

Kadmus was quiet again before speaking. He asked her questions, and she answered them. She was ready to share, to let her brother see the events that had shaped her.

'Even after all of that, you did not want to return here?'

She was lying on her side, and when she blinked, a few tears ran across her nose. 'No.'

He took a moment to think over her answer. 'Promise me you will never go back there. Prince Tyron is right—he can't protect you.'

'I can't make that promise,' she said. 'If he came here tomorrow and asked me to go with him, I'd go.'

'Asked you to go where?'

She swallowed. 'Anywhere.'

After Kadmus had fallen asleep, she tried not to think about Tyron's warm hands, the weight of his arm laying across her, or the feel of his stubble pressed against her forehead. She closed her eyes tight and tried to trick herself into thinking she was actually asleep.

When she opened her eyes, it was still dark, so she waited for the light to arrive. All she could do was wait—wait for the weather to warm, for the lambs to arrive, for the barley to grow. Wait for her life to begin again.

But it could not begin again, because she was still waiting for him.

CHAPTER 17

*T*yron stood with his father in the throne room. Pandarus had just returned from Zoelin and was on his way to meet with them. In the two weeks since his departure, Tyron had been working intensely with Evios, the physician his mother had shipped from Galen to treat him. Even in that short amount of time, he had noticed increased energy levels and improved sleep. The daily sessions had begun with uncomfortable conversations that forced him to delve into dark places he had been trying to shut down, then evolved to a treatment of induced sleep, after which he woke feeling light and calm—a method that would have the bishop praying for his soul if he knew.

The doors swung open and a guard entered. 'Prince Pandarus, Your Majesty.'

Pandarus walked in wearing royal dress and appearing suitably tired. He looked at his father and then at Tyron. No one spoke for a moment.

'Let the queen know Pandarus is here,' Zenas said to the guard.

Tyron stepped forwards and placed a hand on his

129

brother's shoulder. The action felt uncomfortable, but he was aware that Pandarus had been taking care of everything on his own since the incident. 'Sit,' he said to Pandarus. 'You must be tired after the journey.'

Pandarus glanced at the hand on his shoulder. 'I am exhausted,' he replied. 'I see you have finally emerged from your chambers. The physician was worth his hefty fee?'

Tyron withdrew his hand. There was always something in Pandarus's tone that had that effect on him.

The doors opened again. 'Queen Eldoris, Your Majesty,' said the guard.

Zenas gestured for her to be sent in.

Eldoris walked straight to Pandarus and took hold of his face. 'Thank God you are well and safe. I feel as though I hold my breath each time you cross that river.'

Pandarus lowered his head so she could kiss his cheek. 'Is that how you feel, brother?' He glanced a Tyron, his lips curved into a smirk.

'Do not start,' Zenas said. 'We are all pleased to see you safe.'

Eldoris looked between them. 'Of course we are all pleased. What news do you have of the girl?'

It did not go unnoticed by Tyron that his mother never gave the Companions names.

'I need to sit first,' Pandarus said, signalling to the large table.

Tyron pulled a chair out for his mother and sat down next to her. They all watched as Pandarus fell into his chair and exhaled to highlight his fatigue.

'There was a plethora of reasons why she was imprisoned, one of which was attacking a guard who had been ordered to follow her.'

'Good heavens,' Zenas said. 'Does the girl have no sense? What does King Jayr say on the matter?'

'He likes to make an example of people who do not follow his rules. There was talk of beheading her in front of the other Companions.'

Everyone was silent for a moment.

Tyron leaned forwards. 'Where is she now?'

'Now mentoring alongside Hali at Onuric. He agreed to let me speak with her and I pulled her into line.'

Tyron kept his expression neutral. 'You pulled her into line?'

'Yes. I told if her if she ever wanted to return to Syrasan, she needed to perform her role and do it smiling.'

'And she agreed?'

'No. She wanted information on Stamitos in exchange for her compliance. I should have just let King Jayr kill her.'

'Pandarus,' Eldoris said, disapproval in her tone. 'Are you forgetting what she means to your brother?'

'I went to Zoelin to sort out this mess, did I not? We cannot all flail about the castle,' he said, glancing at Tyron.

Tyron let the comment blow past him.

'And what does King Jayr say of Grandor Pollux cutting off Stamitos's hand?' Eldoris asked.

Pandarus shook his head. 'That he is lucky to be alive. What did you think he would say? Stamitos went at the man with a sword.'

They all looked at the table in front of them.

'Perhaps we should request that he release the girl back to us,' Eldoris said.

Zenas sat back in his chair. 'For what purpose? Our son will have lost his hand for nothing.'

'Her safety,' Eldoris said. 'And our son's happiness.'

Zenas waved a hand. 'We sent her away for a reason. Bringing her back now will only prolong the issue. Let us focus our efforts on finding the boy a wife rather than indulging him.'

'What quality of wife do you think we will find for him now?' Eldoris asked.

They would struggle to find a royal partner for Stamitos once word got out of his injury. He was damaged goods in the eyes of neighbouring kingdoms. The King of Braul might be persuaded to hand over a daughter to an invalid for the right amount of grain, but they needed the grain being imported from Galen to feed their own people and to trade with Corneo to maintain the treaty.

'At the very least, one of noble birth,' Zenas said, getting up from the table.

'Where are you going?' Eldoris asked him.

He paused and looked at her. 'Your blame is far too thinly veiled for me to remain seated here.' He walked to the door and exited the room.

Eldoris watched him leave, and then her gaze fell to her lap. Pandarus drummed his fingers on the large table to fill the silence.

'I suggest you search south for a wife. Any noble household will be happy to hand over a daughter right now.'

'Why is that?' Tyron asked.

Pandarus looked at him. 'Because they are all dying of hunger in the south.'

Tyron shook his head. 'There is still plenty of wealth in the south.'

'You have been locked away for too long, brother. Coin is useless to them. There is no food to buy.'

Pandarus pushed his chair back and followed his father. Eldoris and Tyron remained seated alone.

'Are the food shortages in the south really that bad?'

Eldoris's expression softened. 'It is the same every year emerging from the cold season. Crops are being planted. Things will soon improve.' She stood and walked over to him.

'I should have sent food with her, not coin.'

She kissed the top of his head. 'You gave her freedom. You are not in control anymore. Leave her be.'

The clearer his mind became, the more he realised his decision had not solved all of her problems, only presented new forms of vulnerability. One thing was becoming very clear—he was unable to leave her be.

CHAPTER 18

*W*hen Aldara heard the cart pull up, she ran out of the house, face flushed with excitement. 'The first lamb arrived,' she said as her mother stepped down.

Dahlia had been in the village selling the wool they had taken from the sheep a few weeks earlier. 'Thank God,' she said, walking to the back of the cart.

Aldara followed her to help unload the supplies, though it had stopped being a two-person job some time ago. She was surprised to see a wooden crate filled with grain and preserved food. She went still. 'Where did you buy this?'

Dahlia stood next to her, looking at the crate and shaking her head. 'The curate found me in the marketplace and asked me to collect it from the church. I thought it was a letter, but this arrived two days ago. Delivered by the king's men.' She glanced at Aldara. 'I suppose I need not ask who would be sending us food from Archdale?'

Tyron. He had always hated the thought of her being hungry. 'Was there a letter with it?'

Dahlia shook her head. 'No.'

Aldara closed her eyes. She should have felt grateful, but she felt robbed. What harm could a few words do? Then she realised the answer was much. The gesture in itself was almost knocking her legs out from beneath her.

'He has not forgotten you,' Dahlia said, reaching forwards and dragging the crate closer. She picked it up and carried it inside the house.

Aldara still had not moved. She opened her eyes and stared at the space where the crate had been. She could almost feel him in that moment. It was as though he were standing behind her and she was waiting to feel the weight of his hand. A few pieces of hair moved at the base of her neck, and she turned her head to look behind. There was nothing but a few hens roaming in the wide, empty space. He was gone from her then. She reached out and took hold of the cart to balance herself, wondering when the memories of him would fade to bearable.

Later that afternoon, she rode along the boundary checking the fences and came across a broken rail. The culprit was almost always boars. They did not care for fences. She dismounted and picked up the wooden peg that had snapped under the force of the animal. Her eyes moved down the rail to where its hair had become wedged in the splintering wood. They were coming for the lambs. She had seen newborn lambs with their stomachs torn open to get at the milk inside of them. The sheep needed to graze, so they would have no choice but to guard them.

She turned back to Loda to get tools from the saddle-bag, laying her bow and quiver on the grass by her feet. Hopefully she would have time to practice once she had finished her chores for the day. The problem was that they were never finished. She pulled a wooden hammer and peg from the bag and lifted the heavy rail, holding it in place with her hip while she made the repairs. When she was done, she tested the strength of her work using the heel of her boot. Satisfied it would hold, she went to put the hammer back in the saddlebag when Loda took fright, running sideways into the fence.

'Easy,' Aldara said, catching hold of her rein.

The deep growl of a boar came from behind her. She spun around and saw a brown boar with grey tusks, its mouth curved into a sneer, charging towards them. She swooped down and grabbed the bow with one hand, pulling an arrow from the quiver with the other. The bow was loaded and aimed at the boar within moments. A harrowing squeal came from the boar as the arrow pierced its head. Its legs continued to run for a few paces before it collapsed at her feet.

Loda reared and Aldara grabbed hold of her rein again. 'Easy girl. Easy.' The mare's hooves returned to the ground and she let out a few snorts of protest as she stepped back from the dead animal. Aldara was panting and shaking, but also smiling. The realisation that she could protect herself and her beloved mare was more empowering than she could have imagined. 'Let's take him back to the house,' she whispered.

Aldara secured a rope around the hind legs of the boar and attached the other end to the front of the saddle. She made Loda take a few steps to introduce the idea to her. The mare danced sideways, not trusting the movement of the dead animal dragging behind. They made their way back along the fence in search of Kadmus, who had gone to check on the sheep. She was almost at the house when she spotted him. He had already locked the sheep in the barn and was leaning against the fence talking to their neighbour. Byrgus was seventy-four years old and had the only orchard in the area that produced apples. The orchard supplied the few noble households in the south, and on good years sold at market where there was no competition.

Byrgus's eldest son had volunteered as a foot soldier during the recent Corneo war and had died of typhoid a few days before the retreat. A year later, Byrgus's only remaining son died of infection from a minor injury to his leg. The old man continued to work alongside his grandson, who was a year younger than Aldara.

'Good afternoon, Byrgus,' she said when she was close enough to be heard. 'I see your trees have flowered.' She stopped next to them. When he did not reply or look at her, she asked, 'Are you expecting a good season?'

He pushed off the fence, back straight, his silver hair almost glowing with the low sun behind it. His eyes travelled to the dead boar before settling on her. He nodded in her direction, turned back to Kadmus and mumbled a few departing words before turning to leave.

Aldara looked at Kadmus, whose gaze remained conveniently on the boar. 'Should I have not mentioned the apples?'

Kadmus turned to check that Byrgus was out of earshot.

'What's wrong? Are you worried that my words might offend him?' Her tone was clipped.

He finally looked at her. 'Why are you dragging a dead boar around with you?'

'It came at Loda and me, so I killed it.'

He let out a huge breath and shook his head. 'You shot it with an arrow?'

'You sound surprised.'

'Was it standing still?'

She glared at him. 'You're avoiding my question. That man cannot ignore me forever.'

Kadmus walked over to inspect the boar. 'He is an old

farmer who does not understand the way of things anymore.' He bent down and studied the bloody patch of fur where the arrow had gone through. 'Right between the eyes.'

She exhaled. 'You're defending his rudeness. Does he think I sold myself? That when I arrived at Archdale, I was given a choice about how to spend my time there?'

Kadmus said nothing.

'He stills speaks to our mother, who orchestrated the entire thing.' She swallowed and looked down at her feet.

'He does not understand,' Kadmus said, standing up. 'And what do you care what one old man thinks?'

'It is not one old man, is it? It's an entire village. That's why I don't leave the farm.' When her eyes returned to him, she saw pity on his face that made her turn away again.

'You will be mother's favourite child when you return home with this prize.'

She shook her head. 'I could return with a singular of boars and be met with indifference.'

He smiled, and his gaze swept across the bare paddocks. 'They are coming for the lambs.'

She nodded.

'They'll need to be watched when they are grazing from now on,' he said.

She reached out and stroked Loda's head. 'We can take shifts if you like?'

He shook his head. 'Normally I would laugh at you and tell you to remain close to the house, but you have proven that you are more than capable of taking care of yourself.'

His words made her feel warm. 'Yes. It's as though I've just realised it myself.'

He looked at her. 'Are you all right? I hope he didn't get to you.'

'He is not the first man to view me as a harlot, and he certainly won't be the last.'

He nodded and smiled. 'I see something far more fierce than a harlot.'

Aldara glanced at the paddock that Byrgus had hobbled across. 'He better keep his grandson away from me, then.'

Kadmus laughed and clapped his hands together. 'Come on,' he said, draping an arm across her shoulders. 'Let's go show Mother your kill.'

CHAPTER 19

Tyron went to the feast because it was the first social gathering Stamitos had attended since losing his hand. He would normally have found an excuse to be absent, especially when the sole purpose of the gathering was for Pandarus to share news of a flag tournament that could have been announced via a public notice. Instead he arrived late, slipping into the seat between Cora and Salome, who always found a way to have a chair between them. He looked at Salome, who had a hand resting protectively across her bulging stomach.

'How are you feeling?'

She glanced at him, a weak smile on her grey face. 'The sickness never eases.'

Tyron smiled at her. 'Just a few more months and the baby will be here. You will finally be able to eat again.'

'And then a few more children,' Cora added, eyes ahead. 'Especially if it is a girl.'

A worried expression came over Salome's face. 'I am not sure I will survive it a second time.'

Cora looked across at her. 'You do not have a choice.

Even if it is a boy, you will be expected to produce more children.'

Salome turned back to the guests. Tyron glared at Cora and she raised her shoulders in a shrug.

'You know I pride myself on honesty,' she said, turning away from him.

'You might want to tone the honesty down. The virtue has crossed into mean.'

He liked Salome. She was quiet, sincere, and was trying to find a way to survive within his family. He looked across as she picked up her fork and pushed a small piece of quail around her plate. She stood suddenly, hand over her mouth.

'Excuse me,' she said, fleeing the table.

Tyron stood up, watching her plough through the guests towards the door. 'Perhaps you should go after her,' he said to Cora. 'She's quite ill.'

'Her ladies will take care of her. I am the last person she wants hanging about when she is feeling unwell.'

Tyron sat back down and stared at his sister. 'Perhaps if you were not so hostile towards her, she might welcome the company.'

'I am hostile towards everyone. She chooses to take it personally.'

Tyron took a large drink of wine, barely tasting it. He looked out to where Stamitos was moving between guests, his infectious smile gone, but a warming sight nonetheless. So much had changed in the months that had passed. Sapphira was no longer next to him, mirroring his joy and distracting him from his responsibilities. There was no dancing Idalia, no conspiring Hali next to a golden Aldara. Even Astra had lost her shine amid the change and uncertainty.

But the tradition would continue. Tyron had learned

only that morning that his father had purchased the physician's daughter from Nuwien. She had arrived at Archdale and was no doubt locked away, receiving Fedora's special attention. Tyron realised that his father's decision to take another Companion likely stemmed from loneliness. Zenas had the same needs of any other man. Power was not a substitute for a warm body beside you in bed, someone to walk in the sun with, or a smile made from something you said. Unfortunately, the king's actions had a roll-on effect, and the queen was nowhere to be found that evening.

Zenas stood up from his chair, a few seats down from Cora, and clanged his cup with a fork. The guests went silent. He spoke to them of Syrasan's strength and new prosperity, and of Pandarus's foresight and nurturing of alliances. He spoke of peace, but he lacked conviction. Tyron stopped listening. He looked across the room to where Lord Yuri sat with Rhea, listening to the speech. Part of Rhea's role was to identify noble guests who seemed misplaced or lonely. But Rhea could not help Lord Yuri, because like Tyron, he was experiencing the room without the one person who brought meaning to it all. It was not a problem that could be fixed by the attentions of a woman.

When the king had finished and returned to his seat, conversation resumed, music played, and the lies evaporated almost as quickly as they had been spoken.

Cora poured herself some more wine and gestured towards Astra, who was talking to Lord Theon. 'That one barely visits Pandarus's chambers anymore. And when she does, she flees at first light.'

Tyron watched Astra for a moment. 'Is that what your spies told you?'

'Yes,' Cora replied without shame.

He looked at his sister, his eyes moving down to the cut-out sections of her dress around the torso. He had to assume their father had not noticed the dress yet, as he would have deemed it inappropriate for a lady of her standing and sent her off to change it. 'Perhaps Pandarus wants to spend more evenings with his wife.'

She picked up her cup and laughed into it. 'Don't be ridiculous. He has not spent a night with her since she announced that she was with child,' she said, glancing at him over the rim of her cup. 'His new maid, on the other hand…'

Tyron shook his head. 'And here I was thinking the maids were acting as your spies.'

'They are. Just not that particular one.' She took another drink and set her cup down. 'I don't think Lord Yuri is happy with his replacement. He liked the curvy one. I think Pandarus broke his heart when he sent her off to Onuric.'

Tyron glanced again at Lord Yuri and then into his cup. Aldara's heart had also broken the day Hali was sold. 'Why do you pretend not to know their names? You know everything else about them.'

She thought for a moment. 'It keeps the distance between us. I do not want to see the woman beyond the role.'

'Why not?'

She shrugged. 'I might be inclined to feel sorry for them.'

'Would that be so terrible?'

Cora's gaze wandered over to where Panthea was seated with Lord Clio. She was touching her neck as she spoke to him. He said something that made her laugh, and she reached out and brushed his arm with her fingertips. 'They are a constant reminder of what it means to be born

143

a woman. They represent everything I despise about my gender. If I accept them, what message does it send to all the men in this room?'

Her answer surprised Tyron. 'Are you comparing your own life to theirs? That might be a stretch.'

She narrowed her eyes on him. 'One day I will be handed over to a man. No one will consult me, or consider my own feelings towards him. The decision will be a politically advantageous one made by someone else. A male, actually. I have been groomed for that role my entire life. Now look at the women in front of you, the ones allowed in while the wives remain at home. Are we really that different?'

'The women in front of me have multiple levels of appeal. You only have your beauty.'

She waved her cup at him. 'Not true, but it certainly makes Father's plan much easier to implement. Beauty is an easy sell to any man.'

'But your appalling manners add a unique challenge,' he replied, suppressing a smile.

She shook her head. 'Only my beauty, virtue and fertility matter. If you think manners will damage my prospects, then you don't know your own species.'

Tyron thought for a moment. 'Our parents invested as much into your education as they did ours. You cannot deny the fact.'

Cora picked up her cup and emptied it in one gulp. 'The expensive education I received ensured I could speak the language of any future suitor.'

'I recall you learning history.'

She looked at him. 'For the same reason the Companions learn history. To impress men with intelligent conversation. Not women,' she said, filling her cup again. 'Men. I'm no different to them.'

Tyron did not know how to respond because she was right. Before he had a chance to say as much, Leksi walked over and sat in the abandoned chair next to him.

'I think I am getting old,' he said, glancing about the room. 'I am even thinking of leaving here alone.'

Tyron noticed Cora stiffen on the other side of him. Her feelings for Leksi had not changed or gone away with time and age. He knew something about that. 'It is these gatherings that are getting old,' he said, looking over to where Pandarus sat among the wealthy lords of the north, no doubt telling embellished stories that did not belong to him.

Leksi leaned forwards, eyes on Cora. 'My lady, might I say how beautiful you are tonight?'

Cora glanced at him. 'You can say whatever you want,' she replied, keeping her tone disinterested.

Leksi saw through the act, but he played along because he enjoyed it as much as she did. 'Would you do me the honour of a dance? It seems we will be the only ones,' he added, looking around at the seated guests. 'But I'm game if you are.'

She leaned forwards and studied him. 'Can I trust your hands to behave and remain on my dress? I have a reputation to uphold,' she said, glancing at Tyron.

Leksi laughed. 'It will be a difficult task given the lack of material I have to work with. Perhaps you should have worn a different dress.'

She ignored the comment and stood up. The waist of her dress slid a little lower down her hips and Leksi made a point of not looking. 'I just need a moment,' she said, lifting her face to him.

Leksi stood up and gave Tyron a look that suggested he might be in for something. He bowed before stepping away.

Tyron got to his feet so he was eye level with his sister. There was something human in her expression that made him listen.

'I spoke with your Companion before you sent her away.'

Tyron had not been ready to hear Aldara mentioned from his sister's lips. 'All right, I'll bite. When?'

'I had just learned about Stamitos. I was not in a good way.'

'You mean you were drunk.'

Cora gave a small nod. 'You can spare me the lecture, I was just going to say that if I were forced to pick one of them to call by name, it would have been her.'

A wave of something rose in Tyron, making him look away. 'Why is that?'

Cora placed her cup on the table. The action was sloppy. 'Because I see people. Not what they offer up, but the ugly parts they like to keep hidden.'

He swallowed. 'And what did you see in her?'

Her gaze swept the room then. 'The same capacity to see the ugly in people.' Her eyes returned to him. 'And a rare ability to find beauty in them.' She stepped away from the table, her hand outstretched for Leksi to take.

Tyron let his legs fold, landing in his chair with a thud. He picked up his cup and drank, letting the liquid fill the hole in him.

CHAPTER 20

'This is why you shouldn't give them names,' Kadmus said, trying not to laugh. He was driving the cart while their newly-weaned lambs bleated behind them. Aldara sat next to him with her body turned so she could watch them.

'I didn't think we would sell so many,' she said. They had kept a handful of ewes to replace some of the older ones that would be used for food through the next cold season, and one of the larger rams. The rest were sold privately to avoid the uncertainty of selling at market. Dahlia had accepted the offer of a lower price in exchange for the guaranteed sale. 'Who's the buyer?'

'Hagius someone. Works at some manor near Minbury.'

She looked at him. 'Someone from some manor? This is why you needed me to come with you.' She removed her straw hat and turned her face up to the sun. The warmth was glorious.

Kadmus clicked his tongue and the horse moved into a trot. 'It was time for you to leave the farm. It's been three months since you returned. People will have moved on to other gossip by now.'

'I brought my bow in case they come at me with pitchforks.'

They passed an ox grazing at the edge of the road. It continued eating, not bothering to raise its head to look. A small house came into view, an overcrowded vegetable garden enclosed it. A woman was on her knees in the dirt, digging up potatoes by hand. When she heard the cart approaching, she sat back on her heels and placed a hand across her brow to shield the sun as she looked at them. Kadmus raised a hand in greeting, but she did not return the gesture. Her scalding gaze was fixed on Aldara.

'I see not everyone has moved on,' Aldara said. 'She has a son, if memory serves. We can cross him off our list of suitors.'

Kadmus laughed. 'I am fairly confident we will have to look outside of Roysten if you are ever to marry. Though I wouldn't waste too much time thinking on the matter. Mother will choose your husband.'

'A terrifying thought.'

The houses came closer together as they neared the village. The sound of children playing outdoors drifted onto the road. They passed the small church, hidden by trees, and veered off the main road, taking the narrow track behind the blacksmith. Aldara knew her brother was trying to avoid the marketplace to spare her further ridicule, but neither of them mentioned the fact.

The smell of manure and the drone of distressed animals suggested they were close. The sale yards came into view, and Kadmus stopped behind the line of carts at the front. They both watched for a moment as two men stood shouting at one another in a pen full of pigs. Kadmus looked down the line of carts and spotted Hagius standing by the fence, one foot resting on the rail as he listened to the exchange.

'That's him,' Kadmus said, pointing.

Aldara looked at the old man with the rounded back and stooped head.

'Just wait here.' Kadmus hopped down.

She watched them exchange a few words of greeting before Hagius followed Kadmus, on unsteady legs, back to the cart to inspect the lambs.

'Good morning to ya,' he said to Aldara when he reached the cart.

The benefit of doing business with people from other villages was they were not privy to her sins.

'Good morning,' she replied.

Hagius studied the fifteen lambs behind her. 'How many ewes?'

'Eleven,' Kadmus said, pride in his tone as though the gender were somehow his doing. 'Going to breed them?'

Hagius grabbed hold of the closest lamb through the rails and inspected its fleece. It struggled against his experienced grip. 'Might keep a few for it. Got a cart heading to Veanor tomorrow, but these be too young for the journey.' He let go of the lamb and it scurried away to huddle with the others at the other end of the cart.

'Who is your buyer in Veanor?' Aldara asked.

His eyes went to her, looking her up and down before deciding if he should answer. 'Everyone be buyin' in Veanor. Most 'ave the coin for it. Why do you ask?'

She glanced at Kadmus, who seemed to have the same question. 'There's an artillator in Veanor I need to get a message to.'

Hagius eyed her with suspicion. 'Best be letting ya husband take care of business.'

Aldara took a slow breath in through her nose. 'He is

149

not my husband, he is my brother. If I were to supply a letter, could you guarantee its delivery?'

He stepped back as Kadmus opened the cart door. 'I leave the travellin' to the young men. They might take it for a fee.'

She was afraid of that. There was no way her mother would part with coin for such a thing, and there would be no way of tracking if the men had actually delivered it.

'The prince has announced the date for the flag tournament. I'll be headin' to Pelaweth in a few weeks. The noble need feedin'. I could take it that far meself.'

'Aldara here won last year's flag tournament. Perhaps you saw her race?' Kadmus said, reaching out and grabbing hold of a lamb.

'I don't bother bein' a spectator. I don't trust them timekeepers,' Hagius said, glancing at Aldara. 'Women have no business racing men,' he added.

Aldara slid across the seat so the old man would hear her. 'How far is the journey to Pelaweth?'

Hagius pressed his lips together as he thought, making a smacking noise when he released them. 'Takes us a full day with the animals. Sometimes we stop at Archdale and dine with the king,' he said, laughing at his own joke. He held onto the cart while he regained his breath. When he was done, he let go and narrowed his eyes. 'You not thinking of competin' again? Best be also leaving sport to the men.'

Kadmus carried the lamb past them. 'I think my sister will go easy on the men and let them have a turn this year.'

Aldara did not want to talk about the race. She was making plans to see Sapphira's father and tell him in person what had happened to his daughter. He would attend just to get a glimpse of her from across the field, and she knew how his mind would race at her absence.

'The men can have their race all to themselves. There is an artillator I need to see.'

Hagius waved a hand at her. 'Quite a few artillators will be attending. But you best be leaving the hunting to the men also. You get the pride of cooking up the kill.'

Kadmus returned to get another lamb. 'What an honour,' he called to her over his shoulder.

She ignored him. 'Do you need help transporting the sheep to Pelaweth? I would bring my own horse and supplies. I need a chaperone.'

'What are you up to?' Kadmus said, grabbing hold of another bleating lamb.

Her eyes remained on Hagius. She owed this much to Sapphira, and knew her friend would do the same for her. 'What do you say?'

Hagius was studying her. 'You're not one of them castle women, are you? I heard the winner last year was a castle girl. I know 'bout the harlots who seduce their way inside those walls.'

Kadmus handed the lamb to Hagius. 'Do you mind giving me a hand with this one?' He looked at Aldara and shook his head to stop her from replying, then dragged another lamb across the cart floor.

'You don't look like a castle girl,' Hagius said, his voice a low mumble as he passed her with the squirming animal. 'There'll be more of them soon enough from what I hear. All 'bout the place.'

'When is the flag race?' she called to his back.

'It be the fifteenth day of the month,' he shouted, tossing the lamb in the back of his cart. It tumbled, landing on its side next to the others.

She could not stand seeing them thrown about so she jumped down to help. 'What do you say, Hagius?'

"Bout what?'

She picked up a lamb. 'My helping you?'

Hagius shook his head. 'It's not proper for an unwed woman to stay at a public house. Besides, I be delivering the day before and gettin' straight back to things. No time for hangin' about.'

Kadmus gave Aldara a small shove to get her to walk. She reached out her free hand and knocked his hat from his head before walking away.

'Forget the race,' Hagius said. 'Best stay at home and enjoy a spell of peace. Folks 'ave earned it. Boys dying in the east, girls disappearing in the North.'

Kadmus grabbed the last two lambs and carried them off to join the others. When he returned, Hagius took a handful of silver from his pocket and counted it out. He reached past Aldara and handed it to Kadmus.

'You're lucky to be living in the South,' Hagius said to Aldara. 'No one wants the south girls. Too skinny, I suspect.'

'Yes, it's very reassuring,' she replied.

Kadmus pocketed the coin and glanced at her. 'Starvation is a blessing,' he said, laughter in his tone.

Hagius took a long, final look around the yards. 'You best be taking that sister of yours home.'

'Yes,' Kadmus said. 'We don't want her getting in the men's way.'

They walked to the front of the cart. Kadmus held out his hand for her, a smirk on his face. She slapped it away and stepped past him. Hagius gave Kadmus a departing nod as he climbed up next to Aldara. The two of them watched as he climbed back into his cart with great effort, then gave a wave before slapping the reins against the back of his heavy horse. Months of hard work and waiting disappeared down the road.

Kadmus turned and looked at Aldara. She did not look back at him because she knew what he was going to say.

'Why did you ask a stranger to take you to the tournament?'

She watched the pigs in the yard disperse around the men who had settled their dispute. 'Because Mother will never let us both go. You are needed at the farm.'

'Let me deal with Mother,' he replied. 'I have learned a trick or two in your absence.'

She shook her head. 'No you haven't.'

'You're right, I haven't. But leave it to me anyway.' He was not done. 'And if you ever again ask a stranger to take you halfway across the kingdom without speaking to me first, I will make sure you never leave the farm.'

Aldara pressed her lips together to stop from smiling. Her eyes moved over his face. At twenty-one years, his skin already had creases in places usually reserved for men of thirty. She knew he would work himself to his death, the same as her father would. 'What an awful lot of power you think you have.' She faced forwards. 'But thank you,' she added quietly.

He nodded. 'Let's get you back to the farm before you corrupt the village people with your castle ways.'

When they pulled up at the farm, Aldara jumped down from the cart while it was still moving. Her eyes were on the tall chestnut horse tethered in front of the house.

'Judging by that expensive saddle, I'm guessing our visitor is not from around here,' Kadmus called to her.

Aldara was not looking at the saddle, her eyes on the blanket beneath it with the embroidered 'S'. Her heart quickened as she stared at the horse. There was only one place she knew of with horses of that quality.

Leksi appeared from the side of the house where he had been waiting for her in the shade. She felt her blood surge to her head. There was only one reason she could think of why Leksi would travel that far to see her, and she was paralysed by the thought of it.

As he walked towards her, he gave her a reassuring smile. 'Don't look so pleased to see me.'

Her hands were clenched into fists at her sides. She reminded herself to breathe. 'What are you doing here?'

'I was in the area,' he lied. 'I thought I would check in and see how you are doing.'

She glanced about, shaking her head. 'I am... good.'

'You're good?'

'Yes, I'm good.'

Leksi nodded. 'You look good. Thinner, but good.'

Aldara glanced down at herself. Her dress hung a little differently these days. Noticing that her hands were still clenched, she opened them and stretched her fingers. 'Rather less feasting down in the south.'

He smiled again.

Kadmus jumped down from the cart. 'Good day,' he said, walking towards them.

Leksi nodded in his direction. 'Good day.'

Kadmus's eyes went to Aldara. 'Is everything all right?'

She nodded. 'You remember Sir Leksi?'

Kadmus gave a slight bow. 'The indestructible knight I have heard so much about.'

'Your sister exaggerates.'

'He didn't hear it from me,' she said. 'Whenever *I* have mentioned you in conversation, it's always in reference to your wandering eye.'

'The entire kingdom knows of you,' Kadmus said, giving Aldara a disapproving glance. 'You're a hero.'

'I like him,' Leksi said, looking at Aldara.

'I'm going to show Leksi around the farm,' Aldara said.

Kadmus glanced at Leksi. 'All right. I'll be inside if you need me.'

She waited for Kadmus to leave and then looked at Leksi. The worried expression had returned to her face. 'Is he all right?'

Leksi smiled. 'He is all right.'

She was quiet for a moment. 'Did he send you?'

'Does it matter?'

She shook her head. 'I suppose not.'

They walked, passing the barn, feet pressing against the thick, lush grass that now covered the ground.

'Where are all the sheep?'

She turned for a moment. 'Probably in the barn. We've had a problem with boars. I killed one, actually,' she said, glancing across at him. She was not entirely sure why she said it.

Leksi looked at her. 'With your bow?'

'No, with my wit.' She smiled at the ground.

A short laugh came from him. 'You shouldn't make jokes. Wild boars are capable of killing men my size.'

'Only if they are a bad shot. Luckily I had my bow.'

'They are a dangerous animal to hunt, you know?'

'I was not hunting him. He was hunting me.' The last thing she wanted was Leksi reporting events back to Tyron that would have him worrying. And yet there was a small part of her that wanted him to worry enough to come to her himself. Perhaps that was why she mentioned it in the first place. 'We received the food he sent,' she said, changing the subject. 'He need not send anything. I existed

155

in the barren south for sixteen years before he came along. He is no longer responsible for my upkeep. I'm not… his.'

'It has nothing to do with ownership.'

She nodded, eyes on the ground. 'How is Stamitos?' she asked.

'Up and about.'

'And Sapphira?'

'She remains at Onuric.'

'I was hoping they might bring her back. Cheer him up a bit.' When he did not reply, she glanced across to him. 'What is it?'

'I'm not at liberty to discuss the details.'

'I see. What *did* our lordship give you permission to talk about?'

He kept walking, eyes roaming beyond the grassy paddocks to where Byrgus's orchard sat on the horizon. 'I want to hear how you are doing.'

'Because you were in the area.'

'Because I was in the area.'

She exhaled, watching the skirt of her dress move with her feet. 'What would you like to know?'

'Anything. So far, all you have told me is that you killed a boar. Have the people in your village been welcoming?'

A laugh came from her as she swung her arms.

'Ah, not so welcoming, then?'

She looked up at him. 'Were you expecting a different answer?'

'Hoping, perhaps. Has the extra food been helpful?'

'Of course it has. That doesn't mean he should have sent it. Actually, I made the kill the same day it arrived. That beast fed us for weeks. We still have some salted meat if you want some for your return journey.'

He laughed at that.

'What's so funny?'

'I am imagining Tyron's face when I tell him I took your remaining food from you.'

She stopped walking. 'So, you will report back to him, then?' There was a teasing smile on her face.

'Were you expecting a different answer?' he asked, a glint in his eye. 'He sent you away to keep you safe. Naturally, he wants to know you are safe.'

'He is free to write me a letter any time it pleases him,' she said, crossing her arms against the cold.

'Goodness, I don't remember you being quite so pouty as a Companion.'

'I wasn't allowed to be pouty as a Companion. I would have been punished.'

Leksi stopped walking and studied her. 'What would you tell him in your letter?'

She faced him and pressed her lips together as she thought. 'I would tell him that I am thinner and hungrier than I ever was at Archdale.' She opened her callused hands so Leksi could see them. 'That I have never worked as hard as I do now. I am lonely and shunned by people outside of my family. My mother looks at me with the same disappointment Fedora did, because I was meant to live a better life than her and instead I returned here with even fewer prospects because men want to marry virtuous women.' She took a breath before continuing. 'I would tell him I think about him every single day. I keep waiting for the day when I realise it has been a few days since he has come to mind, when I will marvel at my progress. But he keeps blocking me at every turn, by sending food, and sending you, to remind me that he still thinks of me also. I just want one day where he is not in front of me.' She held a hand in front of her face. 'Because he is right there, every day, despite being so far from me.' She put her hand down and shook her head. 'But I would also tell him he made the right decision. He acted bravely in our best interests, something I could never have done. He wanted me safe—I am safe. But that's all I am. That's all we get.'

Leksi nodded and his gaze shifted to his feet. 'I may paraphrase.'

She laughed and her shoulders shook with it. She looked past him to the house where her father had wandered out, pretending to get wood when there was already plenty inside. 'Tell him I am thriving if you think it will help him. Tell him what he wants to hear.'

'I would not be much of a friend if I did that.'

Her eyes returned to him. 'So, what will you tell him?'

He rested a hand on his sword. 'I will tell him you suffer the same.'

CHAPTER 21

yron took a young gelding from the stables and galloped away from the castle. He had no destination, only anger. Weaving through the dense pines, he pushed the eager horse as hard as it could go, jumping obstacles that lay in his way and feeling the sting of low branches as they whipped his face. His horse came to a skidding halt at the edge of a rock-filled stream that was too wide to jump and too hazardous to plough through. The gelding panted hard beneath him, scratches trailing down to his hooves which were buried in the muddy edge of the water.

Tyron folded over the horse's frothing neck, trying to arrange his thoughts into sense and calm. It did not help when he realised where he was. It was the exact spot he had stood with Aldara months earlier when the air had been too cold to satisfy her desires. What had she said that had made his pulse quicken and mouth turn dry? He could not remember. He should have been thankful for the fading memories, but instead it panicked him, because they were all he had left.

There was a selfish part of him that wished she were still at Archdale. She had centred him, calmed him, and been his only source of comfort. She also held the power to undo all of those things, to make him restless, illogical and afraid. The sound of her laughter still rang through the surrounding trees, a haunting reminder that she was still his, despite a piece of paper that said otherwise.

He had sent Leksi south to bring back information he could use to sever the tie. Anything that would save him from his obsessive thoughts. Indifference would suffice, news of a betrothal would have worked, though his head pounded at the possibility. Instead Leksi had spoken of a wasting girl whose dresses were turning to rags. He had almost gone to her himself when told of the boar, but to what end? Instead, he had told Fedora to send dresses he knew she would not wear, and had organised for Lord Thanos to send a working dog that would protect her sheep so she would not have to. He could not bring her back to this life, no matter how much he wanted it for himself.

He needed to focus his energy on his kingdom and people. With grain supplies dwindling, it would only be a matter of time before they fell short of their commitment to Corneo. And then what? Hunger would drive King Nilos's men to the border to take what was his by birthright. Hunger did that to people. They needed the support of the Zoelin army if they were to prevent another war. King Nilos would not be foolish enough to send starving men up against a force that would eradicate them, leaving the throne vulnerable. Every Zoelin soldier was the equivalent of five Corneon men.

But the cost of the alliance was adding up. Each day that passed, King Jayr tightened his inked grip on Syrasan. No one seemed as worried as Tyron. Not true. Tyron saw the shadow of objection in his father. Zenas knew that while the Companion trade might be bringing gold into the kingdom, some costs could not be calculated. But he seemed to have given up, realising that Pandarus's rule was creeping closer, and fighting his son's wishes would not serve the future Pandarus was planning.

Tyron sat up again and closed his eyes while the dizziness passed. He had said no to the trade agreement all along. When Pandarus had asked him long before what he proposed in place of honouring the agreement, he had replied, 'All Syrasan women and children in King Jayr's possession will be immediately returned. In exchange, I will not cross the bridge and disembowel him in front of his family.' He had seen it then, the lifeless expression on his father's face. Zenas did not have it in him to fight that war. He had placed his hands on the table in front of him and said, 'We are not strong enough to fight King Jayr. Pandarus's decisions are difficult for all of us to swallow, but they are the right decisions.'

Tyron opened his eyes and looked down at the running water in front of him. In the past few days, he had felt something dangerous simmering inside of him, something that had been absent for a time. He did not know exactly from where it stemmed, only that if he could turn back time and revisit the day Stamitos lost his hand, he would leave the politics to Pandarus and behave like the soldier he was. He would take the dagger strapped to his leg, aim it at Grandor Pollux, and drive it into the man's throat with precision.

Tyron turned his horse and began a slow walk back to the castle, leaving his thoughts of Aldara amid the ageing pines and letting the breeze fan the flame inside of him.

≈

Aldara walked between the rows of barley with a pail of water, marvelling at the perky seedlings. 'Found you,' she said, sitting on her heels to pick up a grasshopper. She dropped it into the bucket and covered it with the cloth. After all the hard work, she would not let a common pest destroy their crop.

The sound of a dog barking made her stand. She peered out from beneath the brim of her hat, searching for the source of the noise. A cart had pulled up in front of the house and her father stood speaking with the driver. They were both looking down at the dog sitting by the man's feet. Aldara stepped over the neat rows, making her way towards the house. Kadmus had emerged from the barn and was now striding towards them. She watched them, treading carefully for fear of damaging the shoots. The man handed Isadore a letter, nodded a farewell, and then climbed back into the cart. The dog remained sitting in front of her father. Kadmus was next to him now, looking perplexed.

Once she was away from the seedlings, Aldara broke into a run. The dog stood up and let out a single bark to warn of her approach. She stopped still. Kadmus took the open piece of paper from his father and scanned its contents.

'Down,' he called to the dog.

The large, black dog lay down in the dirt, panting.

'What is that?' Aldara asked.

'If you need to ask, that's a problem,' Kadmus replied. 'It's a dog.'

She shook her head. 'No, in your hand.' She gestured towards the letter.

'It's a letter from—' he glanced at the note '—Lord Thanos, with a list of commands that the dog responds to.'

He looked at Aldara. 'Who is Lord Thanos? And why is he giving us a dog?'

Aldara walked over and took the letter from her brother, studying the signature at the bottom of the page. 'I know him. He has a manor in the north and trains dogs there.'

Kadmus and Isadore exchanged a glance.

'And why would this Lord Thanos be giving you a dog?' Isadore asked.

The answer was Tyron. 'I don't know. He is a kind man.'

'This is an expensive, well-trained animal,' Isadore said.

Aldara handed the letter back to Kadmus. There was no point giving it to her father, as he could not read and the action would only cause him embarrassment.

Kadmus whistled at the dog. It leapt to its feet and trotted over to him. 'I think Lord Thanos might have his sights on our Aldara. It's an unusual choice of courting gift, but not entirely inappropriate for the likes of you.'

Aldara shook her head. 'Lord Thanos is married.'

Isadore shifted his weight from one foot to the other.

'It's not what you think,' she added.

'The dog is from Prince Tyron,' Kadmus said. He bent down to rub its head, which was pressing against his leg. 'The food, the dresses, the fancy dog. It's all from him, and it's all for you.' He looked up at Aldara, scrunching his nose in a patronising manner.

'I have heard about a lord in the north that trains these dogs to do remarkable things,' Isadore said, moving the conversation along.

Aldara remembered spending time with Lord Thanos during the last hunt she attended. She recalled the way his dog had sat obediently at his feet amid the chaos. 'Yes. He is remarkable.'

The sound of a cart approaching made them all look up. Dahlia had returned from the village and her eyes were on the dog. She pulled up next to them, squinting against the sun as she stepped down.

'Wherever you got it from, return it. We cannot feed it.' She walked around the back of the cart to retrieve a crate of chickens. They were packed tightly, clucking and flapping their wings in protest. 'I have seen those dogs swallow birds whole.' The dog remained at Kadmus's feet, unfazed by the hysterical birds. 'We are not taking in strays that your father will be forced to dispose of,' she continued. 'No charitable acts until after harvest.'

Kadmus gestured towards the dog. 'She is no risk to the chickens. She's trained to protect stock, and she cost us nothing. A gift,' he said, glancing at Aldara.

Dahlia stood still, eyes on Aldara also. 'A gift from whom?'

'A lord I met while residing at Archdale.' Dahlia nodded and looked away. 'Just an acquaintance,' she added. She did not understand why she felt the need to explain herself. After all, it was the life her mother had chosen for her. 'He is married.'

Dahlia nodded. 'They usually are.'

Aldara glanced at Kadmus and then down at the dog.

'You will have to find a way to feed that thing without taking food from our mouths,' Dahlia said, handing the crate of chickens to Isadore. He carried them off towards the barn. 'If it kills one living thing around here, it goes in the pot. Understood?'

Kadmus bent down and gave the dog another pat. 'Hear that? You can stay.'

After Dahlia had gone inside the house, Aldara and Kadmus remained outside, practicing the commands in the letter and spoiling the animal with ear rubs.

'You should name her Artemis, after the goddess. She was said to be the protector of animals.'

Kadmus nodded. 'Artemis,' he repeated. He stood up and looked at the letter in his hand again. 'According to your fancy lord friend, she is strong enough to take down a boar.'

Aldara's eyes returned to the dog, whose jaw was slack and drooling in the heat. 'Of course she is.'

CHAPTER 22

yron stood with King Jayr beneath the trees in the butts, watching Syrasan archers demonstrate their skills. The king had asked him for a private audience, giving no indication as to what it was he wanted to discuss. Two Zoelin guards waited nearby, smooth chests exposed and faces blank.

Tyron glanced sideways at the king as a stream of arrows was released, taking in the sleeveless leather tunic and muscled arms. It was clear that Jayr continued to train hard despite his position. 'You are free to explore the castle without an escort. You are a guest, after all.'

Jayr kept his eyes on the archers. 'Your army might be half the size of mine, but your men are skilled with a bow.'

Tyron turned back to watch his men. He had fought alongside most of them. 'It is not so small. We have a lot of volunteers, foot soldiers throughout Syrasan who are ready when needed.'

'Untrained common people sent to die before you.'

It was a statement of fact, one Tyron wanted to object to but could not. Hundreds of young men, devoted to their king, poured onto the battlefield with quality weapons and few skills. He closed his eyes for a moment, counted, and breathed deeply. When he opened them, he found Jayr looking at him.

'It is a morbid sight,' Jayr said, eyes shifting forwards again. 'Your men in pieces, the smell of shit and stagnant blood.'

Tyron did not want to have that conversation with the man responsible for the deaths of unarmed Syrasan men. 'What is it you wanted to say that you could not say in front of my father and brother?'

Jayr's mouth spread into a smile. White teeth contrasted his inked face. 'It seems you dislike me.'

It was another statement. Tyron did not disagree with him.

'It does not matter whether you care for me as a man or a king,' Jayr continued. 'The only thing I need is the ability to predict your actions.' He looked at Tyron. 'You may have noticed that I like to be in control.'

'Yes, I have gotten that impression.'

Jayr watched him. 'I never know what to expect from you. It is a problem.'

Tyron's eyes remained ahead. 'It is *your* problem.'

'I see you are an honourable man,' Jayr continued as if Tyron had not spoken. 'And certainly not one to be underestimated.'

A smile flickered on Tyron's face. 'You have been thinking about me. I'm flattered.' He tried to ignore the feel of Jayr's eyes boring into him.

'Why did you send your Companion away?' Jayr asked without warning.

Tyron crossed his arms in front of him, hoping the action covered his surprise. 'Who told you that?'

'She was here during my last visit, and now she is gone.'

Tyron looked at him now. 'So?'

'I understand you cared for the girl.'

He shrugged. 'I care for many when it suits me.' His throat closed as the words left him.

'I hear she was a true prize. Skin like silk.' He leaned in. 'And the softest moans.'

Tyron averted his eyes. The muscles in his neck stiffened with restraint.

'I understand. You were you afraid she might fall into the wrong hands.'

He could not talk about her any longer without breaking the man's nose. 'You did not invite me here to ask about the women I sleep with. What do you want?'

Jayr nodded and looked about. 'You must forgive my intrusive questions. I am trying to understand you better.'

The hiss of arrows sounded in front of them.

'What have you discovered so far?'

'Your loyalties are divided.'

Tyron shook his head. 'You are wrong. My loyalties have always been with my king and the Syrasan people. I want what is best for them, and right now that is peace.'

'Noble of you, swallowing your hatred and inviting me into your home. Sparing the life of my advisor after he cut off your brother's hand. You could have killed him.'

'I wanted to, but my father made his wishes clear.'

'And what of your wishes? You wish me dead, perhaps. And the trade agreement dead alongside me.'

Tyron uncrossed his arms. 'I don't know what sort of confession you are fishing for, but I need to get back soon.'

Jayr glanced down to where Tyron's hand now rested on his sword. 'You may be obedient to your king, but you are not onside. That makes you a threat to my plans.'

'I am too far from the throne to have any power.'

'You have the king's ear.'

'You overestimate me.'

'I overestimate nothing. I see it in his silence and inability to meet your eyes when you speak out.'

Tyron watched the archers reload their bows and take aim. 'It is no secret that I am against the trade agreement. Pandarus should not have signed it.'

'Have you ever asked him why he did?'

Tyron was silent for a moment. 'I cannot imagine you left him much choice.'

Jayr turned his face up to the branches hanging above them. 'To the north of Zoelin is the Asigow empire. Their land spans the distance of Zoelin, Syrasan and Corneo combined. Their armies are six times larger than my own.'

'I know of the Asigow people,' Tyron replied.

Jayr laughed at this. 'You know nothing of the Asigow people.'

'Enlighten me.'

Jayr thought on his words for a moment. 'I see the way you look down on my people. You think us savage men with no laws.'

'You are a liar and a murderer. I cannot speak for the rest of your people.'

'I do what I have to as king, the same as your father.'

Tyron studied his face. 'Tell me, why must you sell Syrasan Companions to Asigow men? What would happen if you told them no?'

Jayr looked at him. 'The reason you know nothing of the Asigow people is because my kingdom behaves as a protective wall.'

Tyron blinked. 'You have been at peace with Asigow for centuries.'

'Because we appease them.'

Tyron laughed then. 'Are you trying to tell me that if you do not provide them with Syrasan women, they will break peace with you? No king, savage or otherwise, would risk war to satisfy a sexual urge.'

'There would not be a war, only annihilation. These men take what they want. There are no civil trade agreements between Zoelin and Asigow.'

Tyron mulled the information over for a moment. 'Do they pay for the women you hand over?'

Jayr sniffed. 'Sometimes with coin. Usually in other ways.'

'Like remaining on their side of the border?'

Jayr turned back to the archers without answering.

'Why are you telling me all of this?'

'Because if we are wiped out by the Asigow people, you will be next. And you will think your quarrel with Corneo laughable.'

Tyron was silent.

'The Asigow people are bigger than us, stronger than us. They worship the sun and do not fear my God or yours. So if they want soft, submissive women with gentle manners and fair hands that barely fill their palms, that is what they get.'

Tyron nodded. 'You give them whatever they want, by whatever means necessary.'

'I believe we have already proven that.'

A bird landed in front of them, collected a bug from the grass, and flew off.

'All right, I understand your motives,' Tyron said. 'But that does not win my approval.'

Jayr shook his head. 'I do not need your approval. I need your compliance.'

'It might be easier to have me killed.'

Jayr's eyes smiled at the corners. 'But you have already proven yourself indestructible when you slaughtered my men in the north.' He looked at Tyron. 'You are a loyal man, not only to your people and your family, but even the women who share your bed. I have thought of a way to ensure your loyalty extends to me for many years to come.'

Tyron frowned at him. 'And what way is that?'

Jayr turned to him and raised his chin. 'You are going to wed my sister, Princess Tasia of Zoelin.'

*A*ldara and Kadmus stood at the entrance of the flag tournament, watching through wooden masks as flames leapt from piled rocks. The four guards shuffled away from the heat as they directed the arriving spectators, their flammable flags merging with the smoke. Aldara looked past them to the elaborate berfroises, which were filling with noble guests. Jewel-laden hands rested delicately on rails draped with heavy velvet. She could just make out the refreshment tables where decorative stuffed birds sat as centrepieces, surrounded by brass cups and trays of imported fruits.

The birds reminded her of the dresses the Companions had worn the year prior. It seemed a lifetime ago. She glanced down at her long-sleeve cotton dress her mother had taken in. All the weight she had gained at Archdale was long gone. Her hair was braided to one side, threaded with fresh flowers she had found on the roadside that morning.

'Let's find the horses some water,' Kadmus said.

They had stayed at a public house the night before to

break up the long journey and planned to do the same on the journey home.

'Keep your mask on,' Kadmus reminded her.

She did not need reminding. The plan was simple: find Sapphira's father, inform him of the whereabouts of his daughter, and get out before anyone recognised her. It was a lot of effort for a simple conversation, but she owed it to Sapphira.

They walked, the horses trailing behind them, heads weighed down with fatigue.

'What is his name?' Kadmus asked.

'Danaus, I think.'

'You think?'

She looked across at him. 'Yes, we were not permitted to talk about our family. From the few hushed conversations we shared about our previous lives, I *think* his name was Danaus.'

Kadmus was quiet as they passed the guards and walked through the entrance. He placed a reassuring hand on his horse as it sidestepped away from the flames.

Once they were inside and out of earshot of the guards, he gestured towards the berfroises. 'They seem to have gone to a tremendous amount of effort. Are there more guests than last year?'

Aldara followed his gaze. 'Yes, there is an extra berfrois this year.' She walked as she spoke. She could not afford to linger.

Grandor Pollux had arrived with some other men she did not recognise and an alarming number of guards. Silence washed over the gathering crowd. News of the events in the north had travelled. Aldara did not know whether they were in awe or fear of him.

'Who is that?' Kadmus said, observing the hushed crowd.

'That is King Jayr's advisor,' she said, looking away. 'Grandor Pollux.'

Kadmus followed her. 'The one who took the prince's hand?'

That was one of his sins. She had not shared everything with Kadmus because no good could come of burdening him with it. 'Yes,' was all she said.

'Stop running, you'll draw attention to us.'

Her feet did not slow. 'I'm not running, I'm getting out of the way.'

Kadmus shook his head. 'I wonder whether Prince Stamitos will attend. What an awkward gathering that would be, drinking left-handed across from the man who cut off your right. Bet you're relieved to be down here this year.'

Aldara glanced over her shoulder at the tall, inked men. She stopped walking when she saw a royal wagon pull up at the step of the berfrois. The noble guests paused their conversations and watched as Princess Cora stepped out, draped in the fur of a white wolf. A fur-covered mask shielded her eyes, and her hair was dotted with small pearls that looked like snowflakes. A long silk skirt spilled across her shoes. She appeared dangerous and breathtaking, and did not so much as glance at the common people waiting to admire her.

'She gets better every year,' Kadmus said.

Aldara glanced at him and then back at the wagon where Princess Salome was stepping down, small, plain, and visibly pregnant.

'That was quick,' Kadmus said, eyebrows raised.

Aldara frowned. 'I can't imagine she was given much choice. Pandarus wants an heir.'

'Might be a girl.'

'What a great disappointment that will be,' Aldara said, her tone dry.

Queen Eldoris was last to step out. Aside from a slim silver mask, she appeared as she always did: understated, elegant, and disinterested.

'Let's go,' Aldara said.

They walked in the opposite direction, swallowed up by the crowd of excited spectators. They did not stop until they were at the far end of the field, where they let the horses drink from a wooden water trough beneath the trees.

Aldara looked about before speaking. 'Let's not stay any longer than we need to.' She felt her breath catching.

'What's wrong?' Kadmus said, narrowing his eyes on her.

'Nothing. I just feel uneasy being here. Danaus will be here somewhere in the crowd,' she said, changing the subject.

Kadmus searched the crowd. 'How do you plan on finding him?'

The spectators began to cheer around them. Aldara and Kadmus looked across the field to where horses, dressed in red and marked with the Syrasan 'S', spilled through the private entrance. A circle of guards formed a barrier around the princes, King Zenas, and King Jayr of Zoelin. Through a flurry of flags, Aldara glimpsed Tyron. Her heartbeat sounded in her head.

'No Prince Stamitos,' Kadmus said. 'A dull afternoon for the noble guests, then.'

Aldara watched as Tyron stopped his horse and stepped down onto the ground. His eyes went to the crowd, scanning the spectators. She felt them brush over her, but she was just another masked face in a crowd of commoners. A groom rushed forwards to take his horse. He glanced up at the berfrois before walking past it, over to the serfs hoping for an audience with one of the princes. She could tell by his body language that he did not want to be there, but he did not have a choice.

Pandarus ignored the waiting men and followed King Jayr into the comfort of the berfrois.

'What's with all the guards? Anyone would think King Jayr afraid of angry northerners,' Kadmus said, a mischievous smile on his face.

'It wouldn't surprise me. People see through the stories fed to them.'

'And yet some are handing over their daughters.'

'Knowledge doesn't feed starving children.' She watched as the kings settled themselves side by side in their overdecorated chairs. 'We need to get moving.'

'You're not going alone.'

'It will be quicker if we split up.'

Kadmus shook his head and tied his horse to the trough. 'It will be quicker without the horses. We stay together.'

She looked at Loda and bit her lip.

'You won't get through the crowd with her once the race begins,' Kadmus said, reading her mind.

A trumpet sounded near them and Aldara jumped. Kadmus took the rein from her hand.

'Yes, it's louder here among the poor,' he said, suppressing a smile. 'Let's go.'

The first rider trotted out into the middle of the field. Aldara remembered how it had felt to ride out with the crowd laughing at her. They had quietened as her time improved. She remembered the exhilaration of the win and how the laughter had turned to cheers. Her mind wandered further, to the ride home with Tyron pressed behind her. She tried to remember the warmth of him as they rode away from all the propriety and wealth.

The second horn sounded and the rider lurched forwards. Her eyes travelled to the berfrois. She found herself searching for him.

'He's not over there' Kadmus said.

She turned away from the field. 'I know.' Her feet moved.

'So, what is your great plan?'

She looked around. 'It's easier than you think. Find the one man here who is not watching the race. That will be Danaus.'

They edged their way along the boundary of trees. People generally preferred to be close to the timekeeper where the action was. Younger families stayed at the back, where their children could run about holding stick swords without fear of them hitting people. Fathers had the smaller ones on their shoulders for a better view. Aldara and Kadmus stepped over crawling babies and woven blankets, trying to find the best view of the berfroises.

Aldara stopped walking. 'This is where I would stand if I wanted to see my daughter.'

The timekeeper's arm went up and the surrounding children jumped up and down with excitement. Aldara turned in a circle, studying the faces around her. And there he was—a still man amid clapping spectators, his face pinched with worry as he stared past the action. She tapped Kadmus and gestured. 'Wait here.'

He glanced at the man and then nodded before turning back to the race.

Aldara took slow breaths as she walked towards him. Clear, calm communication, and then they could leave. 'Excuse me,' she said. 'Are you Danaus?'

The man turned to her and looked her up and down. 'Yes.'

She already knew he was Sapphira's father. They had the same mouth and tucked ears.

'Who are you?' he asked, seeming worried.

'I am a friend of Sapphira's.'

His shoulders lifted at the mention of her name. 'Do you have a message from her? Where is she? I have not seen her.'

A trumpet sounded and the surrounding families clapped and shouted.

'My name is Aldara. I used to be a Companion at Archdale.'

Danaus nodded, waiting for more. 'You know my daughter?'

His hands were shaking, and Aldara remembered what Sapphira had told her of his deterioration. 'Yes. I have travelled from Roysten to speak with you. I wanted to let you know of the... changes that have taken place.'

Danaus's face collapsed a little. 'When I heard about the prince losing his hand, I knew something was wrong. She's not at Archdale, is she?'

Aldara glanced again at his trembling hands. 'I can only tell you what happened before I left.'

He watched her. 'What happened?' His voice was weak. 'Where is my girl?'

She stood with him through two more riders, filling in the parts of his daughter's story she knew. When she was done, Danaus stared at her, wanting more.

'King Jayr cannot be trusted,' Danaus said. 'There are rumours in the north. They may have handed her over to a murderer.' He glanced at the royal berfrois. 'Prince Stamitos told me she would be safe, that he would take care of her.'

She took hold of his hands. 'Prince Stamitos meant every word. He would never have taken her from you if he had known her fate.' She kept her voice low. 'He loves her. You will never hear that from anyone else, but he loves her.'

Danaus face crumbled. 'I miss her. My only comfort came from thinking she was happy in her new life.'

Aldara's eyes burned. 'Your daughter is the strongest woman I know. She is fierce. And she can protect herself in any kingdom.' Another trumpet sounded behind them. 'I'm sorry, I have to go,' she said, letting go of his hands. 'I shouldn't be here at all.'

He nodded. 'Thank you for travelling such a great distance to tell me yourself. Sapphira was selective with friends. Most of them were men.'

'She would have done the same for me.' She smiled and turned from him, walking back to Kadmus who was still watching the race. 'Let's go,' she whispered.

'I was wrong about it being a dull event,' Kadmus said, eyes still ahead.

'What do you mean?'

'Some poor old beggar is having it out with Prince Pandarus.'

Aldara followed his gaze across the field to where a man stood before the royal berfrois, shouting, a finger pointed in accusation. She narrowed her eyes. 'Do you recognise him?'

Pandarus gestured for the guards to take hold of the man.

'No, but this will not end well for him.' He looked at her. 'Go straight to the entrance and wait for me outside. I will get the horses and meet you there.'

She nodded and began pushing between the people. Whatever she was sensing, Kadmus was sensing it also.

There was a feeling in the pit of her stomach that made her feet quicken. When she broke free from the crowd, she exhaled and glanced a final time at the royal berfrois. Two Syrasan guards had taken hold of the man, who was still shouting as he tried to pull himself free.

'I trusted you with my daughter,' he shouted as the guards pulled him back.

Aldara stopped still. She stared at the man, trying to figure out why he was familiar to her. There was a sharp intake of breath as she realised who it was—Felix, Hali's father.

'You promised me she would be safe, and you have sent my daughter to her death. That man is a murderer!' he said, pointing at King Jayr.

'Flog him,' Pandarus said, stepping back from the rail.

'Return her to me, or so help me God, I will ride to Zoelin and get her myself!'

One guard kicked the back of Felix's legs so he fell to his knees. The other tore his tunic so that his back was exposed and then reached for a leather scourge hanging from his hip.

Aldara felt the blood leave her face. She took off at a run towards them. The crowd had fallen silent as they realised what was about to take place. Aldara came to a stop between Felix and the guard preparing to flog him. She held out her hands in front of her. 'Stop, please. Let me take him away. You do not have to do this.'

Pandarus stepped up to the rail again and looked down at her. She felt his eyes transcend her mask.

'Where is my daughter?' Felix pleaded, seeing he had the prince's attention once again.

Aldara kept her palms extended and her eyes on Pandarus. 'Please. Don't punish him for his grief. Let me take him away.'

Conflict flickered in Pandarus's eyes, but then he set his jaw in a way that Aldara recognised.

'Flog him,' he repeated. 'And if the girl gets in the way, flog her also. These people need reminding of their manners.'

Felix's chin fell to his chest with the weight of his grief. Aldara shook her head. Her eyes went to Queen Eldoris's pity-filled face. 'Please,' she said, a private plea. The queen had sought her out to say thank you a few months before, and now she said nothing. It was not because she did not want to help, but rather because it was not her place.

Aldara's eyes ran along all the faces watching her. Cora's blank stare and Salome's confused and curious gaze. King Zenas shifted in his chair while King Jayr watched her with fascination. Amid the noble guests, the Companions stood still, their masks ensuring their expressions remained neutral.

The guard holding the whip shoved her aside. She staggered sideways but remained upright. When the whip went up, she ran in front of it to shield Felix from the blow. It lurched like a provoked snake, striking her arm and collarbone. A roar-like sound came from her.

Queen Eldoris stood up then. 'That is enough,' she said to Pandarus. But he was not listening, only watching.

The guard raised his whip again, but that time when he brought it down, Kadmus caught it mid-air and pulled it from his hand.

Aldara froze as she looked across at her brother. 'No,' she whispered. She wanted to tell him to run, but she knew it would not help him now. The price of his intervention would be higher than her own. Two more guards stepped up and took hold of him. Kadmus's eyes remained on her, resigned but unapologetic. They both knew how the situation would play out. Aldara turned her head to the berfrois, searching for Tyron. He would show mercy to Kadmus if she begged. But he was not there.

Pandarus had grown embarrassed by the spectacle taking place in front of King Jayr. 'Take all three of them away from the crowd and teach them a lesson in respect,' he said to the guards. 'This is a festive event, for God's sake.'

Felix turned his face up to Aldara. 'I am sorry,' he said, his voice weak.

She stared down at him, shaking away the thought of what was to follow. One guard let go of Kadmus and grabbed hold of her arm.

'Let her go,' Kadmus said, trying to pull himself free.

She looked down at the hand gripping her and then stepped towards the guard, striking his throat with her spare arm. He began to cough but kept hold of her. She had not thought the action through at all, reacting on instinct. The guard grabbed her by the hair and threw her to the ground. Her side hit the firm surface hard, knocking the wind out of her.

'No!' Kadmus shouted.

Before she had regained her breath, the guard grabbed hold of her throat and lifted her up. His hand was like a clasp around her neck. She could not breathe through it.

'Let her go!' Kadmus yelled. The guard holding him delivered a blow to his stomach, which made him drop to his knees.

All the self-defence Stamitos had taught Aldara was lost in that moment. She flailed, struggling for air. The guard held her in place with ease, his strong arm as thick as her thigh. She clawed at his hand as he dragged her away from the berfrois. Her eyes still searched for Tyron, but her vision was blurred.

A moment later, the guard let go of her throat and she

fell to the ground, her hands on her neck as she tried to take in air. The guard landed with a thud next to her, eyes closed, face slack against the dirt. She looked up to see Tyron standing over her, panting.

~

Tyron lifted her from the ground, her form familiar in his hands.

He had left with a serf to inspect a gelding. The tournament had seemed far away, the horn a distant plea. He could not sit in the berfrois where she had once stood, a golden finch among larger birds. The place was a swamp of memories.

Leksi had come running up, out of breath. One look at him told Tyron he needed to follow immediately. When Leksi turned and broke into a run, he had not hesitated to match his speed. The sound of cheering had died off in a way that made him run faster. He had arrived from the back, stopping in the shadow of the berfrois to take in the scene before him. Two beats of his heart. That was how long it had taken him to register what was happening. He had propelled himself forwards, both of his feet leaving the ground as his fist came down on top of the guard's head. Aldara sank to the ground, the unconscious guard collapsing face-down into the dirt next to her.

He had her upright now, holding the full weight of her as she trembled on unsteady legs. His eyes went to the weeping wound on her collarbone, the result of being lashed, and then to the finger imprint at the top of her neck. He had sworn he would never let that happen to her again. His chest burned with something resembling rage.

'Are you all right?' he whispered.

She went to speak but began to cough. He kept hold

183

of her.

Pandarus stepped up next to them, jaw clenched and top lip raised in a sneer. He reached out and tore the mask from her face. It was a good thing both of Tyron's hands were holding her up or his fist would have gone to his brother's face.

'I should have known you would be here stirring trouble. What is it with you and this place?' He looked at Tyron. 'I stand by my order.'

'What order?' Tyron asked.

'They will all be lashed for their insubordination.'

The guard on the ground let out a groan, and they all looked down at him. Tyron turned his body around, keeping himself in front of Aldara, one arm behind his back to hold her steady. He spoke quietly to Pandarus.

'This is what is going to happen,' he began.

The guard on the ground let out another groan and lifted his head. The other guards still had hold of Kadmus and Felix. They were exchanging confused glances.

'Take the three of them out of sight and release them without harm,' Tyron said. 'No one else will know. In return, I will cooperate and accept King Jayr's offer.'

'Tyron,' Aldara croaked. 'It's all right.'

He squeezed her arm and she fell silent. King Jayr stood up and walked over to the rail, eyes on them. Pandarus glanced about as he thought the situation through. He looked back at Tyron, shaking his head but eyes resigned.

'I agree,' he said, loud enough so the guests in the berfrois would hear him. 'Let the people enjoy the race. Take these criminals out of our sight.'

Tyron's gaze passed him to where King Jayr stood, watching closely, drinking in the familiar gestures that passed between the pair. Aldara's forehead was resting against his back, her breaths still coming in rasps. Handing her over to the guard who had choked her moments earlier felt like complete betrayal, but leaving the event with her in his arms would draw dangerous attention. His hand kept hold of her, unable to let go. Everyone seemed to be waiting to see what he would do.

'It's all right,' she whispered behind him. Her head left his back, the spot instantly growing cold. 'It's all right.'

It took all of his willpower to step aside so the guard, now upright on unsteady legs, could take hold of her other arm. Tyron's dark expression made the guard loosen his grip.

'Remember your end of the deal,' Pandarus whispered to Tyron through clenched teeth.

Tyron looked at Aldara, whose eyes were on the ground in front of her. She continued to tremble. He blinked. The best thing he could do for her at that moment was walk away without a backwards glance. He could not have King Jayr seeing what was between them. She gave a slight nod. Smart girl; she knew his mind as though it were her own. He released his hold on her and the empty sensation tore through him. He turned away from her.

'Take her straight home,' he said to Kadmus as he stepped past him. 'No stops.'

Tyron heard Pandarus murmur instructions to the guards. He walked towards the berfrois, not looking behind him as she was dragged away. Tyron closed his eyes against the sound she emitted as her arm was pulled too hard for her small frame. Leksi came towards him and they passed one another with a silent nod. No need for words.

A trumpet sounded.

The guests refilled their cups and turned back to their conversations. Tyron's gaze returned to Jayr, but the king of Zoelin was not looking at him.

His eyes were on Aldara.

CHAPTER 24

Tyron and his family gathered in the solar. There were no guards, servants or formalities. They could have been any family in that moment. Tyron was leaning against the bookshelf, staring at his tapping heel—a nervous trait. His father and Pandarus stood close by, lost in their own thoughts. His mother was seated next to Cora, who was slumped in her chair, the previous day's wine intake catching up with her. Stamitos had once again declined the invitation.

'What happy news,' Cora said with mock enthusiasm. 'Another sister to treasure. And just think of all the dark, miniature Tyrons we will have running about the castle, their small hands covered in ink.'

'Cora, please,' said Eldoris, touching her hand to her brow. 'Not now.'

'It was the right decision,' Pandarus said. 'The union will not only strengthen our alliance, but help our people to trust King Jayr.'

'Yes, that way our people will feel better about selling

186

their daughters to a murderous king in a foreign land,' Cora replied, closing her eyes.

Zenas crossed his arms. 'I suggest you follow your mother's instruction and be silent before I offer you up to be queen of Zoelin, as per King Jayr's original request.'

'Some might think us a great match.'

Eldoris stared at her. 'You do not understand what you are saying.'

'Because I am a woman?'

Pandarus held up a hand to silence his sister. 'Before you go off on one of your self-indulgent speeches, let us deal with the issue at hand.'

Tyron was barely listening. He was still thinking about Aldara and what he might do to the guard who had whipped her. Leksi had sent word he was escorting them back to Roysten. She should not have attended the event to begin with, and occasionally his anger swung towards her.

'You are very quiet, brother,' Pandarus said, pulling him from his thoughts.

Tyron looked at him. 'I am confused as to why we are still discussing the matter. I have agreed to the union. The wedding will take place when the princess is of age.'

It had come to light during his discussion with King Jayr that Princess Tasia was in her fifteenth year. Syrasan law stated that a woman could not marry before her sixteenth year.

Zenas cleared his throat. 'Tyron is right.'

'There's a surprise,' Pandarus said, speaking at the ground.

'We must uphold our own laws if we expect others to,' Zenas finished.

Pandarus glanced at Tyron, irritated. 'King Jayr is not a patient man. How do you suppose we convince him that the betrothal will be upheld once the princess comes of age?'

Tyron was coming to the end of his tether. He had been hoping that his father would object to the union, but he rarely said no to Pandarus anymore, and it was clear the proposed marriage had been discussed long before Tyron had heard of it. 'Why are you looking at me for a different answer? I said I would marry the princess, so I will marry the princess.'

Pandarus rolled his eyes. 'Yes, we are all well aware that you are a man of your word. You do not need to convince us of your superior morals. The problem is King Jayr does not share our high opinion of you.'

Tyron looked up at him. 'What would you have me do? I will agree to it in writing if you think it will ease his paranoia.'

'A written agreement will hold little weight given our history.'

'He needs to get over that,' Tyron said, rubbing his temples with his fingers. Leksi would have returned by now, and he was eager to go and find him.

Eldoris came to stand by her husband. 'Sixteen is terribly young for a royal union of that sort.'

'Many her age marry,' Zenas replied.

'Yes, common people, girls who remain close to their families and do not have the added responsibilities of being a princess in a foreign land.'

'You were sixteen,' Zenas said.

Eldoris stared at him. 'I was eighteen.'

'Her responsibilities will not be that great,' Pandarus said. 'All she has to do is uphold her wedding vows and bear children.'

'You make it sound so wonderful,' Cora said, not bothering to sit up.

'I am simply pointing out that she is not expected to fight or do anything of great importance.'

Eldoris narrowed her eyes on her son. 'I suggest you reconsider your words. Raising good men is no easy task.'

A knock sounded, and they all went silent.

'Enter,' Zenas called.

A guard stepped inside and bowed. 'Forgive me for interrupting, Your Majesty. I can confirm that King Jayr has crossed the border.'

Zenas nodded. 'Good. Anything else?'

'Yes. Are you aware that four of his men remain in the south?'

Zenas looked at Pandarus. 'What do you know of this?'

Pandarus held up his hands. 'This is the first I am hearing of it.'

'I want them found and questioned,' Zenas said. 'King Jayr's men should not be roaming my kingdom without our knowledge.' His eyes went to Pandarus. 'The agreement states that every purchase is to go through the appropriate channels. If I find out he is buying women directly from my people, I will be forced to act.'

Pandarus shifted his weight. 'Let's not jump to conclusions.'

Tyron's foot stilled. 'Where were the men sighted?'

The guard turned to him. 'Just north of Roysten, my lord.'

The mention of Aldara's village made Tyron's skin turn cold. He pushed himself off the bookshelf and turned to Pandarus.

'Does that mean something to you?' Zenas asked, eyes moving between his sons. 'What is in Roysten?'

'Not what,' Cora said, opening her eyes and looking at Tyron. 'Who.'

'Who is in Roysten?' Eldoris asked.

Tyron stared at Pandarus. 'Tell me King Jayr would not go after her.'

Pandarus crossed his arms in front of him. 'If he did, it is on you. You were foolish enough to put your feelings on display.'

Tyron wanted to argue the fact but could not.

Cora leaned forwards in her chair. 'King Jayr is smart enough to figure out she is perfect leverage. He sees as I see, thinks as I think. And that is what I would do.'

Tyron's head was pounding. The Zoelin men had probably followed them to Roysten. The fact that Leksi had escorted her would have only confirmed her value. Leksi would have likely returned already, leaving her vulnerable. *'You are not thinking clearly,'* she had said to him, eyes pleading. *'I am safest here with you.'*

CHAPTER 25

*A*ldara sat with her back against the fence post and her knees pulled up. Her boots lay in the grass where she had kicked them off hours earlier. The final heat from the sun warmed her bare feet. Artemis lay close by, always watchful, never off duty. The sheep paid the dog no attention. It had taken them less than a week to accept their new guardian, but Artemis had begun her role as protector immediately, circling the flock at a distance that would not distress them while taking in their scent. She had been with them every day since, returning to the house once the sheep were in the barn.

Aldara called Artemis and the dog collapsed against her, closing her eyes for a moment. She rubbed the dog's silky head and scratched her back the way she liked. It was time for Aldara to face the silence of her family once again. Reckless, her mother had called her. Kadmus had barely said two words to her since the tournament. He was pretending to be angry, but Aldara knew what happened had scared him more than he cared to admit. She had given little thought to the fact that Leksi was escorting them, as

Tyron was always overly cautious. But there was something in Leksi's silence, and the way he had checked behind them, one hand always on his sword, that made her nervous for Tyron. She knew she had put him in a difficult position and he was taking extra precautions for some reason. When she had asked Leksi what Tyron meant when he said he would 'cooperate and accept King Jayr's offer,' he seemed to genuinely not have an answer.

She stood and ran the tips of her fingers along her bruised neck, the same way Tyron had the day before. Her eyes closed. She slid her hand across her shoulder and down her bare arm, taking hold of it, trying to remember the exact feel of his grip. No mark left by him, only warmth where his hand had been. He would be angry at her being there, putting herself at risk, but she could not sit back and watch Hali's father be flogged for his heartbreak. She could picture Tyron, bare-chested in his chambers, pacing the length of the bed, frustrated because all he wanted was to know she was safe. What had he agreed to in order to keep her that way?

Her eyes opened. 'Bring them in,' she said to Artemis. The dog jumped to her feet and ran off behind the flock. 'Bring them in,' she repeated, louder that time. Artemis gave a bark, and the startled sheep began moving in the direction of the barn.

Aldara strolled over, picked up her boots, and slipped her feet into them before joining Artemis. She relished the long walk back under a blazing sky of red and orange, the only noise the bleating of sheep and the familiar pant of the dog. Once the sheep were secured in the barn, she made her way to the house, Artemis trotting at her feet, eager for scraps. The dog knew better than to get under Dahlia's feet. She waited patiently by the door until the rest of the house was fed. What Dahlia did not know was, once everyone was asleep, she would cross the forbidden floor and jump quietly up onto Kadmus's bed for the night.

Aldara was about to go inside the house when the door swung open. Byrgus stepped through it. She stilled, and they looked at one another for a moment. The tired wooden door gave a loud groan of protest as it shut behind him.

'Evening,' he said before rushing past her.

'Good evening,' she replied. It was progress.

She smiled as she pushed through the door. The first thing she noticed when she stepped inside was her mother seated at their small table with Kadmus and her father. Her mother never sat down before food was on the table. They turned their worried faces towards her.

'Goodness,' Aldara said, half smiling to ease the tension. 'Why the sombre expressions?'

Kadmus stood and came towards her. His sleeves were rolled up, his hands still dirty. 'There are Zoelin guards in Roysten searching for you,' he said. 'They're likely already on their way here.'

They were all looking at her, expecting her to have an explanation. She tried to think of one.

Dahlia stood. 'Why? Why would Zoelin guards be searching for you?'

Aldara shook her head. She was feeling a little dizzy. 'I honestly don't know,' she said, glancing at her father.

'Would anyone at Archdale have sent them?' Kadmus asked.

She shook her head. 'No. They would send Syrasan guards to retrieve me.' There was no way Tyron would let Zoelin guards come to her family's farm. Her mind raced. It had to have something to do with the agreement he made with King Jayr.

'Let's not panic the girl,' Isadore said, standing up and

joining them. 'Let's think it through. What are they likely to want?'

Dahlia crossed her arms. 'This is because of the tournament yesterday. You embarrassed the king and forced the prince's hand.'

'They were about to whip a defenceless man,' Aldara said, closing her eyes.

'You should have let them,' Kadmus said, not looking at her.

Isadore raised his hands in a calming gesture. 'All right, all right. We cannot do anything about yesterday.' He turned to Aldara. 'You know more about these men than we do. What do they want?'

Her family waited for her to answer, wanting a logical explanation. 'They are not coming to talk. They are either going to take me with them or…'

'Or what?' Dahlia asked.

Her eyes were welling up. 'I don't know. They saw me with Tyron yesterday. They saw how he was with me. Perhaps they plan to use me against him somehow.'

No one moved for a moment.

'Prince Tyron agreed to something yesterday. Perhaps you are part of the agreement. Maybe he is sending you to Onuric,' Kadmus suggested.

'No,' Dahlia said. 'My guess is Prince Tyron knows nothing about it.'

'Perhaps Pandarus, then,' Kadmus said.

She certainly would not put it past him. 'Even if Pandarus had something planned, he would send his own guards to retrieve me.'

'No one is taking you anywhere,' Isadore said, keeping calm.

Aldara looked at him, eyes wide. 'You do not know

these people. I don't know what brings them here, but I promise you, they will not leave without it.'

Kadmus nodded. 'All right, we prepare for the worst possible outcome. What do we do?'

She slowed her breathing so she could think. 'You do nothing. No one does anything. We ask them what they want and then we give it to them. If you are lucky, you will still have the house, the barn, the crop, and your lives at the end of it.'

Kadmus was staring at her as though she had sprouted a second head. 'Have you lost your mind?'

'She is right,' Dahlia said, staring at the ground and shaking her head. 'If these men want something, they will take it. And they will destroy anyone who stands in their way.'

Isadore was paling. 'So we just hand them our daughter?'

'No,' Kadmus shouted. 'We fight them if we have to. She stays here.'

Aldara stared at him. 'You cannot fight them, Kadmus.' Her voice was almost a whisper. 'They are trained guards with weapons. If you try to fight them, you will die. And they will take me anyway.'

'So we run,' Isadore said. 'We go through the forest and make our way to Archdale. The king will protect us once we tell him what is happening. They protected the people in the North.'

They all looked at each other, bodies stiff with tension. Dahlia nodded as she thought it through. 'We need to leave now. They must be close. Kadmus, saddle the horses. Aldara, you get the bows.' She turned to Isadore. 'Grab the axe, just in case.'

Dahlia returned to the table and picked up the knife that

lay next to the half-peeled potatoes. She glanced at Aldara, who swallowed. It was the first time Aldara had seen the fierce, protective instincts of a mother protecting her young.

Aldara did as she was told. She grabbed the weapons that lay by the door, not bothering to get a cloak or fill a water flask for the journey—there was no time. She followed her parents out of the house where the blood sky had faded to a ghostly grey and the grasshoppers, the ones that had not been drowned in a bucket, vibrated around them.

They went through the small door of the barn. Aldara could just make out Kadmus saddling the horses in the dark. He was smart enough not to light a lantern. She ran to help him, her hands shaking the entire time. His eyebrows were fused together in concentration.

'Mother, you can ride behind me,' he said.

They only had three horses so would have to make do. She nodded and stepped up close to him so she would be ready as soon as he was. Isadore remained near the small door, keeping watch. Aldara's breathing had returned to normal. In a few moments they would be on their way. She knew they would be safe once they reached Archdale. Tyron would protect her family as if they were his own.

The sound of a howling bark reached them. Artemis. They all stilled to listen. Silence for a moment, then another bark, longer and more insistent. She was warning them.

'It might be boars,' Isadore said, clutching the axe with two hands.

Kadmus walked over to the wall of the barn and peered out through a gap in the wood. The sun had disappeared and a blanket of grey light covered the farm. He was about to move to check the other side when the distant whinny of a horse made him freeze. Aldara thought she could hear the pounding of hooves, but it was difficult to hear over the pounding in her chest.

'It's too late to leave,' she said. 'They are already here.'

Kadmus walked over to the small door where Isadore stood, careful not to stir the sheep as he passed. Aldara crept up next to them. During daylight, she could see all the way to the road, but at dusk, she could just make out horses trotting along the road. They would soon turn onto the farm. She looked at Kadmus, eyes wide with panic.

'They're almost here,' she whispered. 'We'll need to leave via the woods.'

A low growl came from Artemis as she took off towards the approaching horses.

'Stop her,' Aldara said. 'They will shoot her.'

Kadmus seemed unsure, but he opened the small door and emitted a short, sharp whistle. A few moments later, Artemis trotted through the small gap in the door, the hair on her back standing up, her ears pricked forwards, listening. 'Stay,' Kadmus said. She let out a small whine before settling at his feet.

'Take your sister and go,' Isadore said. He ran to the other side of the barn and opened the sliding door wide enough for the horses to slip through. 'Your mother and I will stay here and delay them for as long as we can. We'll tell them you are away helping relatives with their harvest. Don't go through the woods. Go through Byrgus's farm and then get back onto the road. But stay off it as much as you can. Go now.'

Kadmus looked unsure. Aldara could not believe what she was hearing. 'We are not abandoning you,' she said, shaking her head. 'Neither of you can defend yourselves.'

'Must you always be the hero,' Dahlia snapped. 'Both of you go, now. Before it is too late to go anywhere.'

Kadmus's face hardened. He took hold of Aldara's arm and dragged her towards Loda. 'Let's go.'

Aldara mounted and glanced at her mother who stood streaked in shadows. Isadore was outside, making sure it was clear before letting them go. He nodded at Kadmus. The two horses slipped through the gap and Aldara turned to see her father's worried face disappear behind the closing door. Kadmus kicked his horse into a canter and led them to the boundary fence before looking around, trying to decide the safest direction. They rode south, away from the road, until they reached a gate that connected the properties. A long, deep bark reached them as Kadmus swooped low to unlatch it. The whinny of a horse came from the woods behind them, causing his hand to falter on the simple lock. Aldara's eyes searched the tree line in the distance. Her father had been right in telling them to avoid the woods. She suspected the Zoelin guards had already covered that exit.

The creak of the gate made Aldara turn around. Kadmus closed his eyes against the noise. As soon as there was enough room for Loda to pass through, she kicked the mare forwards and held it in place so Kadmus could pass. She lifted the gate as she closed it to prevent it from groaning. She would have left it open but did not want to leave a trail.

They cantered through Byrgus's paddocks; trying to find the unfamiliar gates delayed them each time they met a fence. They did not stop until they reached the cover of the orchard.

Only then did Aldara look back towards their house. She could faintly make out the silhouette of horses, but it was too far to establish how many there were.

'Do you think they will leave?' Kadmus asked, sounding doubtful.

'No. Not until they have what they came for,' she whispered. The air had turned cold, and a shiver ran through her. 'Let's go back. We can hide among the trees and use our bows if we need to.'

Kadmus was quiet for a moment. 'No. We need to get you to Archdale.'

Aldara knew he was struggling with the decision. She glanced again at the house and froze when she noticed the gentle glow of a flame. 'What is that?' she said, grabbing hold of the front of the saddle.

Kadmus followed her line of vision back to the farmhouse. 'Fire,' he said. It came like a breath of wind knocked from him.

She recalled the stories Tyron had told her of the Zoelin men burning entire villages in the north. It was a tactic to clear the houses of people so they could take what they needed. She spun Loda around and dug her heels into the mare's sides.

'Where are you going?' Kadmus called to her, but he was already following after her.

He had to stop and open gates while Loda cleared them with ease. When Aldara was back on their property, she resisted the urge to ride out into the open, giving the men what they wanted. Instead, she rode around the barley crop, under the cover of night, and hid in the shadows of the trees thirty yards from the barn. Visible steam rose from Loda, and her front legs lifted off the ground.

'Easy,' Aldara whispered, her voice unsteady.

Kadmus arrived next to her, beads of sweat across his forehead despite the cool air. 'Where is Artemis?' he whispered. She held up a hand to silence him as two men came out of the house, one holding a lit torch. They made their way to the barn and opened the large door at the front. The milking goat ran out, taking advantage of the freedom. The guards drew their swords and watched it pass.

'Come out or we burn it down,' called the man holding the torch. He spoke broken Syrasan with a heavy Zoelin accent. Two more men exited the house and joined them beneath the glow of the fire. After a brief discussion, they split up, two of them circling the barn in opposite directions, no doubt checking for additional exits.

Kadmus shook his head. 'Why aren't they coming out?'

Aldara reached over her shoulder for her longbow and an arrow. She loaded it and looked at her brother. 'Perhaps they got away before the men arrived,' she said, eyes shining.

Kadmus glanced at her longbow and nodded before loading his crossbow.

'We stay here,' she whispered. 'Being hidden is our only advantage.'

He nodded again and raised his bow. 'I'm not sure I can hit a man from this distance.'

Aldara was staring down the arrow in her bow. It was pointed at the man holding the torch. The ink markings on his arm were lit up beneath the flame. He swung the torch back, preparing to throw it inside. She stilled her lungs and then released the arrow. He cried out as it pierced his arm. The torch fell from his hand, landing at his feet, where it continued to burn without spreading. The other guard retrieved his bow, loaded it, and pointed it at the trees. It swung gently back and forth in their direction.

The horses dipped their heads and snorted. Aldara hoped the chaos near the men was enough to drown out the noise of it. She did not want to kill anyone—she wanted them to leave.

The injured guard yanked the arrow from his arm, kicked the lit torch through the open door and closed it again. Aldara pressed her hand over her mouth to stop herself from making a noise. All of their animals remained inside. Kadmus took aim at the second guard and the arrow flew over his shoulder. The men crouched down behind the water trough.

'Where in heaven's name are our parents?' Kadmus asked, growing frustrated.

'They are not in there,' Aldara replied. 'The mare would have been the first to evacuate when the door opened.'

'Why aren't they shooting at us?'

'Because they need me alive.' She watched as the glow of the barn grew brighter. 'All of our stock and supplies are going to be ash in a moment if we do nothing.'

Kadmus looked at her. 'You said staying here was our only advantage.'

She shook her head. 'What is the point of surviving if we have nothing left?' The bleating of sheep drew their attention back to the barn.

'Stay here and cover me,' he said. 'I will try to free a few panels on the side. It might be enough to get the flock out.'

She did not want him to go. 'Once the smoke builds, I won't be able to see you.'

'Just do your best, and stay here,' he said, pulling his horse's head to the right and kicking him into a canter. He rode along the trees for a while before riding out in the open.

Aldara reloaded her bow and swung it between the trough and the other side of the barn. She did not breathe until he had reached the wall and dismounted. She watched as he placed an arm over his mouth and nose, trying to filter the smoke seeping out at his feet. He tested a few panels for weakness, and when one moved, he took hold of it with both hands and used his body weight to tug on it. It was not enough. Aldara glanced at the flames that were now licking the front of the barn. With hay fuelling the fire, it would not be long until there was nothing left to save.

She tried to think through her panic. If she followed, she had to trust they would not shoot at her. Before she could act, a guard appeared around the back of the barn. She would not have noticed him amid the smoke had she not seen the flash of his sword as he drew it. He was creeping towards Kadmus, whose only weapon was on his back as he continued to pull at the wall. She aimed at the man's leg. The injury would be enough to stop him and give Kadmus an opportunity to flee. But her hands were shaking so much she did not have the luxury of choosing a limb. She needed to stop him. The arrow went straight through the side of the guard's chest. He dropped to his knees, his sword clanging on the ground beside him. He tipped forwards onto the warm earth.

Kadmus glanced across at the body a few yards from him and then turned back to the barn, pulling as hard as he could on the wood.

Aldara sat frozen with the bow still raised in front of her. She had killed a man. Someone's brother or friend. Someone's son or father.

The smoke thickened around Kadmus and he leaned against his knees for a moment as he coughed. Aldara reloaded her bow and kicked Loda into a canter. When Kadmus looked up and saw her, he shook his head, but she continued towards him.

'You should have stayed hidden,' he said when she dismounted next to him. 'Now we are both at risk.'

'There's no time to argue about it. Pull,' she said, grabbing the loose panel of wood. He took hold of it and the bottom end came free. He peered inside and saw the sheep pressed together at the back of the barn, the hiss and crackle of flames just a few feet from them now. A few chickens burst through the small gap they had created. At least they would have eggs. They grabbed hold of the plank below and tore it free to make the gap big enough for the sheep to fit through.

Aldara picked up her bow again, loaded it, and aimed it along the wall of the barn. It was only a matter of time before the other men found them.

'I'm going in,' Kadmus said, picking up his crossbow. 'They will be burned alive otherwise. As soon as I'm back, we are leaving.'

It was too dangerous for him to go in, but she had lost the ability to argue. He crawled through the hole and she swung her bow to the other end of the barn, hating the fact that she could not predict which direction they might come from. Something creaked and then collapsed inside, and the horses backed away from the smoke. *No you don't*, she thought, stepping on Loda's rein, which hung on the ground. There was not a chance she would lower the bow. The heat was getting too much, so she edged away from it. Where was he?

A sheep came through the hole and she swung her bow towards it, ready to shoot. Another followed. Two more pressed through at the same time. She got out of their way while continuing to keep watch. After a few steps, she tripped and toppled backwards. She managed to keep hold of the bow and arrow and pointed it over her knees, her adrenaline soaring. There was no one there, only smoke. When she glanced down, she saw that her legs were draped over the arm of the dead guard. The black inked pattern began on the back of his hand and extended up his arm, disappearing beneath her. She turned and saw her arrow still wedged between his ribs. She gasped and pushed back with her feet, her bow pointed at the body as though it would suddenly awaken.

A gentle roar came from the barn as the final sheep escaped. The two horses pivoted and galloped away to the safety of the trees. Aldara lowered her bow, watching their only means of escape disappear into the darkness. She coughed and tried to get her trembling body to still. A figure to her left caught her eye and she swung around, raising her bow again. Her throat was aching as she fought the urge to cough. The crunch of footsteps made her hold her breath. A Zoelin guard stopped just a few feet in front of her, one part of his skull shaved to make room for a single black line that ran around his ear. He smiled.

'There you are,' he said in the Zoelin language.

Her arrow remained pointed at him. Her hands went still. 'Leave here, or I will kill you,' she replied in his language.

He remained where he was, unafraid. 'Do you know how to use a bow?' He was still smiling.

She gestured to the body at her feet. 'Ask your friend.'

He looked down and the smile fell from his face. When his eyes returned to her, they were darker. 'Have you ever stared into someone's eyes and then taken their life? At this distance it will not be so easy for you. Put the bow down and come with me. Then maybe your family will live.'

The string slackened in her hand as she processed his words. She could not trust him. The string went taut again and she glanced at the gap in the wall which was now blocked by flames. No Kadmus. 'I am not going anywhere with you until I know my brother is safe.'

The man's face was lit up by the flames. He glanced at the blazing barn and laughed. 'The only way out of there is at the other end of the barn. *If* he made it out, then my men already have him.'

She looked again at the flames that were now climbing the walls of the barn. 'Where is he?' she screamed, her hands shaking again.

He took a step towards her. 'Put down the bow and I'll take you to him.'

Her finger pressed against her chin, but before she could release the arrow, another came from the side, piercing the guard's neck. His bulging eyes locked onto hers. He gave a large cough that brought blood up with it. It ran down his chin and merged with the pattern on his neck. His body turned slightly as it fell towards her. Her loaded bow remained pointed at him, following him to the ground. Her breath came in short pants and tears spilled down her cheeks. She stepped back until her heel hit the body on the ground behind her. The dead surrounded her.

Through the smoke, another man appeared. He was running towards her. She tasted sweat on her lips as she lifted her bow and aimed it straight at his face. She hesitated—just long enough. Long enough to notice the flash of red that lined his cloak. And just long enough to see his blazing green eyes reflecting the fire behind her.

Tyron came to a stop in front of the arrow. Aldara's face was covered in sweat, tears and floating ash. She stared down the arrow at him, not trusting herself at first. He waited. He would give her as long as she needed. After a few moments, she lowered the bow and let it drop to the ground between them. She did not need it anymore.

'Kadmus,' she said before her legs gave way.

She did not look away from him as she fell. He reached out and caught her before she hit the ground, then slipped an arm beneath her, lifting her and pulling her back from the flames in one motion. He whistled, and moments later two horses came to a stop in front of them. It was Leksi with Tyron's horse in tow. He placed her on top of Otus.

Aldara looked down at him. 'Kadmus went in to get the sheep out, and I haven't seen him since.' Her eyes welled up again. 'He may have gotten out through the door on the other side, but there were two Zoelin men guarding it.'

Tyron drew his sword and turned to Leksi. 'Wait for me behind the house. Eyes open. I have no interest in prisoners.'

Leksi nodded and drew his sword also.

Tyron looked back at Aldara. 'Your parents are safe. We got them out just in time. I was on my way to find you.'

'We saw flames,' she began.

He shook his head. 'I knew you would return here. You never listen, but for God's sake, listen to me now. Stay with Leksi, no matter what.' He waited for her to acknowledge him.

She nodded, clutching the front of the saddle to keep from falling.

He left her and ran towards the fire where he was swallowed up by smoke and the groan of timber. He hated fire more than any other weapon—it soaked up all the oxygen.

He crept around the corner of the barn, keeping a safe distance from the flames while keeping an eye out for the other guards. They would expect one of their own, and Aldara along with him. He glanced at the barn, ablaze. If Kadmus was in there, he was already dead.

He squinted against the smoke and searched around again. He saw him then. Kadmus was tied to a fence post a short distance away, feet bound and mouth gagged. Alive and unguarded. Tyron did not move towards him because something felt very off. If they had intended to kill him, they would have done so already. They were either placing him there as bait, or they were simply keeping him out of the way.

Tyron tried to get inside King Jayr's mind for a moment. He did not want another death toll—he wanted the girl quietly extracted. He could not afford to have more blood on his hands.

Tyron looked at Kadmus, whose wide eyes stared back at him and then past him, probably searching for his sister. She was not with Tyron, and he realised at that moment that he had abandoned the only person those men wanted. Every hair stood up on his body. He turned and ran back in the other direction because every sense in him was screaming.

The house came into view. He told himself she would be waiting with Leksi behind it, just as he had instructed. His pace quickened, feet pounding against the dirt until he reached the shadow cast by the house. He came to a skidding stop and looked about. Leksi lay unconscious on the ground. A drizzle of blood ran down his face, and an arrow protruded from his shoulder.

Aldara was not there.

CHAPTER 26

yron looked up as his mother entered the throne room. She was not usually involved in matters of political conflict. His father was traditional in that sense, preferring to shield her from the vulgarity. But she was very much involved with her children, and his father needed her in the room as they attempted to wade through the mess of the previous night.

No one sat, mainly because Tyron was pacing between walls like a penned wolf. He wanted to break free, but there was nowhere for him to go. He had spent the entire night searching for her, combing the woods and knocking on doors. Eighty men had been sent to the Lotheng River in hope of preventing her from crossing the border, but the river was long and King Jayr had predicted his actions. The following morning, Tyron had returned to Archdale to get a fresh horse and check on Leksi, who was far too proud to die from a shoulder wound and a knock over the head. His father had guards waiting to bring him in. It was one thing to search for her within Syrasan's borders, and quite another to cross the river and start a war. They all knew what Tyron would do next.

'We are wasting time,' he said, turning his eyes to his father.

Pandarus threw his hands up. 'As I have said twice now, the girl has already crossed the border. Now is the time to slow down before we start something we cannot finish.'

'She only got through because you pulled the men I sent to stop her!'

'I recalled them to avoid panic on both sides of the river! Eighty men for one common girl? What were you thinking? You have only reinforced her worth to you.'

'King Jayr should be panicking,' said Stamitos, entering the room unannounced. 'They have gotten away with too much for too long. It is time we show them what happens when they break our laws.'

Pandarus laughed. It sounded unnatural. 'You both need to check yourselves. Are you forgetting that your former mistresses are now at their mercy? We take a fight to them and they will bring those women's heads to you mounted on sticks.'

Tyron had to turn away. He pressed his palms against his eyes.

'We must all remain calm if we are to figure a way through all of this,' Eldoris said, her mouth pinched with worry. 'We do not want anybody else hurt. Leksi is lucky to be alive.'

'It was not luck,' Pandarus said. 'It is clear King Jayr did not want casualties.'

'You seem to know an awful lot about his intentions,' Tyron said, venting his anger.

'Enough,' Zenas said, finally speaking up. 'We have it on good authority from two fishermen that two Zoelin men in possession of a hooded and bound female crossed the

Lotheng River in the early hours this morning. It is no longer an option to go after her.'

Tyron winced despite it being the second time he had heard the news.

'They are banking on us not retaliating,' Stamitos said.

Zenas nodded. 'And they would be correct. Attacking them would be dangerous for everybody.'

'Pity, I would love to fight the bastards,' Stamitos said.

Pandarus laughed again. 'Great, I am sure your left hand will prove very useful.'

'You speak in such a manner again and I will have your father remove you from the room,' Eldoris said.

'I am trying to make him see sense.'

Zenas cleared his throat. 'Perhaps you should tell us how you intend to proceed,' he said, eyeing Pandarus.

'Like grown adults, preferably. We send a messenger and organise a meeting with King Jayr to find out exactly what he wants. My guess is he intends to hold on to the girl until after the wedding.'

A pained noise came from Tyron as he continued to pace.

'Are you suggesting we play along and wait it out?' Eldoris said.

Pandarus nodded. 'What other choice do we have? It is the only way we all get what we want. This could have been avoided if Tyron had agreed to marry Princess Tasia without making a song and dance about her age.'

Tyron stopped pacing and spun around to face him. 'That's a load of horseshit.'

'Tyron, please,' Eldoris said.

'This act is a flexing of muscle. King Jayr wants to remind us who holds the power. You want to just wait and see how it ends?' His hands went to his head, which was pounding. 'He continues to take whatever he wants from us. The problem will not be resolved by giving him more freedom to do as he pleases. God only knows what he is doing to her at this moment.' He turned to face his father. 'What the hell has happened to you? A year ago when those men crossed that river, took women, and burned down houses, you sent me to protect them. Now you are so paralysed by fear you are letting Pandarus make decisions as though you are already dead!'

'Guards,' Pandarus said, gesturing for them to seize Tyron.

Tyron drew his sword and the two guards stopped.

'Everybody stop,' Eldoris said, taking command of the room. 'Tyron, put your sword away this instant.'

He watched her for a moment, trying to rein in all that was loose inside of him, then glanced down at the sword in his hand, returning it to its sheath.

'Pandarus,' Eldoris said, turning to him. 'Your father and king will request assistance from the guards if he deems it necessary.'

The two guards stepped back. Pandarus raised his hands in a mock gesture of surrender. Zenas watched his wife. They were parents again, getting their unruly children under control. Eldoris gave him a nod of support, and Zenas looked back at Tyron.

'If you speak in that manner again, you will not only be removed from the room but from the decision-making process altogether. Is that understood?'

Tyron nodded.

Zenas glanced at Eldoris before speaking again. He was drawing strength from her.

'We cannot start a war for one common girl. Not this war,' he continued. 'We do not just want the girl back—we want her safe. When your anger passes, you will see that retaliation only puts her at risk.'

Tyron's hands went limp beside him, his anger bleeding away. He should never have left her side.

'The girl is collateral,' Pandarus continued. 'She will not be sold off or harmed. They know, more clearly than ever, how you feel about her.'

Tyron's hands returned to fists. He shook his head. 'I sent her back to her family to keep her safe. I made her go.'

'Then she should have remained there.'

Stamitos spoke up at that. 'Aldara is not a prisoner. She is as free to enjoy the tournament as the rest of the kingdom.'

'She was not there enjoying the tournament. The girl stupidly interfered with discipline being carried out by our guards. You would have known that if you had bothered to attend.'

Eldoris went to speak and Stamitos raised a hand. 'It's all right, Mother. You do not have to jump to my defence every time someone speaks against me. I still have my tongue.'

Eldoris turned to Tyron. 'I understand why you feel a sense of responsibility. However, your first responsibility is to your kingdom. You cannot place her safety above your own, or that of your people.'

Zenas nodded in agreement. 'We all admire your heart, but it is Pandarus's ability to think with his head that is required right now. Matters of the heart are a luxury to be enjoyed during times of peace.'

Tyron felt like he was ten years old again, wanting to explore outside of the castle with Leksi, trying to convince his father he could take care of himself and did not require an escort.

'Let us confer with King Jayr before we make any further decisions,' Eldoris said, looking to her husband for support.

'Yes,' Zenas said, coughing into his hand. 'We'll send a messenger.'

Tyron closed his eyes. He had a picture in his head of Aldara bound and gagged beneath a hood. He opened his eyes again to be rid of the image.

'You need to get used to the idea that she might be there until after your wedding,' Pandarus said. 'Possibly longer. King Jayr may wait until his sister is with child. In Zoelin, a union can be annulled if it proves fruitless.'

'One thing at a time,' Eldoris said.

Tyron watched his father. 'I want to be kept informed. You cannot shut me out this time.'

'We will keep you informed, but that is it,' Zenas said. 'You are too emotionally invested to sit in on any meetings.' He looked at his wife.

'Send the messenger,' Eldoris said.

Zenas nodded. 'Send the messenger.'

CHAPTER 27

*A*ldara could not think through her thirst. The hessian bag over her head was wet with perspiration. She was trying to digest everything, make sense of it, and figure out what she could have done to save Leksi, her brother, and herself. She did not even know if Tyron was all right, though her instincts told her he was. He had to be.

Leksi had led her behind the house, sword in hand, surveying their surroundings the entire time. She should have held on to the bow. It was easy to think that in hindsight.

A sharp groan had come from Leksi, and his sword had fallen to the ground. It had taken her a moment to realise there was an arrow lodged in his shoulder. In that time he had already dismounted, picked up his sword with his other hand, and was running towards her. The other guard had appeared then, from the other side of the house, sword flashing. She had watched from on top of Tyron's horse, her warning coming too late as the hilt of his sword came down on the top of Leksi's head. His eyes had rolled back and his legs had given way.

Shock had prevented her from acting. She could have turned Tyron's horse and galloped from them, but there was a confused part of her that remembered the promise she had made to Tyron to stay with Leksi no matter what. *He will be here soon*, she had thought. *He will return with Kadmus and fight the men and save Leksi's life. He will know what to do if I wait a little longer.* Then the large hands had been on her, pulling her from the saddle, covering her mouth in case she mustered a scream.

Everything had gone dark.

As they rode north, her thighs rubbing the back of the saddle and her hands tied and pulled forwards so her head collided with the rider's broad back, she felt suffocation in every form. *He will find me soon*, she told herself. He had a way of doing that. But when the sound of flowing water reached her, she had to let go of those thoughts. The horses trotted down the sandy banks of the Lotheng River and waded into the cold water. At that time of year, some sections of the river could be swam across on horseback.

If anyone was coming for her, it was too late.

The water enveloped her legs, and she kept shifting between being fearful of drowning with her hands tied and tempted to lower her head to try and drink. The guard in front took hold of her as they crossed so she neither drowned nor drank. When they emerged on the other side of the river, the men watered the horses and allowed them a short rest. They said nothing to her as she waited on Zoelin ground while they relieved themselves and refilled their water skins. When they did not offer her a drink, she asked in Zoelin, 'Can I please have some water?'

'You kill our comrades and then ask us for water?' replied one man.

She did not ask again.

The sun was rising in the east, its glow seeping through

the hessian, but not strong enough to stop her from shivering as her wet dress clung to her hips and legs. The men mounted their horses, that time placing her behind the other rider who did not bother pulling the rope tight to secure her. She was in their kingdom now, with no one behind them.

They burrowed into the dense Zoelin forest that smelled of moss and walnut trees, their pace much slower. Aldara was grateful for the head cover as the low branches struck her face. Sometime around noon, the sound of the horse's hooves changed from quiet padding on soft, leaf-laden earth to the clop of a firm road. She could feel the temperature dropping as they continued north, up into the hills. She wondered if they would take her to Onuric—or rather hoped they would. Sapphira and Hali would pull her out of the nightmare.

They passed through a village where she could hear children playing. It sounded the same in any kingdom and any language, the sound of carefree joy. No one in the village asked questions of the men with the pale-skinned prisoner, though she was certain they would have seen her. They went about their work, no doubt with their eyes down.

Later in the afternoon, she heard the crunch of fine rock beneath them. She hoped this meant they were close. Her head was pounding from dehydration, back and legs aching, wrists rubbed raw from the rope. She wondered how much longer she could remain upright and what would happen when she inevitably fell.

The horses stopped, and she listened for the sound of a portcullis. Instead she heard the creak of iron gates.

'Tell him we are here,' she heard one of them say.

When a guard finally pulled her from the horse, her legs did not work. She collapsed at his feet and fought the urge to lie down on the uneven stone. Someone took hold of her arm and pulled her to her feet. They led her up more steps than she could manage and through several doors, each one guarded. The silence rang in her ears and the ground was smooth beneath her boots. The air smelled of rose oil. Its overpowering scent made her nauseous.

They came to a stop and someone pulled the cover from her head. She took large, greedy breaths of air, her eyes closed against the brightness. When she tried again to open them, many faces came into view. She looked between them, hoping to recognise someone. One face held her attention. She blinked and focused. It was King Jayr. He was watching her, his expression neutral.

'Can I have some water, please?' she asked him in Zoelin. Her tongue felt swollen in her mouth.

King Jayr gestured to a nearby servant, a man in a mid-length leather vest and a closely shaven head. He walked to a nearby jug, filled a brass cup, and took it over to her. Her hands were still bound, so he helped her keep hold of it as she drank. She could taste blood from a split in her lip. She emptied the cup, but her thirst remained.

'What is your name?' Jayr asked her in Syrasan.

Aldara squinted against the radiance of the white marble floor. 'Your men have gone to great efforts to bring me here. Two of them died during their attempt. I hope my answer does not disappoint,' she replied in Zoelin.

He smiled, but it was not friendly. 'I suggest you address me as King. Please answer the question, as I would hate to see you lashed upon arrival. Prince Tyron is not here to save you this time.'

She glanced at the guards next to her before looking back at him. 'My name is Aldara, Your Majesty.'

He signalled for the servant to get her more water and then waited for her to drink it. 'I remember you from the tournament,' he began. 'The fierce common girl standing in front of armed Syrasan guards twice your size.' He paused for a moment. 'And then came Prince Tyron, appearing from nowhere. I believe he would have made his way through an entire army if he suspected that you were on the other side of it.'

Aldara swallowed and looked around. There were guards kneeling by the door, eyes to the floor. 'Why am I here, Your Majesty?'

He smiled at her again. 'There will soon be a wedding that will unite our kingdoms.'

Some hair was clinging to her face. She used her shoulder to free it. 'Congratulations,' she said, her tone flat. 'I am not privy to royal news as I live and work on a farm in the South—as you are aware.'

Jayr studied her. 'Yes, but you were not always a farmer, were you?'

She kept her face blank. Fedora would have been impressed with her efforts. 'I apologise for being direct, but you did not bring me all the way here to break the happy news. What is it you think I can help you with, Your Majesty?'

'Prince Tyron certainly has unusual taste in women. I can only assume that you were not this outspoken when you were his Companion at Archdale.'

She said nothing.

'My sister, Princess Tasia, will make for a refreshing change when she becomes his wife,' he continued. 'She knows her place.'

The word hung in the air between them. *Wife*. She swallowed again, mouth still dry. 'I am afraid I cannot comment on their suitability. I have never had the privilege of meeting the princess, but I pray their union will be a happy one.'

Jayr regarded her coolly. 'It does not need to be a happy union. We are not writing stories for children. We are building an empire.'

Aldara blinked. 'Historically, empires have existed under a single monarch.'

His mouth tugged at the corners. 'We are writing history every day.' He picked up his cup, took a drink, and set it down again. 'In answer to your question, you will be my guest here at Drake Castle until after the wedding.'

She was at Drake Castle. The water rumbled in her stomach and her lip began to bleed again. 'Your guest? Guests are invited and are free to leave. I have to assume you mean prisoner.'

'Call it whatever you like. It changes nothing.'

She nodded as she thought. 'I am afraid that you may have overestimated my value to the prince. He is a good man, an excellent soldier, and he takes the protection of his people seriously. But in my experience, his choices are made for the greater good, and he does not respond well to threats.'

Jayr pushed himself out of his chair and walked over to her. He stood examining her for a moment as though trying to decide if he was attracted to her or repulsed by her. Without warning, he grabbed hold of her hair, pulling down on it hard so she gasped. He bent down so his lips were against her ear. 'Who do you think you are talking to? You are in my kingdom now,' he whispered. 'The only reason you, and your worthless family, have not been slaughtered, is because I have a temporary use for you. So you better pray to your God that I have overestimated nothing because your life depends on it. If Prince Tyron does not marry my sister the day she turns sixteen, the only part of you that will return to Syrasan will be your head. Missing its tongue.'

She kept as still as she could under his grip.

He released her with a shove of his hand. 'Get her out of my sight,' he said to the guard next to her. 'Tell me when the Syrasan messenger arrives.'

The cover went back over her head and darkness swallowed her again.

CHAPTER 28

Tyron spent an unhealthy amount of time imagining all the different ways he could kill King Jayr. He was not normally a violent man, but he had been lately. The Zoelin King had sent Grandor Pollux to Archdale to discuss recent events. Tyron remained outside of the throne room because his father knew better than to let him inside. He understood why—just the hum of Pollux's voice on the other side of door pushed him from angry into rage territory. Another man he wanted bleeding out at his feet. It seemed his mind was planning a massacre.

The door swung open and Tyron stepped back to let the Zoelin guards pass him. Pollux emerged next, alert eyes shifting to him. His hand went to his sword and Tyron held up his hands to show he was unarmed. Pollux's shoulders dropped slightly.

'I hear your friend is recovering well,' Pollux said, speaking Syrasan.

'No thanks to your men who shot him.'

Pollux's eyes smiled. 'Stop crying. Two of mine are

dead. An arrow through the shoulder renders a man useless. In Zoelin we call it a graze.'

'We call it something else here. You are lucky your man was a good shooter, or we would be having a very different conversation right now.'

Zenas and Pandarus had stepped outside now. His father gave him a look of warning.

'Let us not keep Grandor Pollux from his long journey,' Pandarus said, stepping between them.

Nobody moved.

'I was just telling your father that we should ink your hand after the wedding,' Pollux continued. 'King Jayr is eager to mark you.'

Tyron smiled, but it did not reach his eyes. 'Perhaps I will mark him instead.'

'Enough,' said Zenas. 'Step aside, Tyron, before I have the guards help you.'

'It seems there is something your son wants to say. So say it,' Pollux said.

Tyron's body was rigid. 'I am growing tired of looking over my shoulder, wondering what harm your king will cause next. You better make sure nothing happens to those in your care, because I take the protection of my people seriously.'

Pollux stepped closer to him now, eyes flashing. 'Corneo is emerging from one of its longest food shortages in history. The only reason they do not slaughter your army and rape your fertile lands is because we stand alongside you. What is one common girl in place of the Corneon army lining the east border?'

'Your king's actions make me question my choice to unite with his sister.'

A smile stretched across Pollux's face. 'It is no longer a

choice, is it?' He faced forwards then and stepped past him, following after the guards.

Tyron looked between Pandarus and his father. 'You have welcomed King Jayr into our kingdom and into our home. We will continue to suffer. Our people will suffer.' He shook his head. 'You have welcomed the devil.'

Before either of them could respond, Pero came striding down the corridor towards him. 'Forgive the interruption, my lord, but there is someone outside of the castle demanding to see you.'

Tyron narrowed his eyes. 'Who is it?'

Pero glanced at the king before replying. 'It is Kadmus, my lord.'

'Who is Kadmus?' Zenas asked, taking in Tyron's falling expression.

Tyron blinked. 'Aldara's brother.' His gaze returned to his father. 'He will be looking for his sister.'

Tyron and Stamitos sat by Leksi's bedside, staring down at their outstretched feet.

'You are both hands down the worst patient visitors ever,' Leksi said. He was propped up by pillows and his right arm was in a sling. 'When I visited you in your hours of need, I was always armed with distasteful jokes and funny stories. Look at your faces. You will put me in an early grave.'

Stamitos regarded him. 'Do you remember that woman you spent the night with who was so pregnant you had to help her off the bed the next morning?'

'What I remember of that story is you were angry because she didn't tell you she was married,' Tyron said, crossing his arms in front of him.

Stamitos laughed. 'The bulging stomach wasn't a hint?'

'She carried it well for her size,' Leksi replied. 'I stand by my reaction.' He looked at Tyron as the laughter died down. 'What did you tell Kadmus?'

Tyron shrugged. 'The truth.'

'I bet that went down well,' Stamitos said.

'I gave him my word that I would bring her back.'

Leksi raised his eyebrows. 'To Archdale or to her family?'

Tyron swallowed. 'To her family, once I know she will be safe there. In the meantime, I have sent men down south to assist in rebuilding the barn.'

'Eighty of them?' Leksi asked.

Tyron tilted his head. 'Very funny.'

He had been surprised when Kadmus had agreed to let him handle the situation. He seemed to trust that Tyron would get her back. It probably had more to do with the fact that Aldara trusted him, and Kadmus had little choice at that moment. He liked Kadmus; he was a lot like Stamitos.

'What are you scheming in that dark mind of yours?' Leksi asked, pulling his attention back.

'Nothing. This is my tired face.'

'You only have one face, and it isn't cheering me up right now.'

'You still have both of your hands. I don't know why you are complaining,' Stamitos said.

Leksi's eyes remained on Tyron. 'Don't do anything stupid until I am out of bed.'

'Don't do anything stupid at all,' Stamitos said. 'You are the best fighter this kingdom has—'

'Second best,' Leksi said.

Stamitos ignored him. 'So when the opportunity comes, you better be ready to fight. You let them take Sapphira.

And then you let Pollux ride away after he cut off my hand. I know why you did, but I also trusted you had a plan to get her back, the same way Kadmus is trusting you.'

'This just got heavy,' Leksi said, leaning back into his pillow haven.

Self-loathing weighed Tyron down in that moment. In his efforts to be compliant and avoid conflict, he had forgotten one of the main reasons he fought. 'I'm going to get her back.'

Stamitos regarded him through bright, youthful eyes. 'Who? Aldara?'

'Yes, and then Sapphira.'

Stamitos nodded. 'How?'

'I don't know yet, but I promise you I will.'

CHAPTER 29

*A*ldara stopped counting the days. She stopped asking the guards questions, growing sick of their silence. She stopped imagining her family's grief, the conversations people may have had about her disappearance. Stopped imagining what Tyron might be doing, or not doing. She just stopped, only taking the food, the water, the clean dresses and the blankets.

Each morning the guard would come and unlock her cell door. She would follow him past her unruly neighbours, their vile propositions following her down the narrow stone steps of the tower. She would step into the small courtyard at the bottom and listen to the door lock behind her. Circles. That was all she could do—walk circles along the edge, keeping close to the walls to absorb the warmth from them.

She would walk until another guard came in the afternoon to collect her. Then she would amble ahead of him, back up the dark, narrow stairs, devoid of warmth, and try not to look at the other prisoners who leered and shouted until the guard pounded his mace on the bars. Each time

Aldara's body would jump and her eyes would close. She preferred the words to the loud noise of weapons hitting iron.

She had a window. If she stood on her bed, she could see the courtyard she paced around each day. It seemed even smaller from that height. Opposite she could see the guard tower, connected by two curtain walls. She never saw the sun. It had abandoned her, passing out of view, casting only shadows.

For some time, she had tried to remain positive, telling herself that she could have been placed in a dungeon, or stripped of all comforts. But loneliness had a way of destroying logic. And she was completely alone.

One morning she sat on the cool stone in the court-yard, her back against the wall which no longer held heat, tired of walking nowhere. She was watching the shadows grow tall on the east wall. When she looked up, she saw a woman standing at the top, the sun on her face, staring down at her. Aldara got to her feet and stared up. Her feet moved towards the wall, but once the woman realised she had been seen, she turned and walked back towards the guard tower. Aldara's chest grew heavier, if that was possible. The rattle of keys sounded behind her. She turned around, feeling hopeful for some absurd reason, but it was just another guard, waiting to return her to her prison. Up the steps. Clang, clang. More shouting. The clink of doors locking behind her.

How much longer could she survive?

The next day, as she paced in the courtyard, she watched the top of the walls, but the woman did not appear again. In the afternoon, she went with the guard. There was silence when she reached the top of the stair-well—no shouting, no crude comments, only subdued prisoners watching her pass. Her mind grew alert. When she arrived at her cell, she found a woman standing in the doorway, peering in. The woman from the wall. Aldara guessed her to be around seventeen years. Her skin was the colour of dark honey and the insides of her wrists were patterned with ink. She wore a backless, cream dress with a thick gold chain around her neck, each link the length of a finger. Her black hair was pulled into a tight bun, revealing another small pattern of ink on the back of her neck. A petite gold crown balanced on top of her head.

The guard escorting Aldara bowed. Aldara remained upright, watching her.

'Who are you?' she asked, using her voice for the first time in days. She barely recognised the deep, broken tone.

The woman's gold-painted eyes blinked at her. Aldara could not tell whether she was beautiful or just beautifully presented.

'I have some questions for you, if you do not mind.' She spoke in Syrasan but the Zoelin accent was thick.

Aldara continued to stare at her. 'Who are you?' she repeated. 'I would prefer to know who I am speaking with before I say another word.'

The woman nodded, her brown eyes unblinking. 'I am Princess Tasia of Zoelin.'

Aldara felt small next to the guard. 'King Jayr's sister?'

'Yes.'

Tyron's betrothed. Aldara's eyes swept over her once more. She was everything his wife ought to be. 'You obviously know who I am.'

'Yes,' Tasia replied. 'You are the royal Companion.'

Aldara repeated the words in her mind. It had been true once. Now it seemed ridiculous. 'Not anymore,' she said, her voice clearing.

'I came here to ask you about him. To find out who he is without his crown.' She spoke quietly.

Aldara had spent so much time blocking him out that she was not sure she could let him back in. 'Who?' she asked, hoping she would say another name.

'Prince Tyron, of course. My betrothed.'

She said his name, and just like that, he poured back in. The face she thought she had forgotten, the hands, the voice, the warm breath behind her, in front of her, consuming her. She took a small step sideways. 'What is he like?' She could only repeat the question.

'We are yet to meet. Syrasan law does not permit women to marry before their sixteenth year.'

Aldara took her in. 'How old are you?'

'I am two months past my fifteenth year.'

'Oh.' It was all she could manage.

Tasia linked her hands together in front of her. 'I suppose I should not be surprised you love him. He is a prince, and you shared his bed for some time.'

Yes, she had at one time, but that was not why she loved him. 'Forgive me. I do not get a lot of visitors nowadays.'

Tasia looked away, giving her a few moments before speaking again. 'Is he a good man?' she asked. 'My brother is not generous with details. And I am not sure I would trust his appraisal.'

Aldara saw a glimpse of a smile. She fought hard to remain composed. 'He is a great man.' Her voice was once again unrecognisable. 'There is no better husband in any kingdom, I assure you.'

Tasia exhaled, relief on her face, her youth evident for the first time. 'I am pleased to hear it. It is a long life to live at Archdale with a cruel man.'

Tyron was incapable of cruelty. She was having difficulty resenting the union of two like-minded people. 'You have nothing to fear,' she said, looking down.

Tasia went to leave but stopped next to Aldara. 'It is a

good sign you are here at Drake Castle. It means you will leave here one day. Prisoners who go to Onuric never leave.'

She had stopped breathing. 'I have friends at Onuric, mentors. Have you seen them?'

Tasia shook her head. 'I have not been outside the walls of Drake Castle since my brother became king.'

Aldara was still and unsure how to respond.

'He has big plans for our kingdoms, and I am his only recognised sister.'

Aldara nodded. 'I see.'

Tasia hesitated before speaking. 'Do you have enough food? Enough blankets?'

Aldara glanced across at her cell. 'Yes, thank you.'

Tasia gave a slight nod and then continued walking. Aldara turned to watch her descend the stairwell. The guard gestured for her to move. She glanced at him, wondering what he made of the conversation, if he cared. Blank eyes stared back at her. She walked into her cell, over to her bed, and curled up on it. Her back faced the guard as he locked the door. The tray of food sat untouched next to her. The thought of eating it made her stomach turn.

She had no idea if she slept that night, or if perhaps her vivid thoughts resembled dreams. In the morning, the door unlocked and the guard stood waiting for her to get up, but she did not move.

'What is wrong with you?' he asked. 'Are you sick?'

She shook her head and pulled the blanket around her. 'I do not want to go out today.'

He hesitated before locking the door and leaving.

She stared at the patterns on the bricks in front of her. One conversation with his future wife had torn something inside of her, rendered her useless. If she was going to survive, she would need to shut him out again, build walls around her heart higher than those she lived within. There was still a chance she would go home to her family, so she needed to survive for them. She had made a life without him once. She could do it again. Shut him out.

But lying on that bed, she knew she could not do it. There was no closing her heart against him.

Tyron was in a permanently agitated state. It did not help that his father had him followed. It was as though his footsteps echoed. When he rode his horse, the sound of hooves trailed behind him. He went through short periods of cooperation, but occasionally he found himself riding north, never sure how far he would get before he turned back, or someone stopped him. What made him return was not the guards but the need for a plan that would not put her life at risk. How far was he willing to go? Who was he prepared to betray? The lines in his head were blurring, and she was not there to centre him.

One day he rode as far north as Soarid. He stopped outside of the village, in the middle of the road, thinking through hypotheticals. Four Syrasan guards lined the road behind him. They would keep their distance as long as he remained inside Syrasan's borders. He knew he could escape them if he wanted to, kill them if he had to. They knew it as well but would still follow orders.

That morning he had trained with Leksi in the butts, as his friend was worried about being out of shape. They had circled one another, wooden swords coming together between words.

'You are waiting for a failsafe plan,' Leksi had said. 'There is no such thing. Someone is always at risk.'

'It cannot be her.'

The air had begun to cool, the mornings bringing occasional frost.

'I wish there was a way I could communicate with her,' Tyron continued. 'I have no proof she is even alive. I don't know how she is being treated, where she sleeps, what she eats, if she is cold. I wonder what King Jayr tells her.'

'Probably nothing, and I doubt she would listen anyway.' Leksi took advantage of Tyron's distracted mindset and, in a few swift movements, knocked the sword from his hands. 'You just lost to a cripple.'

'There is nothing wrong with you.'

'I have emotional scars.'

'I can recommend a physician for that.'

For once Leksi did not laugh. 'The easiest way to get her back is to marry the princess sooner.'

'You think I haven't thought of that? I'd be marrying a child. I'd be a criminal.'

He kept swinging back to the idea and then remembering all the men his father had locked up for that exact crime.

Otus shifted beneath him, pulling him back to the present and the waiting guards behind him. Tyron turned the horse and faced the watchful men. As he approached, they parted to let him through. He loosened his reins and began the journey back to Archdale.

CHAPTER 30

*W*hen Tyron learned of the planned feast to announce his engagement to Princess Tasia, his first question was, 'Will King Jayr be attending?'

Zenas frowned at him. 'I thought you would ask me if your future wife will be attending. I imagine you want to meet her.'

'Will she?'

'No. At least not this visit.'

'But King Jayr will be?'

Zenas folded his arms over his chest. 'Yes, so you will need to be on your best behaviour, prove to King Jayr that we are all moving in the same unified direction.'

Tyron watched his father, who seemed unsure of the words he spoke. He nodded. 'I promise you I will do whatever it takes to get Aldara back.'

'I think we can both agree that the less time she remains at Drake Castle the better, but the focus should be a safe return.' There was a warning in his tone.

That was Tyron's *only* focus. 'How do you know she

remains at Drake Castle? Perhaps he has sent her to Onuric by now.'

'He will be keeping her close.' Zenas narrowed his eyes. 'Whatever plans you might be making in that mind of yours, forget them. King Jayr is well aware of your attachment to the girl. He is keeping her close for good reason.'

He shook his head. 'Have you forgotten what it feels like?'

'What?'

He almost could not say the word. 'Love. The consuming kind.'

Zenas stared at him as though he had said something treasonous. In a way, he had.

'Have you forgotten Idalia?' Tyron said, barely a whisper. 'Do you remember the loss of her? The regret? The feeling of helplessness?'

'We existed within boundaries, something my sons seem to lack.'

Tyron looked at him. 'This life killed Idalia. I sent Aldara away so she could live, and it still wasn't enough. *Your* ally broke my boundaries, so do not lecture me.'

'He is Syrasan's ally.'

He shook his head. 'No. That man is not my ally, and he is not an ally to our people. He is a constant threat.'

He walked away from his father, not bothering to bow, and strode down the south corridor towards Stamitos's chambers. Fragments of thoughts came together in his mind.

Stamitos's squire stepped aside, letting Tyron enter unannounced, like usual.

'I think I have a plan,' Tyron said, not bothering with a greeting.

Stamitos was seated at the table under the window, his tunic hanging on the back of his chair. He looked up from the letter he was writing and leaned back to observe Tyron. He nodded. 'All right. What do you need me to do?'

Tyron leaned against the wall of the great hall, watching the hands of noblemen slide into forbidden nooks of the Companions' dresses as they danced. It was one of the few occasions wives had been invited to attend. They stood in a private huddle at the far end of the room, pretending not to see their husbands' indiscretions, but their discomfort showed beneath their well-rehearsed smiles. He glanced about the room and spotted Stamitos talking with Lord Clio. His brother met his eyes, and they nodded at one another.

King Jayr broke off his conversation with Pandarus and made his way over to where Tyron was standing. They stood side by side, silent for a moment.

'Are you trying to make me nervous by hiding in the shadows?'

Tyron glanced at him but did not move. 'Is it working?'

Jayr laughed. 'No.'

Eldoris was seated at the high table. She looked over at them, eyes wary. Tyron held her gaze for a moment.

'I imagine she would have been a vision in this environment, far removed from the filth of farming,' Jayr said. 'I can see the appeal for a man like you.'

Tyron did not take the bait. If there was ever a night he needed to exercise self-control, it was that night.

Cora joined them, filling the uncomfortable gap in the conversation. 'Good evening, Your Majesty,' she said, curtsying in front of Jayr while balancing a cup of wine. She rose and took a delicate sip. The jewels on her arm made a chiming noise as she moved.

Jayr gave a small bow. 'Are you here to tell me your father has changed his mind and that you are to be my queen?'

She smiled mischievously. 'Today we celebrate another happy union. We are all so eager to meet her. Is she looking forward to the tour?'

Jayr raised his eyebrows. 'The wedding tour?'

Cora took another sip of wine before speaking. 'In Syrasan, it is tradition for the betrothed to tour the kingdom prior to the wedding. They visit each village, collecting the good wishes of the common. It is believed to sustain the marriage.'

'Is that so?' Jayr said, glancing at Tyron.

Before Tyron could respond, his father stood, tapping his cup with a fork. The crowd fell quiet.

'Here we go,' Jayr said, raising his cup towards Tyron in a private toast.

Tyron stopped listening. It was easier that way. Judging by the moderate applause, the guests were not fooled by the stories being fed to them anyway. There was an update on the Companion trade—a trade the nobles were happy to support as long as their own daughters were never a part of it. And then came the announcement. Zenas's smile seemed unnatural.

'Tonight, we gather here in peace, to celebrate the joining of our great kingdoms before God through the marriage of Prince Tyron of Syrasan to Princess Tasia of Zoelin.'

Zenas started the applause, encouraging the room. All eyes went to Tyron, pressing down on him. Jayr watched, plain-faced and calm. Cora's eyes twinkled at him from behind her cup. She was enjoying herself.

Tyron stepped forwards and raised his cup. 'To my future bride, Princess Tasia, who will stand with me in ensuring that justice is served, that honour is rewarded, and that the laws of Syrasan are upheld.'

Leksi appeared next to him and placed a hand on his shoulder. 'My lords and ladies, join me in wishing Prince Tyron of Syrasan and Princess Tasia of Zoelin a long and happy future, blessed by God.'

Everybody raised their cups. 'Hear, hear,' came the chorus of guests.

Tyron took the cup his sister offered him and drank as the applause sounded around him. He had known the announcement was coming, and yet every step he took in the direction laid out by King Jayr felt like a betrayal to the people in the room.

The music began and Rhea walked to the middle of the room to sing a traditional Syrasan song. His father joined his new companion, Ellarosa, for a rare dance. Violeta and Panthea both moved towards Leksi, but he was already heading for the door. He had somewhere to be. Some of the men collected their wives to join in the dancing. Tyron looked at Stamitos, who watched him from the other side of the room. Pandarus walked up to them, drunk, with one arm draped across Astra, who appeared uncomfortable beneath the weight of it. She was subtly trying to keep him steady as he leaned on her.

'Excellent speech, brother,' Pandarus said. 'The future looks bright.'

Tyron glanced across at Cora. She raised her chin and turned to King Jayr.

'Would you like to dance, Your Majesty?' she asked.

King Jayr gave a small nod and offered his hand to her. She slipped hers into it and the two of them walked off to join the others.

Tyron felt his senses heighten. He stretched his fingers and let his left hand brush across his sword, watching as the pair stepped together and then apart. He watched their palms connect, hands swapping mid-step. He waited for that small gesture, that inappropriate touch that would justify his next action. Cora glanced at him as she stepped around Jayr. When they came together the next time, she took a larger step so her hip brushed his. Tyron saw it then, a change in Jayr's face that meant she had his full attention. Their hands came together again, eyes locked. Cora was wearing one of her gowns with pieces of fabric cut out above the hip, and Jayr could not help himself. The next time the young king stepped around her, his fingertips slipped across the exposed skin as she passed him.

That would do it.

Tyron glanced at Stamitos to make sure he was paying attention before making a move towards them. He counted the number of Zoelin guards, estimating how much time he would have. He was a few steps away from them now.

'What do you think you are doing?' Tyron said, coming between them. He stepped up into Jayr's face and Cora took a few paces back. 'You think you can come into my home and put your hands on my sister?'

Jayr seemed a little taken aback but pleased by the reaction. 'You better watch your temper in front of your guests.'

'Tyron, we were just dancing,' Cora said.

'Stay out of it.' His eyes remained on Jayr. 'Do you honestly think you can just take whatever you want? I think enough Syrasan women have suffered at your vile hands, don't you?' He stepped closer again, pushing into Jayr's space.

The other people dancing looked over. A few people stopped to watch. His father was yet to notice.

Jayr leaned in closer, so his lips were at Tyron's ear, and

whispered, 'You have no idea the things I have done to that girl. And you know I never take no for an answer.'

Trigger.

Tyron's hand went to his sword. Jayr stepped back, drawing his weapon as he did so. A few of the women who had been dancing gasped and moved away. When Tyron's sword went up, Stamitos grabbed hold of his arm to stop him.

'Tyron, no!'

Zenas noticed the conflict then. His eyes widened. 'Guards!' he shouted.

Syrasan guards descended on Tyron like a pack of wolves moving in for the kill. Two Zoelin guards stepped in front of Jayr, ready to defend their king. Jayr returned his sword to its sheath, watching Tyron through the gap.

'You animal!' Tyron shouted as four guards dragged him from the room. 'I'm coming for her! And then I'm coming for you! I'll see you at Drake Castle, you bastard!'

The entire room was still and confused by the display. Some of the noblemen held the hilt of their elaborate swords while their wives stood, hand over mouth. Tyron knew they would talk about it for weeks to come. He had just drawn his sword on the King of Zoelin and made a public threat on his life. He had just committed a crime.

He struggled against the guards all the way to the tower, shouting threats and profanities along the way. Only once he was locked in a cell did he go quiet.

He hoped it was enough, because it was the only plan he had.

Stamitos and Leksi arrived in the early hours of the morning. It was still dark, and the torches on the walls cast flickering shadows across their faces. They came to a stop in front of his cell. He stepped up to the door.

'Well?' he asked, waiting.

'He just sent a messenger,' Leksi said. 'I followed the rider for a while to ensure he was heading north.'

'One of Cora's spies saw King Jayr hand it to him in person,' Stamitos said.

Tyron exhaled and took hold of the bars. 'He'll arrive at Drake in the evening. They won't move her overnight, it's too hazardous.'

Stamitos looked sceptical. 'Are you sure about all this?'

Tyron nodded. 'Yes, the first thing he will do is move Aldara to Onuric. He knows Father cannot keep me locked up forever, and he knows I will make good on my threat. He believes I will come to Drake Castle.'

'We'll cross the river near the Corneo border,' Leksi said. 'Ride north through the woods and intercept the party. No one needs to die, unless they want to.'

The click of shoes on stone made them all turn. Cora and Eldoris stepped into the light, unfazed by their surroundings.

'Seeing you in here is so enjoyable. Must we release you?' Cora asked.

'Not until tomorrow,' Tyron replied. 'We mustn't panic King Jayr by letting me out too soon. He needs to feel confident enough to move her, and he will want to do that while I am locked up.'

Eldoris's hands were clasped together. 'You are lucky King Jayr did not kill you during your little performance.'

'He is not a fool,' Tyron said. He looked at Cora again. 'Thank you. I'm sorry to have used you as bait, but protecting your honour was one of the few justifiable reasons I could come up with for drawing my sword.'

'Not true,' Leksi said. 'I could think of a few other justifiable reasons.'

'Yes,' Eldoris said. 'However, we needed one that would ensure my son was released from this place.'

Cora touched her forehead. 'Do not thank me, I had nothing to do with it. Especially if Father asks.'

'I cannot believe I agreed to help you,' Eldoris said, shaking her head.

'You didn't,' replied Stamitos. 'You agreed to help *me*, because I have one hand and you have trouble saying no to me now.'

'Really?' Leksi said. 'I say no to you all the time.'

Tyron's eyes ran across the people standing on the other side of the bars. He felt overwhelming affection for them in that moment. They had come through for him, supporting his insane plan to get Aldara back into Syrasan.

He pressed his forehead against the cold iron bars. *Hold on*, he thought. *Just a little longer. I'm coming for you.*

CHAPTER 31

'Get up' came a voice.

Aldara's eyes snapped open. A guard stood next to her bed.

'Put this on. You are leaving,' he said in Zoelin, thrusting a cloak towards her. When she did not immediately take it from him, he let it drop on the bed.

She sat upright, staring at the thick garment. 'Where am I going?'

'Not a word for weeks and now you have questions?'

'Just one question,' she replied, still not moving. 'Where am I going? To Syrasan?'

The guard picked up the cloak again and shoved it into her hands. 'You are being moved. Put the cloak on or we will leave it behind.'

She climbed out of bed and wrapped it around her. She had heard the guards say there was snow on the mountains. The cold season was closing in. 'Why am I being moved?'

'Enough questions. Move.' He gestured towards the

242

open door with his free hand. The other rested on his sword.

She slipped into her boots, which were as icy as the floor they sat on. They walked down the familiar steps and into the courtyard. She glanced at the shadows on the wall to gauge the time. It was early morning. A heavy door opened beneath the guard tower as they approached. They entered a dark walkway where another door opened as the one behind them banged shut. Aldara glanced at the tall guard behind, but his eyes were looking past her.

They stepped through the doorway and out onto a frost-covered lawn. It was the first time she had seen grass in almost two months. It was a vibrant green, wet and spongy beneath her feet. She stopped and breathed in the clean air, a welcomed change from the damp, mouldy smell of the tower. At the edge of the lawn, she could see stables.

'Keep moving,' the guard barked.

They walked across the lawn towards the scent of hay and manure, their footsteps leaving a trail.

'Are we leaving the castle?' Fear crept into her voice. Or perhaps it was fatigue. She had not eaten properly in weeks and her legs were unsteady.

The guard was next to her now. He glanced sideways at her. 'What does it matter? You can be a prisoner here or a prisoner there.'

'There?'

A groom was waiting with two saddled horses at the end of the lawn. The smaller horse was tethered to the larger one's saddle. Aldara looked past them to the training yard where a young horse was cantering in circles along the fence while a man stood in the middle, flicking his whip at its legs.

'Show me your hands,' said the guard. He was holding a

rope and had a black woollen hood tucked under his arm. She held her hands out for him, her eyes remaining on the bag. When he was done, he held it in front of her face.

'Do you need this? Or are you finished with the questions?'

'I am finished.'

The groom helped her into the saddle while the guard mounted the other horse. It shifted under the weight of him. They trailed along the castle wall until they reached the large iron gates at the front of the castle. Aldara counted eight guards, six at the gate and two on the wall. The two on the wall did not even glance down.

The horses trotted along the road to the bottom of the hill before slowing to a walk. Aldara stiffened in the saddle when they veered off the road into tall pines hidden by thick fog.

'Why are we moving off the road?' she asked.

'I still have the bag.'

She went silent, looking up at the cloud-covered sun to gauge the direction they were travelling. East. Syrasan was south. Her family was south. So was Tyron, but there was no room in her mind for him. Onuric Castle was in the East. What had Princess Tasia said? Prisoners who go to Onuric never leave? A part of her felt warm at the prospect of seeing Hali and Sapphira, but there was a chance neither of them were there, or she might not be permitted to see them anyway. There was also the possibility that the guard was not taking her to Onuric. Perhaps he was leading her out into the woods to dispose of her. Was it possible that King Jayr no longer needed her alive?

Her mind repeated one thought. *Run.*

She studied the guard's weapons: a bow and quiver on his back, a sword on his left hip, and the handle of a dagger poking up from his right boot. She tested the rope around her wrists. It was tightly bound, and she was unfamiliar with the knot he had used. She knew she could wear through it if she could find something to use for friction, but there was no time or opportunity. She glanced again at the dagger sticking out from the guard's boot. If she was to have any chance of escape, she needed her hands free. She needed that dagger.

It took around half an hour to formulate a plan and another half to work up the courage to implement it. In front of her, the guard appeared relaxed, with a loose rein and one hand hanging by his side. The head cover was tucked in a saddlebag. Her heart quickened as she realised what she was about to do. There was an opening in the trees coming up on the right that she could fit through. There was still enough cloud cover to help her get away. Would he shoot her? It depended on what his orders were. It was too late for fear; her body was readying itself. Her muscles were tight, her hands damp. The moment would be critical.

When she reached the opening, there was no time for procrastination; she had to take the opportunity or risk not having another one. Her heels spurred into the horse's sides and the mare lurched forwards. She slid her hand up the neck of her horse and pushed the top of the bridle over its ears. The leather strap slipped down the face of the alarmed mare and swung to the ground at the same time the guard turned around. Aldara was already at his side. In one swoop, she snatched the dagger from his boot.

'Ha!' she shouted at the mare, digging her heels in again.

The guard's eyes widened as he realised what was happening. He lay his studded boots into the ribs of his horse. The horse heaved under the force of it. He was only a few paces behind her, reaching for his bow.

'Halt!' he shouted. 'Or I will stop you by whatever means necessary.'

Aldara leaned right so the mare turned into the gap between the trees. No bridle meant she had to rely on legs and body weight to direct the mare while trying to outrun an armed guard with two weapons. She hoped he needed her alive, because there was no way he would miss her at that distance. The trees came closer together but she did not slow down, ploughing between them, her body wrapping the mare. An arrow struck the tree in front of her and she knew from the height he was either a bad shot or had been aiming for the horse. She had not considered the fact that he would take down the mare if it meant stopping her.

There were no tracks or familiar landmarks, only small pockets of space she was forced to fit through. Manoeuvring them slowed her—but it slowed the guard more. The problem was her horse was only allowing enough room for itself, meaning Aldara's legs kept snagging the tree trunks. She squeezed the inside leg to try to widen the gap around each tree, but the mare was not Loda and, confused by the signals, she sped up. Aldara clipped a tree and it pulled her from the saddle. She landed on the mare's rump and grabbed hold to stop from sliding off the back of the horse. The dagger slipped from her hand, instantly buried by the forest debris kicked up behind her. The mare slowed when she pulled herself back into the seat of the saddle.

A backwards glance. The guard was further back now. He had put his bow away to better navigate the trees. She leaned right and moved into the dense shrubs that grew in the shade of the larger trees, lying flat across the mare's neck to avoid the low branches. When she reached her bound hands behind her, feeling for the hood of her cloak so she could cover her head, her arms collided with a branch. She felt a sharp sting across her left arm, followed by the warmth of blood. She tucked them beneath her and peered behind to see if the guard was still in pursuit. There was no sign of him. She checked the other side. He was not there either. Hopeful she had lost him, her legs relaxed a little and the horse responded by slowing down enough to enable her to sit upright again. The mare was tiring, but she could not afford to slow her pace any more. She knew it was at least four hours of hard riding to the border, and she needed a much bigger gap between her and the guard.

She turned her face up the sun to ensure she was still moving south, then looked down to inspect her bleeding arm. The sleeve of her dress was ripped to the elbow. It had taken most of the impact, but a long, haggard cut ran from her elbow to her wrist. She pressed it against her stomach to stop the bleeding. No dagger, no bridle, useless hands. It had been a risky plan even with those necessities. As she was, even if she made it to the river, she would probably drown trying to cross it.

An hour later, the mare slowed to a trot, ignoring Aldara's heels in her sides. Exhaustion had won. Aldara looked about, listening for the other horse. A bird took to flight in front of her and she gasped. Her hands went up to cover her mouth, and she winced as her injured arm pulled away from her dress. She glanced down at the bloody line across her front which had been a makeshift bandage. At least the arm had stopped bleeding.

The guard could not arrive without her. She was certain he would hunt her all the way to the border, so she needed to get absolute control of herself.

The sun was high in the sky when she slowed to a walk. The mare's neck was lathered with sweat, her breathing laboured. Aldara took a moment to get her bearings. She had veered east, wasting time she did not have. Her wrists stung where the harsh rope had been rubbing. Still, she did not stop. She had to get across the river before night held her prisoner.

Mid-afternoon, the sound of hooves reached her. She leaned back in the saddle, releasing the grip of her legs. The horse stopped, its head hanging with exhaustion. Their only cover was the trees. Aldara sank deeper into the hood of her cloak, remaining still as she peered between tree trunks. Mounted Zoelin soldiers cantered past in single file. She held her breath as she counted them. Thirty-two. Thirty-two soldiers riding south. She realised at that moment that she was only twenty yards from the main road. And now there were men in front of her.

Once they had passed, she did not move for some time, partly because she wanted to grow the distance between them and partly because fear anchored her. Her horse needed water. *She* needed water. It drove her forwards, slowly, so she could listen to her surroundings. It was no longer a race to the border; it would be a crawl, a game of hide and seek. She thought about all the things Fedora had taught her, all the lessons she had sat through on Zoelin geography, history and culture. She knew every custom and tradition, but she did not know where to source water or what foods you could access if you found yourself starving and dehydrated in the woods. So much time spent practising manners for men who had none.

Tears threatened to spill over, but she breathed through them. There was no time for self-pity; she needed to figure a way past the men hunting her. They were stronger, much stronger, so she would need to be smarter.

The first thing she had to do was free her hands because she had a river to swim across. She watched the ground for something to cut through the rope, finding a fist-sized rock on the ground ahead. She dismounted and dropped to her knees, thankful the mare was too tired to flee. She picked up the rock and examined it. It had some jagged edges. Her father had once told her that a rope under tension could be cut with almost anything. She pressed her wrists against the trunk of the closest tree to create as much tension as she could, then angled the rock in one hand so the sharpest edge of the stone was against the rope.

At first, not much happened. She rubbed as best she could while keeping the tension in the rope. Her hands tired, and the rope burned against her wrists, but she persisted. Kadmus's voice was in her head telling her to stop complaining and get on with it. The rope frayed, and the more it frayed, the quicker the progress came. When the final pop sounded and her hands were freed, she had to stop herself from laughing with relief. She slumped against the tree and studied the cut on her arm. It was difficult to gauge how bad it was with all the blood that had dried on her skin. She looked away, trying to focus on what was next.

She glanced down at the rope lying next to her. Picking it up, she examined it to see if it could be used. There was just enough to make a simple head collar for the mare. When she had finished, she tore the loose fabric off the sleeve of her dress and used the rock to rip her skirt into strips. She tied them together to make a set of reins, which she then attached to the collar. At least she could tether the mare if needed.

The air was cold on her exposed legs. She looked up at the sun once again. It was sinking west. Despite her progress, she felt the familiar press of panic on her chest. She mounted and rode south, making sure she maintained a good distance from the road. Her tongue moved in her mouth, recognising thirst. The cooling air was no compensation for liquid.

Keep moving towards water. That was as far as she let her mind go. She could not let herself think beyond reaching the river, because if she did, she might realise there was no guarantee of safety on the other side. What if they handed her back?

She blinked away the thought and Tyron's green eyes flashed in her mind. If she could just reach him, she knew he would hand her over to no one.

One moment at a time. It was all she could manage.

She had to make it to the river.

CHAPTER 32

The sun was beginning its ascent and Tyron was waiting to be released from his cell. He was leaning against the door, his arms threaded through the bars, feeling caged. The feeling might have overwhelmed him had Aldara not likely been in the same situation for the previous two months. He was expecting his brother, sister, mother, or Leksi to arrive. What he did not expect was his father.

King Zenas strode towards him, flanked by guards, a fed-up expression etched into his face. He stopped in front of Tyron, his gaze moving past him to the damp walls and the string cot.

'I am surprised your mother did not have more comfortable furnishings brought in for you.' There was a definite note of sarcasm in his tone.

Tyron stepped back from the door. 'Any longer and she may have.'

Zenas looked at him then. 'I was so disappointed by your behaviour,' he began. 'I kept wondering what on earth would make you draw your sword before a visiting king.'

Tyron opened his hands. 'I lost my temper. I'm sorry.'

His father shook his head. 'I don't think so. I have been trying to figure out what would lead you to make such a spectacle of your emotions, as you are the most closed off of all my children.'

'And what did you discover?'

Zenas watched him for a moment. 'I realised that your actions served another purpose other than simply venting your anger.'

'What do you mean?'

His father crossed his arms and exhaled. 'Do you want to know what confirmed my suspicions?'

He waited.

'Your mother and sister were completely silent on the issue. I had you imprisoned, and they said nothing on the matter. It reeked of something.'

It was true, his mother would never leave one of her children imprisoned without saying something about it.

'I realised that whatever you were planning, they were likely a part of it. Last night, I visited the queen in her chambers.'

That was not good. 'And?'

'And your mother remains highly effective in the art of persuasion, because I am about to release you knowing that you will cross the border and take back the common girl.'

It seemed no one liked to use her name. He took in his father's angry expression. 'You decided this last night and left me in here?'

Zenas laughed. 'You are damn right I did. You embarrassed me in front of our guests. I would have left you in here another week if your insane plan was not time-sensitive.' He shook his head again. 'Do you really think you can you pull this off with discretion?'

Tyron nodded. 'Absolutely. No one need die. You have my word.'

'I have witnessed the mess a man can make without taking lives.' Zenas gestured to the guard to open the gate. 'You understand what will happen if this goes badly.'

The door swung open but Tyron did not move. 'I cannot leave her there, and I cannot marry Princess Tasia before her sixteenth year. King Jayr has left me with no choice.'

Zenas unfolded his arms, observing his son. 'I have not forgotten what it is to love, because your mother acts as a constant reminder. Have you ever seen a mother's love more fierce?'

He shook his head. 'Never.'

'Go. The girl will have departed for Onuric by now.'

Tyron raised his brows. 'How do you know?'

'Because your mother and sister are not the only ones with spies. And mine extend beyond these walls.' He stepped aside so Tyron could pass.

Tyron stepped through the cell door and stopped in front of him. 'And King Jayr?'

'Yet to emerge. I sent two Companions and some excellent Galen wine to his chambers last night.'

Tyron bowed before his father and king. 'Thank you,' he said, placing a hand on Zenas's shoulder as he rose.

'Stamitos stays here. You come back with one girl. Am I understood?'

It seemed his father had a more thorough understanding of the situation than he initially thought. 'I understand.'

≈

They had stayed off the roads, moving through the familiar Syrasan woods at a steady speed. When they neared the river, they observed the bridge from the cover of trees and were surprised to find it guarded.

'It's easy enough to cross downstream at this time of year,' Leksi said.

Three additional men waited on horseback behind them. Tyron had hand-selected them himself. He needed strong fighters who would follow orders without question, and the men behind him had proven their skills and loyalty many times over.

He glanced at the sun to gauge the time. It was almost noon. If they did not cross soon, they risked not reaching her in time. He glanced downstream and saw two more guards on horseback, trotting along the tree line on the other side.

'It seems King Jayr is expecting us,' Leksi said.

It was possible, but it made little sense that he would remain at Archdale, indulging in women and wine, while Tyron waited at the Zoelin border. He observed the guards on the bridge whose eyes swept north.

'Look at that,' Tyron said.

'What?'

'The guards on the bridge.'

Leksi watched them for a moment. 'They are not looking south to Syrasan. Their eyes are searching north. They are not keeping us out.'

'They are keeping someone in,' Tyron finished.

'Do you want me to go downstream and see how far down the river is guarded?'

Tyron shook his head. His stomach had grown tight. 'We cannot waste time travelling west and then making up the distance.'

The clap of hooves reached them and their eyes moved

across the river to see a horse emerge from the trees. Its rider barely slowed as he approached the bridge. The guards stepped aside to let him cross.

'Messenger. Shall we find out what is going on?' Tyron asked, glancing at Leksi.

'After you.'

The five men turned their horses and wove through the trees towards the road. They waited until the rider came into sight before bursting out of the trees in front of him. The galloping horse came to a skidding halt and the young Zoelin rider looked between the men, his wide eyes coming to rest on Tyron.

'I have an urgent message for King Jayr.'

The five horses had formed a circle around him.

'I'm sure you do,' Leksi said, moving closer to him. 'Hand it over.'

The Zoelin rider shook his head and withdrew his body. 'I am to deliver it into the king's hands.'

Leksi laughed. 'I'm not sure if you have noticed, but you are on Syrasan soil now, and Prince Tyron here would appreciate it if you would hand over the message.'

The rider glanced at the other men, whose hands rested on their weapons.

'What is going on here?' came a voice.

Tyron turned to see King Jayr and his party approaching at a walk. He glanced at Leksi, who all but rolled his eyes. Jayr came to a stop in front of Tyron. He looked between the prince and the Zoelin messenger.

'I see your father let you out.'

Tyron gave a half smile. 'Your Majesty,' he said, nodding at the king. He watched as Jayr's men formed a larger circle around them. Then came the collective sound of swords being drawn. Tyron and Jayr kept hold of their reins, letting their men handle the rising conflict.

'I am surprised to find you this far north,' Jayr said, a knowing smile on his face.

Tyron glanced down the road. 'Yes, we had reports of Zoelin men along the border and were sent to investigate. Do you mind telling me what is going on?'

The messenger squeezed between Tyron's men and handed the message to his king. Jayr kept his eyes on Tyron as he opened the letter and then looked down to read it. A muscle pulled in his jaw. When he was finished, he tucked the note inside his vest and his eyes returned to Tyron, his smug expression gone.

'Well?' Tyron asked. He had good instincts about these things, and his instincts told him Aldara was involved somehow.

'Nothing for you to concern yourself with. You and your men can relax.'

'Relax? With Zoelin soldiers combing our border?'

They continued to look at one another. Tyron wondered if she might have escaped, if that was even possible. It would not be the first time he had underestimated her. Perhaps her escort had underestimated her also. She had an advantage on horseback, but even if she had gotten away, she would have no supplies or means of defending herself. Assuming she outsmarted them, she would freeze waiting for the opportunity to cross. Then there was the water. It was close to freezing temperature now. There was every chance she could drown trying to cross it.

'Who are your men hunting?' he asked.

Jayr considered his response for a moment. 'An escaped prisoner. We are trying to save her from her own stupidity.'

The horses shuffled, growing restless. The other men watched each other, swords ready.

'If any harm comes to her, I'm coming for you.'

Jayr kicked his horse into a walk. 'You and your four men?'

Tyron shook his head. 'No. Just me.'

Jayr stopped his horse and turned in the saddle. 'I want to make something clear. You are not permitted on Zoelin soil until an invitation is extended. So I suggest you return to Archdale before you get yourself into more trouble.'

Tyron swung his horse around. 'Since we are establishing rules, Your Majesty, ensure your men understand that if your prisoner happens to be Syrasan, and she reaches that water, she will be protected by our laws, and there will not be a damn thing you can do about it.'

Jayr turned and kicked his horse into a canter. 'Then we understand each other,' he called over his shoulder. His men returned their swords to their sheaths and followed the king, the messenger fleeing with them.

'Now what?' Leksi asked, resting his hands on the front of his saddle. 'Even if we make it across, there is no clean path to find her. She could be anywhere by now.'

Tyron knew the odds of her making it to the river were not great, but if there was one woman in the world capable of defying odds, it was her—small and indestructible. 'Aldara will make it to the river. And when she does, we will be waiting for her.'

Leksi nodded. 'All right. Any ideas where that might be? The Lotheng River is long, in case you have forgotten.'

Tyron thought for a moment. 'Drake Castle is in the west of Zoelin. The fact there are men already at the river means she escaped early in the journey.'

Leksi glanced at the woods to his left. 'You think she will show up west of the bridge.'

Tyron nodded. 'She would have fled south, forced to

keep west of the main road in order to avoid the guards. That halves the search area.'

'That's something.' Leksi turned back to him. 'Let's go find her.'

They moved their horses off the road, disappearing into trees and chasing the sun on its journey west.

There was no abandoning her this time.

CHAPTER 33

The sound of rushing water was torture. Aldara sat crouched behind a group of large rocks, watching Zoelin guards pass along the riverbank. She gripped the reins of her horse because survival instincts were drawing the mare to the water. Her own survival instincts told her to remain where she was, but her thirst was consuming. She counted between sightings of the men. They appeared to be the same riders arriving in intervals of two minutes and twenty seconds from each direction. Two minutes, twenty seconds. It would not be enough time to get to the river and cross it; plus she would be forced to let the mare drink—another time leech. She was at least eighty yards from the bank and could not risk going any closer.

Two minutes, twenty seconds.

Water.

The sun was sinking in the west. Soon night would arrive and she would not be able to see. She pressed her palms against her eyes as she tried to think past her thirst. Move farther down the river and try to find another safer place to cross—assuming there was one, and the river was not guarded all the way to the Galen border.

Water first.

She mounted and the exhausted horse swayed under the weight of her small frame. As soon as the guards came into sight, she began to count. Two minutes, *ten* seconds. They were either riding faster or her mind had slowed. Either way, she had to get in and out as quickly as possible.

More waiting. The next time, she kicked the mare into a slow canter as soon as the men were out of sight. They did not move quite at the speed she had envisaged, but they were moving. It took thirty-five seconds to get to the edge of the tree line, a few more to check her surroundings, and then eight seconds to get to the water's edge. The horse was drinking before she had even dismounted. She had around ten seconds before they turned around and made their way back. Aldara scooped up the icy water with her hands and drank greedily, her eyes on the bend in the river where they would appear. She was back in the saddle and heading for the trees twelve seconds later, her heart pounding as she raced for cover. The horse came to a halt behind the rocks and Aldara leapt from its back, crouching behind the rocks. She peered through the small gap. It was almost another two minutes before the soldiers passed at a walk. Her eyes closed with over-whelming disappointment. She could have crossed in that time.

The mare nibbled leaves from a low-hanging branch. Realising they were not to her taste, she bobbed her head, trying to spit out the ones stuck inside her mouth. Aldara looked around to see if there was anything more appetising close by. The only other green offering was the moss painted across the rocks, so she picked up a stick and began to scrape at it. She held the small collection in the palm of her hand. The mare sniffed at it before eating it. Aldara would have to go hungry.

When night came, the guards rested their horses and lit fires for warmth. Aldara led the mare west, inwardly cursing as she navigated forest debris, tripping every few steps under the cover of darkness. The glow of another fire shone through the trees, and she tried to stop herself from crying. It was as she had thought—they were all along the river, and they knew she would not attempt to cross without vision. It was risky enough in daylight with water temperatures close to freezing.

She turned and moved east again, stopping in the middle of the two groups and slumping against a tree trunk. Now and then the wind would carry the sound of their voices to her, a reminder they were close. The cold rose from the earth and seeped through her clothes. She wrapped the cloak around her bare legs and thought through all her options while the mare dozed in front of her. At first light, she would ride west until she found a narrow section of the river where she could cross safely.

Hunger rolled inside of her. She cupped her icy hands over her mouth and breathed warmth into them as she thought. She tried to remember if she had passed anything edible, then recalled there had been blackberry bushes by the river. Had there been berries on them? She could not remember. It was likely too late in the season, but her hunger drove her to check.

With the mare tethered, she crept through the trees towards the water, stepping lightly, cloak wrapped tightly to avoid snagging. She stopped at the edge of the tree line, listening. Nothing but the soft roar of the river. She crouched low to the ground and observed the guards upstream, warming themselves by the fire. Turning back to the water, she thought about crossing at that moment, but fear of drowning alone in the black water stopped her. Her eyes moved along the river. It was fierce and wide as far as she could see.

She glanced downstream to the other campsite. There were at least three men—two seated, one looking about. The cloud cover helped her remain invisible. She crawled on her hands and knees, so she might be mistaken for an animal if spotted. She felt the familiar prickle of a blackberry bush against her arm and winced as she tried to find fruit among the thorns. There was no fruit, but the bush still held leaves which could be fed to the horse. She gathered them in the skirt of her dress, picking as many as she could hold.

Voices came from the woods behind her. She froze, dropping her skirt and sending leaves fluttering to the ground around her. Slowly, she lowered herself until she lay flat against the wet sand, eyes searching the tree line. She heard the low whinny of a horse, followed by the pounding of hooves and tinker of armour. Torches blazed through the trees.

'She is here,' one of the men said in Zoelin. 'Find her.'

Her makeshift bridle would have given her away in an instant.

The torches cast a surprising amount of light as the men separated and searched for her. Aldara remained perfectly still. The wet earth beneath her was soaking through her dress and her body began to tremble. Soon, all the guards in the area joined the search. Her horse was led away. She panted against the ground as the realisation that she would be on foot crushed her.

Her self-pity was stifled when a guard stepped out from the trees and lifted his torch higher to look around. She pressed her face into the ground and held her breath as the light danced on the ground in front of her, threatening to touch her. When it retreated for a moment, she rolled her body towards the blackberry bushes, continuing until she was tangled beneath the prickly branches. Another torch. Two men were speaking to each other. The combined light spread across. She buried herself deeper beneath the bush, hoping it was enough coverage.

Footsteps came closer, and the light drenched the ground where she had lain just a few moments earlier, reaching all the way to the water. The two men walked closer, bringing more light with them. She pushed herself farther still, the rustling of the branches drowned out by the sound of the water. Something scurried away from her, and she covered her mouth to prevent herself from making noise. She hoped it was only a rat. She managed a daring glance to see how well she was concealed. As well as she could be. The thorns clawed at her bare legs. Another scurry, and she turned her head to see a terrified hare burst from the bush she was hiding under. She panted into her hand.

Light spilled over the bush and she held her breath, turning her face from it. At that moment, she could not afford to move or make any sound. Tears were running down her face and she had no control over them. She kept waiting for a hand to reach through the shrub and grab hold of her. They would drag her out into the open by a limb—and then what?

The light faded. The footsteps moved away, but fear kept her still.

More men arrived, combing the woods in pairs. She could hear them swinging their swords through the bushes. At one point a sword hissed above her head. Her small cry was muffled by the hood that covered her face. Still, she did not move.

An hour before sunrise, the tired men gathered in a

large group upstream, next to the river. The morning breeze carried their voices to her.

'She must have crossed,' said one.

'Then she is dead,' said another.

'We will resume our search at first light.'

The men lit fires and cooked fish they speared in the river. The smell reached Aldara, but she was too nauseous to appreciate the aroma. Bellies full, some of the men dozed by the fire while others kept watch. Aldara remained awake, shivering and numb from cold and fear. At one point her eyes sank shut, but a bird landed on the bush above her and they flew open again. She needed to move before the sun rose.

The small campsite downstream had been abandoned. She could walk farther downstream now and try to cross before she ran into the next group of guards. *Move.* Her body was stiff and sore as she emerged from her hiding place, wet dress clinging to her skin. She glanced upstream. The two guards on watch were facing the woods, talking. She took a deep, sobbing breath and ran for the trees. When she reached them, she steadied herself against a trunk and glanced upstream to see if they had noticed her. They had not. She walked downstream, her ears aching in the cold, her wet hood doing little to help. The water grew quiet, the current slowing as the river widened. She stopped walking just as the sun kissed the horizon. Any wider and she would never make it across before her limbs froze up.

She checked her surroundings before stumbling down the sandy riverbank. About twenty yards downstream, there were piles of stones on the other side of the water. Tyron had once told her that he had smashed apart the bridges connecting the kingdoms after the attacks in the north. She wondered if that pile of stones had been one of them. If he could work through blizzards to keep his people safe, she could surely survive one cold swim to save herself.

She stood on the gentle slope and stared into the dark water. The sun made little difference to the colour when the water was that deep. There were no visible rocks, and the riverbank on the opposite side allowed an easy exit from the water. She removed her boots with trembling hands, stepped into the shallow water so it covered her feet, and counted. Within a few seconds, her feet were throbbing with a sharp pain. When she stepped back, the skin on her feet felt as though it were burning. She took a final look around her before pulling the hood of her cloak farther over her head. Soon the soldiers would arrive searching for her. Perhaps there were men already checking the water for a dead body.

She covered her mouth with her hands and breathed into them one final time, enjoying the warmth of her breath. Then she picked up her boots and threw them into the river. They bobbed on the surface for a moment before sinking, the river carrying them away. She did not want to leave a trail for them to follow. Her feet were already aching and had changed to an eerie shade of red. She took a final breath, but as she was about to step in, the sound of hooves whispered across the water to her. She crouched down, eyes searching as she prepared to dive in and swim for her life. The sound grew louder.

Go.

But her feet would not move. She checked left, right, behind her, turning in panic as she searched for riders. Five Syrasan soldiers on horseback came to a stop on the other side of the river. A brief moment of relief was replaced by panic when the men drew weapons. She swallowed and stood up. There was nowhere to hide anymore. She was out of ideas. The fight was gone from her.

The hood of her cloak slipped back and her hands hung limp by her body as she stood there, exposed. There was nowhere for her to run to if Syrasan was not an option.

'Aldara!'

The water carried his voice, familiar and warm. The river between them seemed to narrow. She felt as though she could reach out and touch him. One empty hand lifted instinctively towards him. He raised his loaded bow and aimed. The four men with him did the same. Five arrows pointed at her. Her outreached hand fell to her side and she shook her head. At least when she died, his face would be the last thing she saw.

The creak of a bow behind her made her turn. More arrows pointed at her. Three Zoelin soldiers stood ten feet from her. Four more arrived behind them, pointing their bows across the river at Tyron and his men.

How had she not heard them?

Because all she had taken in was him.

Tyron's heart drummed in his chest. It would only take one of those arrows to kill her. He glanced at her again. She was pale, and one of her arms was bloodied. Her dress was torn at the bottom and her shivering was bordering on convulsing.

'I am Prince Tyron of Syrasan. Lower your bows!' he shouted in Zoelin.

Unsurprisingly, the men did not lower their bows.

'Our orders come from King Jayr,' one of them shouted. 'The girl is to return with us.'

Tyron moved his horse to the water's edge. 'Aldara, step into the water.'

She blinked at him, confused maybe, or perhaps untrusting. He could not blame her for that. But when the three Zoelin guards moved towards her, she stumbled back into the river, the icy water biting at her calves.

He looked back at the men. 'Unless you want to start a war between our two kingdoms, I suggest you lower your bows. The girl is no longer on Zoelin soil.'

The Zoelin men glanced between themselves, unsure, bows still raised. He had to play it carefully if he was to get her out in one piece and keep his word to his father. How easy it would be to kill them.

'She comes with me if you lower your bows, and she comes with me if you do not,' he continued. Otus stepped into the water. 'We cannot kill you, but we can injure you in ways you cannot imagine.'

The guard closest to Aldara took a few steps towards her. Tyron aimed at the man's foot and pierced it with his arrow. The man roared, his bow falling at his feet. A spray of Zoelin arrows flew across the river at Tyron's men, landing short of them. Zoelins were excellent swordsmen, but not strong archers at great distances. His men did not retaliate, but they were ready. The creak of bows sounded behind him.

'Our orders are clear,' said one of the guards. 'The girl is to be retained and returned to Drake Castle.'

He stepped forwards, reaching for Aldara. An arrow pierced his arm and the bow dropped to the ground as he clutched it. Aldara stepped deeper into the water. Tyron put his bow away and drew his sword. His horse was submerged in the water now, swimming towards her.

'Do nothing stupid,' he warned the Zoelin men, whose arrows turned on him. 'The rest of you can leave here in one piece and tell your king she got across the river before you could get to her. Or you can shoot at me and leave with arrows through you, like your friends here.'

Tyron kept moving through the icy water. No one would have guessed the temperature as the large gelding paddled through it at a slight angle to compensate for the current.

'You are not permitted on Zoelin soil!' yelled one man.

The gelding found his footing on the sandy slope and stopped, chest deep in the water. Tyron held up his hands. 'I am not coming any farther,' he reassured them.

The Zoelin men watched Aldara down their arrows as she backed away from them. She turned, eyes closing, no doubt expecting an arrow in her back. Tyron watched the guards closely, trusting the men he had brought with him to keep her safe. She waded towards his outstretched hand, stumbling in the water, eyes blazing. He reached out, willing her forwards.

As soon as she was within reach, he grabbed her arm and pulled her into his lap like a child, trying not to wince at the feel of her wasting arm beneath his grip. She gasped as her small frame sank down into the icy water. He pressed his face against the top of her head before glancing once more at the Zoelin men.

'Tell King Jayr that I await his invitation to Drake Castle.'

He turned his horse and Aldara pressed her shivering body against him as they sank deeper into the water. Another sound as the cold climbed her body. She could barely hold on, but it did not matter because he was not letting go.

The Zoelin soldiers lowered their bows, remaining at the river's edge, watching them. Otus groaned as his stiff, aching body came out of the water, steam rising from his neck and rump.

'Hold on,' Tyron whispered to Aldara as they leapt up the bank of the river. He rode up to the waiting men whose loaded bows were still pointed across the river. 'Let's go before they change their mind.'

Leksi glanced across at Aldara. 'Hold your position,' he said to the other men. He lowered his bow and took off his cloak, throwing it to Tyron.

Tyron wrapped it around her, eyes moving over her body and stopping on her injured arm. 'You're hurt.'

Her empty face watched him. 'Just cold,' she said through blue lips.

'Are you able to hold on for a while?' He cupped her head, noticing the blackberry thorns tangled in her hair.

'Yes,' she replied.

He knew she would hold on if he asked her to.

'I'm all right,' she said, teeth clenched.

He tucked the cloak tighter and wrapped his arm across her. 'I've got you.'

She exhaled and closed her eyes, her body going limp against his chest.

'I've got you,' he said again.

CHAPTER 34

*L*ord Yuri's manor was a few hours east of Veanor. It was the safest place Tyron could think of to take her, and Lord Yuri was one of the few men he trusted to be discreet. They rode through the opening in the wall and past the manicured lawns and gardens, scaring the few sheep that were grazing near the road before stopping at the bottom of the steps. Leksi dismounted and went over to take Aldara from him. As soon as Tyron was off his horse, he gathered her in his arms again and glanced up at the large stone house with its sharp rooftop. He did not wait for an invitation; he walked up the steps with Aldara shivering in his arms and met Lord Yuri as he came out of the house. The surprised expression on his face was replaced with one of concern when he saw a trembling and blue Aldara.

'Dear God, what has happened?' he asked, rushing forwards to assist.

Tyron kept firm hold of her and continued past him. 'I apologise for imposing, but I need use of a hot bath and a warm room. If you do not mind, I will explain everything once she is taken care of.'

'Of course,' Lord Yuri said, following behind him. 'Straight up the stairs to the left. I will send the maid to assist you at once.' He turned to the nearby servant. 'Have the groom come and take the horses to the stables, and bring the men in to refresh themselves.'

The maid's name was Odele, and Tyron immediately liked her. She clucked around the room, grabbing everything she needed, narrating her actions aloud as she did so. She moved with efficiency while instructing the much younger maid who was running frantically between rooms with pails of hot water. Tyron stood empty-handed next to the bed where Aldara lay shivering, eyes closed.

'That's enough hot water for now,' Odele said to the young maid. 'We need to bring her body temperature back up, but we need to do it slowly.'

She unfastened Aldara's cloak and peeled it off her. There was a collective silence as their eyes ran over her body. Her legs were covered in scratches, plus a long cut along her arm and deep, raw bruises around each wrist. When Odele lifted Aldara's hands to inspect the cut, Tyron had to look away. The fact that she had been bound made his stomach twist.

'We'll take it from here,' Odele said, glancing sideways at him. She then waved her arms, shooing him from the room like an unwelcome child.

He stood on the other side of the wooden door which had long before closed in his face, listening to the old woman's words of reassurance as the women helped Aldara into the tub.

'She is in good hands,' Lord Yuri said, coming up behind him.

Tyron turned. 'Yes, I see that.'

'Please, come.' Lord Yuri gestured with his hand. 'I have a room made up for you. Wash, rest. We can talk later. I can have food brought up to you if you would prefer?'

Tyron tried to smile. 'Thank you.' Fatigue and cold had caught up to him. They had spent the entire night searching for her along the river. It was not until he saw a group of guards across the water doing the same that he realised she was close. When they discovered the abandoned horse, he had been ready to cross and search for her, until Leksi had convinced him to wait until daylight. They had watched all night from the trees as the men searched the area, swinging their swords about. In the morning, they had made their way to the water. He had not recognised her standing on the water's edge, barefoot, her tiny frame dwarfed by an oversized cloak.

Tyron closed the door to the bedchamber Lord Yuri had prepared for him and looked at the clean clothes laid out on the bed. Near the window, steam rose from a large basin. He stepped out of his wet clothes and washed himself with the hot water. Before he dressed, Odele burst through the door carrying a tray of food. She placed it on the table next to the basin of water while he hopped around trying to cover his nakedness. She took no notice.

'Eat up,' she said, not even glancing at him. 'We can't have you getting sick.' She padded back towards the door and closed it behind her.

Tyron shook his head and stepped into the dry trousers. He ignored the spoon on the tray and drank the hot broth straight from the bowl, pausing only to tear off pieces of bread. Then he slipped the shirt over his head and left to check on Aldara.

'She is fast asleep, my lord. I suggest you do the same,' Odele said in a hushed voice, blocking the door with her body.

He got a brief glimpse of a sleeping Aldara, layered with blankets, before the door closed in his face again. He walked back to his chambers and forced himself to sleep. When he woke, the sun was blazing through the window. He shielded his eyes as he sat up. There was a fresh tray of food next to his bed. He picked up the cup of water, emptied it, and went off once again to check on Aldara. She was still asleep, so he wandered downstairs in search of Lord Yuri. He found him in the hall, seated at the long table talking with Leksi and the other men.

'Ah, there you are,' said Lord Yuri, standing. 'Feeling better?'

Tyron's men got to their feet and gave a small bow before leaving them. Leksi patted his arm as he passed.

'Much,' he said. 'I appreciate you opening your home to us. I feel I owe you an explanation, even if it is a little late.'

'Nonsense,' said Lord Yuri, feigning offence. 'You owe me nothing. I am honoured to help my king and those who serve him.'

Tyron hesitated before speaking. 'I suppose you remember Aldara?'

Lord Yuri smiled. 'I was fortunate enough to spend time with her at Archdale.' He crossed his arms in front of him. 'I heard rumours she had been taken from her home in Roysten some months back. I am not one for rumours, as you know. It is upsetting to see there may have been truth to the story.'

Tyron nodded. 'Yes. King Jayr is keen for me to marry his sister, so he found a way to ensure I kept my word.'

The two men sat down at the table and Lord Yuri poured them both some wine. 'By the appearance of her, I am guessing she was not voluntarily returned by King Jayr.'

Tyron shook his head and looked into his cup. 'She escaped, like only she could.'

'What will you do now?'

Tyron blinked. 'Now I figure out a way to ensure they never go near her again.'

Lord Yuri let the wine sit in his mouth for a moment before swallowing. 'I wish you luck. King Jayr has a reputation for getting what he wants. His father was a fierce king, but at least he was predictable.'

Before Tyron could reply, Odele walked into the hall and began clearing dishes.

'The lady is awake, my lord. I swear to you, the moment her eyes opened, she asked for you. I told her she needed to eat something proper first if she is to keep from getting sick—she was frozen through, after all. I've never seen a person eat so fast. It's a good thing we got her out of those wet clothes when we did or we'd be starving a fever right now.' She glanced up from the table and saw Lord Yuri seated alone. 'Oh I see.'

The door was ajar when Tyron reached her. He peered through the gap, watching her for a moment. She was standing next to the bed, chatting to the young maid, a blanket wrapped around her shoulders covering her white cotton nightdress. Her hair was out, waves of it spilling over her left shoulder. Her cheeks were rosy from the roaring fire.

She looked up, meeting his gaze through the crack in the door.

Aldara sensed him before she saw him watching her through the gap in the door. The maid picked up the empty tray and left, stopping to curtsy in front of Tyron as she passed him in the doorway. He did not enter the room.

'My lord,' Aldara breathed, wrapping the blankets tighter around her. 'Please, come in.'

He stepped inside, remaining near the door. 'Are you feeling better? Did you eat?'

She watched him. 'Yes, and yes.'

He nodded, still not moving towards her. 'Why were your wrists bound?'

She glanced down at them. 'Straight into the interrogation, then?' she said, a weak smile forming.

'I'm sorry.'

Her smile fell away. 'It was only during transportation. Seems it was justified. Perhaps they should have tied my feet also.'

Tyron blocked the image from his head. 'That is not funny.'

'You're right. It has been a long time between jokes. I am out of practice.' She looked about the room. 'I hear you are to be married.' What had seemed like casual conversation in her head sounded very much like an accusation out loud.

His eyes closed for a moment.

She shook her head, wishing she could take back the words. 'Sorry. You do not have to explain yourself. It was always the plan. Perhaps I should have started with congratulations.'

He was silent for a long time before he spoke. 'Should we begin with how you escaped from Zoelin guards, the largest men I have ever fought against?'

'Large, yes. Not very bright though.'

He exhaled. It could almost have passed for a laugh. 'Where did King Jayr keep you?' he asked, taking a step forwards.

She noted the pain in his tone. 'It was a step up from

the farm as far as comfort is concerned.' She could tell by his expression that he did not believe her.

'Your family are safe and well. I had the barn rebuilt for them.'

Aldara had known he would take care of her family whether she was there or not. 'Thank you,' she said, taking a few steps towards him. 'It was one thing I did not have to worry about.' She looked away from him.

'What did you worry about?' he asked, taking another step.

If she reached out, she could touch him. Her hands opened and closed again. 'Just about everything else. I had a lot of time to think and not much to do, which is never a good combination for me.'

He swallowed. 'No.'

She saw his eyes move briefly to her lips.

'You will stay here for a few days while you recover. I will return to Archdale in the morning to sort out this mess once and for all.'

She nodded, eyes trailing down him. 'I see. And what about tonight?'

'What about tonight?'

'Where will you be tonight?'

His eyes moved to her lips again and her entire body responded to the small gesture.

'I will stay here. Lord Yuri was kind enough to have rooms made up for me.'

She knew she was not the only one resenting the remaining space between them. 'Do you want to spend the night in the rooms that Lord Yuri has made up for you?'

His lips parted and his breath caught. She closed the gap between them and his familiar scent wrapped her.

'Clean cotton and pine needles,' she said.

He swallowed again. 'What?'

'You always smell like clean cotton and pine needles.'

He lifted a hand and ran a finger over her lips. 'And you always smell like horse and forest debris.'

She laughed and he withdrew his hand as though she had burned him. But she knew he could not walk away from her in that moment. She took another small step and reached for his hand, returning it to her lips. The timid Companion from years earlier was gone. The time she had spent in Zoelin had seen to that. Tyron reached his other hand up and touched her hair, rubbing it between his fingers in that familiar way.

'It is the cleanest I have ever seen it.'

She leaned in and pushed against him. He stepped back and she moved with him, all the way to the door that Tyron pushed closed with his back. For a moment neither of them moved. Her hands were resting against his chest, his were holding her face. His breath was coming in pants now. She wrapped her arms around his neck and the blanket fell to the ground as she pulled herself up with her good arm. He took hold of her legs as they wrapped him. A groan came from her when his mouth landed on hers. He walked her over to the bed, wearing her like a skin.

And the healing began.

She was crying and he could not continue. He could not even touch her. He lifted her and laid her on the bed next to him, then sat on the edge with his head in his hands, hating himself.

Aldara pushed herself up, her hands returning to him.

'Look what I have done to you,' he said.

She brushed away the tears but more came. 'I'm sorry. I'm not normally a crier.'

He turned his wet face to her. 'I just keep failing you. I wanted to protect you.' He held up her bandaged arm. 'Look at you!'

She flinched, shaking her head. 'This is not because of you.' Her mouth returned to him. She had never felt so hungry for him. 'It's all right,' she whispered into his open mouth.

He pulled back from her, his face pained as he gathered his words. 'Did anyone touch you?'

Her expression softened as she understood the question. 'No,' she said. 'No one touched me.'

Her nightshirt was too big and hung down one arm. He pressed his face into her bare shoulder and she held his head.

'We're no good apart,' he whispered against her skin.

'I know.'

'It doesn't get easier.'

'I know.'

He tilted her back on the bed and moved on top of her. The suffocation was just what she needed.

'I gave you up because it was best for you.' He kissed her, lifting the nightdress with his hand. 'Everything I have done since the moment I met you has been for you. It is always for you.'

She cried because she knew it was true.

He rolled off her, onto his back, and pressed his fists against his eyes, trying to block out her pain. There was no comfort for either of them. When she could, she crawled to him, wrapping herself around him, burying her face in his familiar neck. His hands gripped her back, and they did not leave her that time.

The sky turned black outside. They did not move from the room, and no one in the house disturbed them. Even Odele knew better.

'I met her, you know,' she said. She was laying behind him, her lips on his warm back. He was silent, listening. 'She came to me, knew who I was. She wanted to know about you. Find out who she was marrying.' He said nothing. 'I was expecting her to be like King Jayr. Perhaps I was hoping she would be, so I could hate her. But she is not like her brother, in the same way you are not like yours.'

He turned, kissing her wet face. 'Tell me what you want and I'll do it. If you tell me not to marry her, I won't.'

She watched him, her cheeks puffy and lips swollen. 'Did you agree to marry her at the flag tournament to stop me from being lashed?'

'That was when I agreed to it out loud.'

She blinked. 'It is what your father wants?'

'It's what Pandarus wants, which is the same thing these days.'

The conversation was painful, but neither of them turned away from it.

'He wants to strengthen the alliance?'

Tyron ran his hand up her. 'Yes, but not for the reasons I first thought. King Jayr is acting out of fear.'

She raised her eyebrows. 'I thought he wasn't afraid of anything.'

'He is afraid of Asigow rising against them, more than I realised.'

She thought for a moment. 'If Asigow takes Zoelin, what happens to us?'

He shook his head. 'I don't know. The alliance strengthens both kingdoms against Corneo and Asigow. As much I hate King Jayr, we both need allies.'

She touched his face, running a finger along his jaw. 'Marry her. You are the people's prince, a man who puts the needs of his kingdom ahead of his own. If it benefits Syrasan, marry her.'

'I can't see past you right now.' He closed his eyes. 'What will you do?' he asked, threading his fingers through hers and bringing them to his mouth. His eyes opened as he kissed the scratches on them.

She smiled. 'Knowing my luck, Mother will sell me back to the Zoelins.'

'Again, not funny,' he said, silencing her with his lips.

She pressed her body against his and then pulled back to look at him. 'I wish I could be your Companion. I wish it were enough. But I see now you were right. I don't belong there. It would be a painful existence for both of us.'

His hands were moving over her now. 'I can't live without you. It's like living half a life.'

She kissed him, soaking up the feel of his hands. 'I'm yours until death, even if I'm not with you.'

As the room lightened, they lay watching each other.

'If there is ever a time in your life when you need it, I want you to think of me and feel comforted. There is no end to the way I love you. No limits. No conditions.'

He pulled her hand to his lips. 'I'm not sure there is life after you.'

'When Pandarus is king, your people will need you more than ever. That is your purpose.'

'Will you need me?'

'Always.' She tried to smile. 'One day you will ride through Roysten, its name bringing memories, and I will be just another old woman in an adoring crowd.'

His eyes closed. 'In my mind, you will be eternally young, stumbling down the path towards me.'

Somehow, they fell asleep. Exhaustion won.

Aldara woke with a start and looked across at Tyron sleeping next to her, his arm tucked beneath his head. Nausea bubbled inside of her. They had skipped a few meals, and now her empty stomach was filled with nothing but grief. She hoped he would continue sleeping so he would not leave. Her plan was ruined when Odele walked through the door carrying a tray.

'Morning,' she sang, bringing the food right up to the bed. Tyron's eyes snapped open and he sat up, forming a barrier around Aldara with his arm.

'Easy, soldier,' she whispered, kissing his shoulder.

'Now, I have put a little of everything on here as I wasn't sure what you felt like. Eat up,' Odele said, placing the tray on the small table next to the bed. 'I'll bring fresh water for the basin.'

Aldara held the sheet up, covering herself as the woman collected the water jug before waddling from the room. When the door closed, she turned to Tyron.

'She has no sense of propriety, but I like her,' he said.

She smiled and glanced at the closed door. 'Me too.'

Lord Yuri was in the hall eating with Leksi and the other men when Tyron and Aldara came in. Everyone stood and Tyron gestured for them to return to their seats. They sat and waited for him to speak. Aldara remained next to him, dizzy with exhaustion. Or perhaps not from exhaustion.

'Lord Yuri, my men and I will depart this morning. If it is all right with you, Aldara will remain here for a few days while I sort out matters at Archdale.' He did not look at her. 'I will send an escort as soon as I am able.'

Lord Yuri smiled at her. 'You are welcome here as long as you need.'

'Thank you, my lord.' She tried not to choke on her words.

An hour later they stood at the bottom of the steps alongside the horses. Otus was dozing when Aldara walked over to him and rubbed his head.

'Thank you,' she whispered to the gelding. 'It was very

cold water and you displayed true chivalry.' His eyes opened, and he pushed his muzzle against her.

'I was in that water too, you know,' Tyron said, watching her.

'Yes,' she replied, not looking at him. 'I believe I thanked you last night.' A smile flickered and vanished.

Lord Yuri said a brief farewell before returning indoors. The other men mounted their horses. Leksi nodded at her before leading the others away to give them some privacy.

Aldara held on to Otus's bridle for balance. 'What will happen when you return?'

He forced himself to step up to the horse, step up to her. 'I don't know.'

'I'll pray for miracles.'

'You never pray.'

'I would if I thought it might help.'

He watched her. 'What miracles would you pray for?'

She laughed. 'How much time do you have?'

He rested a hand on Otus's neck. 'Give me your top three.'

'All right. I would probably start big. End the Companion trade with Zoelin.'

'Just end it?'

'If everyone is afraid of the Asigow people, why on earth are we sending Syrasan women there?'

'Excellent choice of miracle. Number two?'

'The next is not a miracle but an outcome of ending the trade. No trade equals no need for mentors. Hali and Sapphira return to Syrasan.'

'As Companions?'

'As whatever they choose.'

He nodded. 'Free. That would be a miracle. Next?'

'Stamitos and Sapphira marry.'

He raised his eyebrows. 'What about something for yourself?'

She shrugged. 'What more could I want than to see the people I love happy?' There was no point in making them feel worse than they already did.

His expression turned serious. 'You're right. It is enough.'

She let go of the bridle. 'I wouldn't wish any of it away, even the ugly parts. It was a handful of moments, but they are ours to keep.'

He stepped up to her, cupping her face, and kissed her mouth. She was a little taken aback as he was not one for public displays of affection.

'I love you,' he said, pulling back from her. 'Whatever happens next, whatever miracles come or falter, I love you.'

She wiped away the first tear that escaped, but they kept coming. Soon they were bleeding out of her. She gave up wiping them and rested her hands on his wrists. 'I think very highly of you also.' She laughed, but it was more of a sob.

Tyron kissed her once more before releasing her face, then mounted Otus and turned the gelding, kicking him into a trot. He did not even glance at her, and she could not blame him. Watching him leave was difficult, but she forced herself to look because it was another memory of him. The sobs that erupted took her by surprise. They tore through her as he disappeared behind the wall. The sharp intake of cold air made her insides ache.

She held onto her arms to steady herself. A small snowflake landed on one of her hands, disappearing. Turning her face, she watched as the first snowfall of the cold season fell. She let the flakes mix with the tears on her face.

CHAPTER 35

The air in the throne room was unbreathable. King Jayr had sent Grandor Pollux on his behalf, and he was using up far too much.

'This is quite a mess we have,' Pollux said.

He was seated across from Tyron, and Pandarus was beside him. They presented a different kind of alliance. Zenas was leaning forwards on his chair.

'No borders were breached by my men, and we cannot be held responsible for the actions of a prisoner,' he said. 'Need I remind you the girl should not have been imprisoned to begin with?'

The fact that Pollux sat opposite, casting disapproving glances across the table, did not sit well with Tyron. When he had arrived at Archdale, Stamitos had told him the advisor had arrived a few hours before him. It seemed King Jayr had received his message.

'King Jayr considers Prince Tyron's actions a breach of his trust—'

Tyron stood, his chair sliding backwards. 'Enough.'

Pollux's eyes turned up to him and the guards behind him shifted their weight.

'Grandor Pollux, could you give me a moment alone with King Zenas and Prince Pandarus?'

Pollux pressed his fingers together 'You want me to leave?'

Tyron placed his hands on the table. 'Yes. I want you to get out of your chair and wait outside until we are ready to talk to you. Your guard dogs can wait with you.'

'Tyron—' Pandarus began.

'We will talk in a minute,' Tyron said, cutting him off.

Zenas sat up straight. 'You heard my son. Please wait outside.'

Pollux stood and walked over to the door, his guards in tow. The doors closed behind them.

'What are you doing?' Pandarus said, standing up.

Tyron pushed off the table and walked towards him. 'What the hell are you doing?' The burning pit inside of him was bubbling over. 'Are you going to let that piece of shit come into our home and speak to your king and father like that?'

Pandarus shook his head. 'Have you lost your mind? We are trying to clean up your mess.'

'This is not my mess. I have been out there protecting the people you are failing!'

'Lower your voice,' Zenas said.

'Why? Because we might hurt Pollux's feelings?'

Zenas leaned back in his chair and looked at Tyron. 'You wanted a private audience, so speak.'

Tyron took a breath. 'You need not do this.'

'What?' Pandarus asked.

'Any of this. King Jayr has led you to believe he holds all the power, and he doesn't.'

Pandarus linked his hands on top of his head. 'I think

the girl you pulled from a freezing river might disagree. How was her time in Zoelin, by the way?'

Tyron kept his eyes on his father. 'King Jayr needs this alliance as much as we need them. If he wants this alliance, then he needs to accept our mutually beneficial terms.'

'Good luck with that,' Pandarus said.

Zenas ignored Pandarus. 'You are being vague,' he said to Tyron.

'Yes,' Pandarus said. 'Tell us more of these mutually beneficial terms.'

Tyron's eyes pleaded with his father. 'You have been king for nearing thirty years. Anything I have to say, you already know. The trade agreement was a bad idea and you knew it. That is why you broke it.'

Pandarus threw up his hands. 'Are you suggesting we break it *again*?'

Tyron shook his head. 'We don't have to. King Jayr broke it when he removed a common girl from Syrasan without using the appropriate channels, and without the consent of her family.' He looked between them. '*He* broke the agreement, and now we are free to walk away from it.'

Pandarus walked past Tyron and came to a stop in front of Zenas. 'If we walk away, we risk another fight.'

'He won't fight,' Tyron said. 'Because he still needs allies, and we can offer that.'

Zenas cleared his throat. 'Meaning you are still prepared to marry Princess Tasia?'

'Yes, on our terms.'

'Which are?'

Tyron exhaled, recalling Aldara's list of miracles. 'As already mentioned, the end of the trade agreement.'

'Are you prepared to fight if they come for the women anyway?' Pandarus asked.

'Yes,' Tyron said without hesitation. 'As a matter of fact,

I have never felt stronger and more prepared for a fight. This one matters a great deal. We are not talking about land or grain here. We would be fighting to protect Syrasan women and their families.'

'Go on,' Zenas said.

Aldara's laughing face flashed in Tyron's mind. 'The next term is an outcome of the first. The mentors and women remaining at Onuric are returned to Syrasan.'

Pandarus leaned on the table. 'You cannot be seriously considering this,' he said to Zenas.

'Silence. Anything else?'

Tyron had made Stamitos a promise. The next miracle was for his brother. 'I have one request. Give Stamitos your blessing to marry Sapphira. He is forever changed by this, and his marriage prospects are dismal at best. Please, let some happiness stem from this mess, and I will fight and marry whoever you need me to.'

Pandarus slammed his hands onto the table. 'I knew when I met that girl she would be trouble.' His eyes were on the table in front of him but his words were aimed at Tyron. 'I hanged a man in her village that day. A criminal. And she stood before my horse, knee deep in mud, judging my actions. I should have trodden over her instead of stopping.'

'She sees people,' Tyron said. 'You were forced to look at yourself that day, and what you saw made you uncomfortable.'

Pandarus shook his head. 'But she didn't find fault in you, did she?'

Tyron stared at him. 'Is that why you gave her to me? To find faults?'

Pandarus laughed, glancing between Tyron and Zenas as he did so. 'There are no faults. Even after all that has happened, you stand before your king as the perfect son.' He looked at Zenas. 'Isn't that right, Father?'

Zenas raised his head and linked his fingers over his stomach. 'Tell Grandor Pollux we are ready to see him now.'

Lord Yuri introduced Aldara to his library. Companions had not been permitted into the library at Archdale; books were accessed through Fedora. Aldara enjoyed the novelty of selecting a book from the high, polished shelves. She ran her fingers along the leather spines, reading the titles aloud as she did so, selecting a book on the history of Corneo. She sat on a wide cushioned chair in front of the small fireplace, skimming the text and studying the portraits and painted landscapes. Lord Yuri sat at the table writing letters of business. It had been two days since Tyron had left, and the snow had not stopped falling.

When she finally closed the book, Lord Yuri looked across at her.

'Do you ever hear from Hali?' he asked.

She shook her head. 'No. I doubt she would be permitted to write.'

'I suppose not.' He was quiet for a moment. 'I went to see her at Lord Clio's manor before she left for Zoelin.'

Aldara frowned. 'I did not know. How did she seem?'

He considered his words. 'Afraid, but she was trying to be optimistic. She was always a fountain of light, that girl.'

She smiled at the memory of her friend. 'Yes, she really was.'

'I wish we lived in a different world, one where we did not have to say goodbye to those we love so frequently.'

Aldara looked at the flickering fire. 'I know what you mean.'

'I was lucky enough to marry for love many years ago,' he said.

When Aldara glanced at him, he was staring ahead, quill poised.

'When I lost her, I thought I might die also. Grief does that to you. It is as mysterious as death itself.' He turned to her. 'I understand now that grief is a corridor you pass through. You cannot stay there as I did. Hali taught me of new beginnings. Even after great loss, there are still unexpected gifts to be found in life.' He fell silent again, dipping his quill in ink and continuing his letter.

Aldara turned back to the fire and closed her eyes. She hoped he was right.

A servant arrived in the doorway. 'Pardon the interruption, my lord, but Sir Leksi is here requesting an audience with Aldara.'

'Send him in,' Lord Yuri said, standing to leave. 'I will be outside if you need anything.'

Aldara stood and smiled at him. 'Thank you, my lord.'

When Leksi walked through the door, she could not hide the disappointment on her face. A childish part of her had hoped for a miracle, the one she had not mentioned because it was pointless and they had both been in pain.

Leksi joined her next to the fire and gestured for her to sit. She normally would have remained standing, but her legs threatened to give way.

'How is he?'

Leksi's gaze swept across the bookshelves. 'Would "good" be too strong?'

'Not if it's honest.'

'It's always hard to tell, and I'm a terrible judge of his mood. Perhaps he elaborates in his letter to you.'

He pulled a note from his tunic and handed it to her. She stared at it as though it were a weapon. It took her a moment to work up the courage to take it.

'I'll be outside with Lord Yuri when you are finished.'

She nodded, fingers running over the edges of the paper. 'Thank you.'

Dearest Aldara,

This is my sixth attempt at writing this. How does one open such a letter? Perhaps Fedora could give me some pointers.

If you are reading this, then Leksi has arrived to take you home. You are likely wondering if it is safe for you there given recent events. You will be safe. I have made sure of it. We are making changes to ensure Syrasan is safe for everyone.

Aldara, your prayers were answered. You prayed, correct? Of course you did. That is why I am able to write and tell you that we are making miracles happen.

First, the Companion trade with Zoelin is no more. As of today, it is illegal to sell women outside of Syrasan's borders. Any unsold Companions at Onuric Castle will be transported back to Syrasan within the next few weeks. I have purchased two mentors, and since we do not have a place for them at Archdale, I have granted them their freedom. As for your third miracle, I'm afraid that one is out of my control, but given that King Zenas has given his blessing for Stamitos to marry a woman of his choosing, I suspect you may be pleased with later outcomes.

Thank you for bringing back my strength, for waking my mind and rejuvenating my body. Thank you for reminding me that my actions should always be in the best interests of the Syrasan people, even if those interests do not align with those in power. I swore to protect them until my death, and I plan on upholding that promise at whatever personal cost. And the cost is great.

I will keep praying for one more miracle.

When trying to come up with final words for you, nothing sufficed. So instead, I leave you with a final gift that says everything I cannot.

Your prince,

Tyron

Aldara stared at the words on the paper. When the men came back into the room, she stood and looked at Lord Yuri.

'Hali is returning to Syrasan,' she said, glancing again at the letter.

Lord Yuri appeared stunned, and then his face filled with emotion. 'That is wonderful news.'

Her hands went over her mouth for a moment, but then she remembered herself and returned them to her sides. 'Yes, it is.'

The old maid packed an assortment of items for Aldara to take on the long journey. She handed it to Aldara along with her well-wishes and an encouraging, firm squeeze of her hands. Aldara put on her cloak and followed the men outdoors into the cold. She turned to Lord Yuri before descending the steps.

'Thank you,' she said. 'Not only for your recent hospitality, but your kindness over the entire period I have known you.'

He took both of her hands in his. 'I wish you a long and happy life. I truly hope we meet again.' He bowed and then nodded at Leksi before returning inside.

Aldara followed Leksi down the snow-littered steps towards the waiting horses. When she saw Otus standing with the groom, she looked up at Leksi, confused.

'A final gift for you,' he said.

Her hands went over her face and she cried.

'That is an entirely appropriate reaction. I tried to tell him retired horses are not suitable gifts for women. The gelding cannot plough, by the way, but his battle experience may come in handy next time Zoelin soldiers visit your farm. He practically does the fighting for you.'

A laugh escaped her.

'Too soon?'

'Much too soon,' she replied, brushing aside the tears freezing on her cheeks. She rushed over to the gelding then and buried her face in his long grey mane.

He had given her all he could.

EPILOGUE

*R*oyal weddings were big events in Syrasan, lavish celebrations that extended across months. Tours enabled everyone to join the celebration in some small way. The couple would travel the kingdom, collecting the good wishes of the common people who lined the roads to see them. They would visit each village, waving and smiling from their wagon, while their loyal servants offered heartfelt blessings.

Stamitos and Sapphira's wedding was no exception. It did not matter to the Syrasan people that Sapphira was common, at least not to those outside of nobility. If anything, it breathed new hope into the kingdom. Every young girl grew hopeful, believing they could be crowned and draped in heavy velvet one day. They made pretend crowns from scraps of fabric and decorated them with flowers, held pretend weddings and took turns being the princess. They tried to involve the boys, but the boys preferred to play knights, battling pretend enemies with their stick swords.

When the couple visited Roysten before taking their

vows before God, Aldara and her family made the journey into the village to pay their respects. They stayed well back from the road, as Aldara did not want to disrupt the procession or create a scandal. She only wanted to see their happy faces from a distance and feed off the memory for years to come.

Her plan was disrupted when she returned home with her family and found Stamitos and Sapphira waiting for her at the farm. Aldara leapt from the moving cart and wrapped herself around Sapphira, her vision blurred with tears, laughter mixing with sobs. She pulled herself free to curtsy in front of Stamitos. He bowed before pulling her into his arms. She looked between them, shaking her head, happiness spilling over.

'Princess Sapphira,' she said.

Stamitos laughed and Sapphira covered her ears, but she could not cover the vibrant smile that lit up her face.

'Someone had to keep this one safe,' Sapphira said, pointing to Stamitos and scrunching her nose at him.

After they had something to eat, Stamitos volunteered to teach Kadmus how to use a sword, so Aldara and Sapphira wandered the farm under light snowfall, catching each other up on the last few months.

'Is there any news of Hali?' Aldara asked. She had heard nothing since her return.

Sapphira smiled. 'Yes.'

Her smile was contagious. 'And?'

'She did not return to Arelasa.'

Aldara frowned. 'I don't understand.'

'Because she is living with Lord Yuri at his manor outside of Veanor.'

Aldara buried her face in her hands.

'Don't cry! It's happy news.'

So many tears. What was wrong with her? She raised her tear-streaked face. 'It's very happy news.'

Sapphira wrapped an arm about her. 'She will write soon, I'm sure of it. Perhaps you could go visit her.'

Aldara shook her head. 'I don't think that's a good idea.'

Sapphira looked at her. 'Why not?'

'Because it would not be appropriate. I'm not part of that world anymore.'

Sapphira rolled her eyes. 'You are such a snob.'

'Yes, a true farm snob.'

When it was time for them to leave, Aldara cried like a child, surprising herself more than anyone. Kadmus wrapped an arm around her as they watched the wagon disappear.

'I thought you would be happy,' he said, squeezing her shoulders.

She was. Everything was as it should be.

Winter raged on, bringing heavy snowfall and gusty winds. They avoided the village for a period because the roads were too dangerous for the cart. And then for another reason.

When the snow finally eased, Kadmus talked Aldara into coming with him to Roysten for supplies.

'I suppose I have to face them sooner or later,' she replied.

'Before you leave, I have finished your dress,' Dahlia said. She stood, holding it against her daughter.

'It's lovely,' Isadore said, winking at Aldara.

She smiled at him.

'Buy more fabric,' Dahlia said, not looking at her. 'You will need one more dress for the warm season.'

Aldara was quiet on the trip in. They went to the market and bought the fabric, some grain, preserved vegetables, bread, sweet buns, sewing supplies, paper, and a large bottle of ink. Tyron had ensured she would never go without, and she let him do whatever he needed to.

Everywhere they went, people were talking about the wedding. Someone knew someone who was supplying something for the lavish event. Aldara smiled to herself as she watched the excited children playing in the snow, daisy chain crowns on their heads. They watched her also, their curious gazes falling on Aldara's bulging stomach. She did not mind. She preferred their inquisitive expressions to the disapproving glances of the adults.

Aldara remained on the farm for the final months of her pregnancy, allowing the rest of the kingdom to enjoy post-wedding celebrations. She did not want to intrude on their fairy tales by parading the darker side of Companionship to them. Instead she worked, trying to maintain the parts of her life she had control over. Chores kept her out of the house, away from her parents' worried expression whenever they thought she was not looking. She was so grateful for the indifferent face of her brother.

When the sun showed itself once again, she spent her time in the fields, watching the land come alive with the warmth. When their first lamb was born, she sat in the grass a short distance away, one hand on her own kicking belly, watching in amazement. Afterwards, she lay down in the grass and imagined the birth of their baby. She was grateful for this final gift from him.

She often imagined what it would be like to tell him the news. He would not wish it away—she knew him far better than that. When she closed her eyes, picturing him in her mind, he would smile and place his gentle hands on her belly. Lift her off the ground and kiss it. He would forbid her to go riding and insist she eat more than she could. He would spend every night with her, his warm breath on her, hands drawing circles on her stomach. In another world, that was how it would be.

'If there is ever a time in your life when you need it, I want you to remember me and feel comforted. There is no end to the way I love you. No limits. No conditions.'

'I am not sure there is life after you.'

She cradled her bump, the part of him she would have forever. Lord Yuri had been right—even after great loss, there were still unexpected gifts to be found in life.

ACKNOWLEDGMENTS

I would like to express my gratitude to the many people who contributed to this book. What started as a pregnant dream, has now grown into a series.

My biggest thank you goes to my readers. Without readers I would not get to do what I love. Next, a huge thank you to my rock star husband who supports and encourages me even though my writing takes time away from him. A big thank you to Saltwater Writers for your feedback and support each month. A shout out to Dr Timothy Blake for checking all the medical components of the story. Thank you to Kristin and the team at Hot Tree Editing who polished the manuscript into something beautiful, and to my proofreader Rebecca Fletcher for catching everything I missed. Thanks to my beta readers for your honest (and at times hilarious) feedback and to MiblArt for another gorgeous cover. And finally, a huge thank you to my Launch Team for your encouragement, honest reviews and being the final set of eyes on my work. Your support is much appreciated.

This book is dedicated to my mum who hates to read, but supports her children at any cost, even if that means reading an entire novel. I love you.

ALSO BY TANYA BIRD

You can find a complete list of published works at

tanyabird.com/books

Made in the USA
Columbia, SC
20 June 2024